PRAISE FOR
EARTH FORCE RISING

"A richly detailed, highly imaginative world and a cast of clever, creative kids. Readers will be eager to bound into the next book."—Shannon Messenger, author of the Keeper of the Lost Cities series

"A joyful space adventure full of humor, friendships, and action . . . This is a great sci-fi adventure for boys and girls alike. I had so much fun reading it!"—S. J. Kincaid, author of the Insignia series and *The Diabolic*

"Fans of *Ender's Game* will feel right at home in this fast-paced debut. . . . I read it in a day, unable to put it down, and look forward to more from this promising new author!"—Wesley King, author of *The Incredible Space Raiders from Space!* and *OCDaniel*

BOUNDERS
BOOK 2

THE TUNDRA TRIALS

MONICA TESLER

ALADDIN

New York   London   Toronto   Sydney   New Delhi

This book is a work of fiction. Any references to historical events, real people, or real places are used fictitiously. Other names, characters, places, and events are products of the author's imagination, and any resemblance to actual events or places or persons, living or dead, is entirely coincidental.

ALADDIN

An imprint of Simon & Schuster Children's Publishing Division
1230 Avenue of the Americas, New York, New York 10020
First Aladdin paperback edition December 2017
Text copyright © 2016 by Monica Tesler
Front cover illustration copyright © 2016 by Owen Richardson
Back cover illustration copyright © by Thinkstock
Also available in an Aladdin hardcover edition.

For information about special discounts for bulk purchases, please contact
Simon & Schuster Special Sales at 1-866-506-1949 or business@simonandschuster.com.
The Simon & Schuster Speakers Bureau can bring authors to your live event.
For more information or to book an event, contact the Simon & Schuster Speakers Bureau
at 1-866-248-3049 or visit our website at www.simonspeakers.com.
Cover designed by Karin Paprocki
Interior designed by Mike Rosamilia
The text of this book was set in Adobe Garamond Pro.
Manufactured in the United States of America 1117 OFF
2 4 6 8 10 9 7 5 3 1
Library of Congress Control Number 2016955905
ISBN 978-1-4814-4596-2 (hc)
ISBN 978-1-4814-4597-9 (pbk)
ISBN 978-1-4814-4598-6 (eBook)

For Gabriel

1

AFTER BREAKING INTO PRISON CELLS
and battling aliens, you might think Cole and I would have
no problem with Addy's plan to bust into an apartment
building's mainframe tonight and take its elevator for a
joyride, but you'd be wrong. She's been pestering us ever since
I agreed to let her tag along as I show Cole around our district.

"Jasper says you're an ace hacker." My younger sister narrows her eyes at Cole and pushes into his personal space. Even
though they're about the same size, Addy seems twice as big as
she looms over him on the bench.

"I never said that," Cole stammers. His gaze dodges in every
direction except at Addy. He leans so far back I'm worried

he's going to fall off the bench and land in the grass of the green block where we're killing time before heading back to the apartment.

Cole's not going to be happy with me. He definitely does not like to be called a hacker, although there's really no other way to describe his mad skills at system manipulation. And I doubt being pushed around by my little sister was high on his wish list when he decided to come stay with us for a few days before we leave for our second tour of duty with Earth Force.

"It doesn't matter what you said." Addy transfers her hands to her hips. "It only matters if it's true. This whole plan hinges on you breaking into the lift system. Can you do it or not?"

"How do you know it will work?" Cole asks.

"Do I really have to go through this again?" Addy rolls her eyes, reminding me of our pod mate, Lucy. "Mason's dad works in lift maintenance. He told Eric, who told Larina, who told Molls, who told me. Execute the Lift System Maintenance Protocol and the lift dead drops until the safety tether engages. Easy."

"And we'll free-fall all three hundred floors of the apartment complex," I remind Cole before he chickens out. "Think of the speed! I overheard some older kids talking about it on the rails. It's supposed to be awesome!"

"Fine," Cole sighs. He won't look at Addy, but he shoots me a stern stare.

Yep, he's mad.

"Great!" Addy says, sitting next to Cole on the bench. "Then it's all set. The plan goes down tonight! While we're on the subject, I have a couple other ideas that could use Cole's hacking genius."

I laugh. "You're all about the danger and thrills these days, Ads."

Cole turns his back on Addy. "Speaking of that, Jasper, you better keep your sister away from Marco when she starts at the Academy next spring. They'd make a scary combination."

"No kidding," I say. Our pod mate Marco is the walking definition of thrill seeker. He could teach Addy a thing or two, and from the way Addy's been acting lately, she would definitely go along for the ride.

Addy clears her throat. "Ummm, I can hear you. I'm standing right here. And I can take care of myself at the Academy, thank you very much."

Cole looks at his shoes. He must be struggling to keep his mouth shut, just like I have since I got home from the EarthBound Academy.

This past spring we were part of the first group of Bounders to be sworn in as Earth Force cadets and sent to space for training. Before we were born, Earth Force discovered a link between brain structure and quantum space travel. They reintroduced the Bounder genes into the population and—*Bam!*—twelve years later they had the first group ready to be trained as quantum aeronauts to pilot the ships that can bound across the galaxy in an instant.

We weren't at the space station long before we realized Earth Force wanted the Bounders for more than traditional space travel. They'd stolen biotechnology from an alien race—the Youli—and were convinced the Bounders could master it. And they were right. Now Earth Force is training Bounders to be the front line in their secret war against the Youli. Cole and I have a battle under our belt to prove it.

Addy's completely in the dark. She still thinks the Academy curriculum is learning how to pilot the quantum bounding ships. Cole and I are under strict confidentiality orders to keep it that way. Revealing the truth about the Academy to anyone is a grave violation of the Earth Force Code of Conduct.

Unfortunately, Cole's the worst at keeping secrets, and he's about to blow our cover.

"What?" Addy says, ogling us with an evil stare.

Cole and I stay silent.

"Seriously, what?"

"It's just . . . ," Cole starts.

I elbow Cole hard in the ribs. "It's just nothing. Tell us about those other hacking ideas."

"Uh-uh, Jasper." Addy shakes her head. "You know I can

spot a secret from a mile away. What are you guys keeping from me?"

"Like I said, nothing," I spit out quickly so Cole doesn't have a chance to even think about telling the truth.

Addy nods at Cole. "Then why is he squirming around on the bench?"

She kneels in front of Cole and tries to make him look her in the eye.

"Cut it out, Addy," I say. "Leave him alone. It's just Academy stuff we're not supposed to talk about. That's it. You'll find out soon enough."

"You must be joking!" Addy springs to her feet and throws her arms in the air. "I'm a Bounder, too, remember? The whole world knows we're Bounders, J. No more secrets!"

While we've been arguing, the green block has filled with workers on their lunch breaks. And now it seems we're their prime dining entertainment. That is the last thing we need—an accidental announcement to all of Americana East that we're at war with a technologically advanced alien race.

"Go home, Addy!" I shout. "No one asked you to tag along!"

Addy's cheeks color pink like my words slapped her skin. Then the muscles in her face move, morphing from shock to hurt to rage.

I expect her to lash out. Addy is rarely one to give in.

Instead, she spins on her heels and races up the block.

"Why did you do that?" Cole asks.

"Really?" I remember the nosy diners and lower my voice to a whisper. "You were about to spill the beans, that's why!"

"You mean about the—"

Before Cole can say another word, I grab his arm and drag him off the bench. I pull him by the sleeve off the green block and into the thick of pedestrian traffic. After a few twists and turns, I duck into an alleyway and spin to face him.

"What the heck, Cole? What part of *top-level security clearance* don't you understand?"

"I know, but . . ."

"No buts! I've lived in the same apartment with Addy for the last four months! I've kept my mouth shut all that time! Never once did I come as close to caving as you did just then."

"But she's . . ."

"I said no buts! Geez, Cole. Did you tell everyone in your district about the Youli?" As soon as the word slips from my mouth I cringe. Scanning the alleyway, I'm relieved there's not a single person remotely in earshot.

"I didn't tell anyone," Cole says. "I swear! I basically kept to myself the entire time. But something about being here with you . . . and your sister is a Bounder, too . . . and . . ."

"Look, I get it," I say, "but we need to be careful. If word got out, it could be a huge problem."

MONICA TESLER

And now I have another huge problem on my hands: Addy.

"What do we tell your sister?" Cole asks.

"The same thing we should have told her before. Absolutely nothing."

Cole bounces on his toes. He's nervous. He really is the worst at secrets.

"Seriously, Cole. Not a word to Addy about the Academy. If she tries to pry it out of you, bring up *Evolution* or something."

Cole's eyes light with a fire only *Evolution of Combat* can ignite. He's a genius, like a total game master. I've never known anyone who came close to Cole at his *Evolution* skills. All summer we've been syncing up our game modules remotely, and he's been leading the Battle of Berlin. Just last month, we won World War II. It took Cole more than a year to defeat the level.

"You must have made it further than anyone by now," I continue.

Cole shrugs. "Now that we're in the Cold War, the game has changed. There's a lot of behind-the-scenes human psychology to factor in. That's not my strength."

I choke down a laugh. "No kidding. Maybe Lucy can help you," I joke. Lucy would never help. She hates *Evolution*. But Cole thinks I'm serious.

"Maybe," he says. "She can be annoying, but she's really good with rallying troops." Cole shoots me a side glance. "On the Paleo Planet—"

"Shhh!" I say, scanning the alleyway again. "I know what you're talking about! You don't need to say it." I press my back against the stone wall and slide down until my butt hits the ground. Cole crouches beside me.

I close my eyes as my brain takes me back to the battle. Lucy rallies the Bounders while Cole issues the marching orders. Marco takes off in his blast pack, charging the Youli on the cliff. His body goes rigid as the alien seizes control of his atoms. For a second, Marco hangs suspended in space, then the Youli flings him across the valley directly into the herd of mammoths. Next thing I know, I'm tackling the alien on top of his ship as his words slip inside my brain. Then Mira bounds amidst the herd of charging wildeboars.

"I'm scared." I wouldn't tell most people, but I know Cole understands. All my pod mates understand.

"Earth Force has a huge incentive to protect its military assets," he says.

Cole offers this factual nugget to make me feel better. It kind of does. But by *military assets*, he means me. Us. The Bounders. The soldiers they bred to fight their war with the Youli. The next evolution of combat.

"That's something, I guess." I stand and brush off the back

of my jeans. "Let's get back. My mom will be worried."

And Addy will be mad.

And we'll still be soldiers.

At least we're shipping out tomorrow for our second tour. And when we return in the spring for our third, Addy will be twelve and coming with us. She'll find out the truth soon enough. She'll learn what it really means to be a Bounder.

· *EF* ·

Cole and I beeline for my room as soon as we get back to my apartment. I slam the door and sink into the beanbag I begged my parents for after my first tour. If I close my eyes, it's almost like I'm in our pod room at the Academy with its green grass carpet, starry ceiling, and groovy light sticks. Unfortunately, the hum of Addy's violin is blowing a hole straight through my imagination. Her sad song is proof that I'm in my bedroom and not in space, and a vivid reminder that I'm the world's meanest brother.

Cole lays his tablet on my bed and the projection for *Evolution of Combat* fills the air space above my blanket. "Let's mess around on some old levels. How about the Middle Ages?"

"Sure, as long as we can joust." I toss my tablet on the bed, activate, and sync up.

I select my armor, weapon, and horse for my avatar, but Addy's music won't let me go. Her notes drift through the walls and down my throat where they take shape as one of those close-to-crying lumps.

I don't know why I haven't told her the truth. Like Cole said, she's a Bounder, and she'll find out soon enough. But when I got home from the Academy, everything was shaken up, including me. I didn't know how to be Jasper who fought the Youli while being Jasper, Addy's brother, background boy, klutz. Plus, Mom was so sure that everything would go back to normal with me at home that I didn't want to disappoint her. So I left the new Jasper at the space station and went back to my old self. I keep my mouth shut and say *Huh?* and *Oops!* and *Sorry* all the time like I used to. It's as if I'm in a perpetual holding mode, hovering like a passenger craft waiting for clearance to land, but in my case, I'm waiting to get back to the Academy.

"Hey!" Cole says. "I thought you wanted to joust!"

"Huh?"

"The game, Jasper."

In the *Evolution* projection, my very dead knight stays upright on his horse only because he's skewered by Cole's lance at the tournament of champions.

"Oops! Sorry." At least I won't be in a holding pattern much longer. "Do you mind playing on your own for a few minutes? I'll be right back."

Cole doesn't respond, but I know he'll be fine. I grab

my clarinet from the top of my duffel bag and head into the hall.

When I knock at Addy's room, the music stops, but she doesn't answer. I crack open her door.

She shoves her violin into its case and pushes back her chair. "What do you want?"

I open the door the rest of the way and lift my clarinet. "How about a duet?" Her poster of Maximilian Sheek, the celebrity aeronaut, still hangs above her desk. She probably would've taken it down if I'd told her what a coward Sheek was on the Paleo Planet.

"No." The word's a dismissal. She steps to her closet and ducks inside. "Things have changed, Jasper."

She's right. Things *have* changed. I've changed. And even though I've tried to hide it, Addy knows.

"Can we talk, then?" I walk into her room and sit at the foot of her bed.

Addy emerges from her closet, arms crossed tightly against her chest. "What? You've finally decided to tell me all your secrets?"

This isn't going to be easy. "Look, Addy, I get it. You're mad. You have a right to be mad. But I'm in a tough spot. The admiral was crystal clear about one thing: confidentiality. We're under strict orders not to talk about certain things, even with our families."

"But I'm not just family. I'm a Bounder. Isn't Earth Force going to share these secrets with me, too?"

"Yes, but not until next spring, when you go to the Academy."

She throws her hands in the air. "I don't get it. If they're going to tell me anyway, why can't you tell me now? Am I not important to you anymore? How come you're choosing them over me?"

Huh? "That's not what I'm doing! You'll always be important to me, Addy."

"Maybe. But you're loyal to them. To Earth Force. Not to me." Addy's voice grows quiet. She climbs onto her bed—careful to keep a meter between us—and snuggles with a purple elephant Dad won at the fair a few summers back.

This is not going well. How do I make her understand without unloading everything I know about Earth Force? "Look, Addy, it's stuff you need to experience for yourself. And most of it's pretty amazing! As for the other stuff . . . well . . . I'll be there to help you through it."

Addy huffs. "What's that supposed to mean? What other stuff?"

"I told you about the confidentiality order, Ads. And I'm really not trying to be cryptic, it's just . . . there was this girl at the Academy. Mira. There was so much to take in, and

MONICA TESLER

she helped me. I want you to know that I'll be there for you, like Mira was for me."

Addy's face is all crumpled. I can't tell if she's thinking, or fuming, or about to burst out laughing. She squeezes her elephant so tight I'm sure the stuffing is going to explode all over her bed.

"I'm not happy you're keeping secrets," she finally says, "but I'm glad you talked to me. It's hard enough that you're leaving again. I don't want the night before you go to be filled with fighting."

I relax a little. "Good." I push up from the bed, and my mind jumps ahead to my jousting match with Cole.

"Not so fast," Addy says with a sneaky grin on her face. "Let's hear more about this girl. Mira."

Oh no. I should have seen that coming a mile away.

"She's just a friend," I say.

"Sure." Addy's clearly not buying it.

"No, really. She plays the piano, and we played this duet together once, and . . ."

Addy jumps to her feet. All the anger and frustration of moments before, now long gone. "I can't believe you didn't tell me you had a girlfriend! That's the biggest secret of all!"

"Shut up!" I grab a pillow from her bed and deck her with it. "She's not my girlfriend. But maybe this will give you a clue about why I don't tell you everything."

"Fine. She's not your girlfriend." The smirk on Addy's face tells me she doesn't believe it for a second. "Can I meet her tomorrow at the launch?"

Oh geez. No way. The last thing I need is my sister steam-rolling quiet Mira. "No. She's . . . she's not what you'd expect. You can meet her next spring when you come to the Academy."

"Uh-uh, Jasper. I'm meeting her tomorrow, whether you like it or—"

The doorbell rings.

"Who's that?" she says.

"Let's find out!" Saved by the bell, I leap off the bed and dash out of the room.

An Earth Force officer stands at the open door. Mom blocks his way into our apartment. Her hands are on her hips, and she's shaking her head.

"I'm sorry, ma'am," he says. "Those are the orders."

"What's going on, Mom?" I ask.

Mom reluctantly steps aside to let the officer enter. She turns to face me. "It seems you and Cole are departing a bit early for your second tour. Make sure your bags are packed. You're leaving tonight."

"THIS WASN'T THE PLAN," COLE SAYS TO
my dad, who walked in from work to be greeted by Officer
Owens and the news that we're leaving a day early for our
second tour. For reasons Owens either doesn't know or can't
disclose, our pod is meeting at our pod leaders' labs beyond
the scorch zone and departing for space directly from there.

"I know, but there's nothing we can do," Dad says to Cole.
We had just called his parents to let them know of the change,
and Cole could barely talk. Dad assured them we had it all
under control. "Everything will be fine," he tells Cole.

I've seen Cole fired up, but never quite like this. I punch
him on the shoulder. "We need to get changed." When he

doesn't move, I haul him by the sleeve back to my bedroom. "I know this wasn't the plan, but it's the plan now! You heard Officer Owens. We need to go! The hovercar is waiting."

Cole sits on my bed, his back rigid. That's how he always sits in the pod room, like he has a pole through his spine. I have no idea how he can sit super straight like that.

"I don't like it when plans are changed unexpectedly." Cole's teeth are clenched, so he sounds kind of like this creepy ventriloquist that performed at our school once. "It makes me very uncomfortable."

"Obviously," I say, "but I don't get it. You weren't freaked like this during the Youli attack—plenty of Bounders were, and you weren't—and that was certainly unexpected!"

"First, I was, in fact, freaked," he says, thankfully giving the ventriloquist voice a rest. "Second, that wasn't entirely unexpected. When you're on another planet, you have to leave room for a wide range of unknown variables. Here, you don't. When they say you'll depart on a certain date from the Americana East Aeroport, that's the plan."

"Wait . . . what? You're saying an alien attack was in the range of variables you accounted for?" Now *that* has *me* freaked.

"Not really. Just forget it. We need to go, like you said."

Despite this proclamation, Cole shows no signs of moving. He sits on my bed and jiggles his knees while clenching and unclenching his fists. I'm not sure what to do, but then the jiggles start to slow and his hands soften. He takes a deep breath and blows it out like he's trying to extinguish an enormous candle.

A few deep breaths later, he climbs off my bed and rummages through his Academy duffel bag. "Let's see. Cross-country travel? That means dress formals, per Earth Force code, section 17.6."

"Of course." Cole's mind is a deep vault of seemingly useless information that somehow always proves useful.

Ten minutes later, we emerge from our room fully dressed, duffels in hand. As I stand in our living room in my indigo shirt with its orange Earth Force insignia, everything seems right. I feel more confident, more like the real Jasper, than I have all summer.

Addy hops off the couch when we walk in.

She scoots to my side and leans her head against my shoulder. "I'm sorry I was a pain today," she whispers.

"Don't be," I whisper back. "I really wish you were coming with us."

"Me, too." She steps back and nods at Officer Owens. "I can't believe you'd go to all this trouble just to avoid pulling off the elevator prank. Or is this so you don't have to introduce me to your girlfriend?"

This again? "For the hundredth time, I don't have a girlfriend!"

"Does he have a girlfriend?" Addy asks Cole.

"I don't know," Cole says.

"That means yes!" Addy shouts.

"It means no," I say.

"It means I don't know," Cole says. "Don't either of you understand plain English?"

Before Addy can further dissect Cole's literalisms, Dad walks over. "Time to go." He gives me a sad smile before pulling me in for a hug. "I thought we'd have a bit more time, but sometimes quick good-byes are easier."

"See you in six weeks, Dad."

He nods and then points at Mom, who leans against the counter in the kitchen.

"Bye, Mom," I call.

She rushes over, straightens my collar, and smooths the cowlick in my sandy hair that I can never wrestle down as well as she can. "I can't believe how old you look," she says, blinking back tears.

"You know what I look like in uniform, Mom. Same as last tour."

"It's not the uniform. It's your eyes. They look like they've seen things I can't imagine. Things that have made you old and wise."

"I guess that's space travel for you." In other words, I'm certainly not getting into the whole soldier-in-an-alien-war topic right now. "Love you, Mom."

18

"I love you, too, Jasper." She places her hands on my shoulders and bows forward so our foreheads touch. "Be safe," she says, then kisses the top of my head.

Mom's words stay with me as we leave the apartment and board the lift that lowers us along the outside of the apartment tower. The buildings of America East grow tall as we shrink to the ground. You're right, Mom. These eyes have seen things hardly anyone can imagine. And as an officer of Earth Force, I suppose it's my job to keep it that way.

· *EF* ·

The lift opens to our building's loading dock. Behind a second row of supply vehicles, I spy the official Earth Force hovercar. The vehicle looks more like a tank than a standard hover, and it's nothing like the open-air cruisers we rode on the Paleo Planet. The craft is boxy and black, with dark-tinted windows that wrap all the way around. The orange Earth Force insignia—the letters *EF* in the middle of a circle ringed by smaller circles—is stamped on the door. The engine is mounted underneath, so you have to climb a few steps to board. It's the kind of craft that says someone important is inside.

"Nice ride," I whisper to Cole.

He nods. "A Model 330 EX."

The front door opens and another officer gets out. From what I can see when he opens the door, there's a front compartment with the drive console where the officers sit, and a large rear compartment for passengers. The second officer takes our duffels and tosses them in the trunk.

"Time to make pace, kids," Owens continues. "Load up." He opens the side door and gestures for us to enter.

I grab the sides of the hover, haul myself up the first step, and . . . stop.

Another pair of shoes stares back at me from inside the hover—Earth Force cadet standard-issue brown lace-ups connected to indigo-clad legs.

Is Marco making the ride with us? He told me last year he traveled up from Amazonas the night before the launch and stayed at a portside hotel. Maybe they picked him up first.

I duck my head inside the hover.

Mira sits on the bench in front of me.

I freeze.

I can't believe she's here. The last time I saw her, she was walking off the passenger craft at the end of our last tour. I'm not ready to see her. I haven't thought of what to say, how to act. Every scene I've played in my head was at the launch, at the aeroport, not here, in a hover, in my building's filthy basement.

She looks up, and her brown eyes suck me in. I blink to break the trance, but I'm frozen on the hover steps, staring at her tall frame, her thin pink fingers, her long blond braid.

She's tied her hair in indigo ribbons, just like Lucy taught her last tour.

My brain sends the word *Hi!* to my mouth, but as the greeting tries to slip past my lips, my tongue twists in my throat. All that comes out is a strange grunting sound.

Could I be more of an idiot?

Cole whacks my back. "Get in!"

Ouch. Apparently, pain can break a trance. I tear my eyes from Mira for the tiniest of seconds and climb the rest of the way into the hover. Good thing my legs cooperate better than my tongue.

Cole slides in behind me. "Oh," he says. "Hi, Mira."

Mira shifts her gaze to Cole, then locks her eyes on me.

Act normal. Act normal. Act normal. I open my mouth to try the whole speaking thing again, and out comes, "Hi!Howareyou?Howwasyoursummer?" all in one big word-breath.

Mira doesn't reply, but I think a whisper of a smile lifts her lips before she turns to look out the window. I claim the bench across from her, and Cole sits in the rear.

A glass panel separating the compartments slides down. "You kids okay back there?" Owens asks. When Cole and I say yes, he continues, "Once we clear the city limits, we should make good time. We'll reach the base by mid-morning, and then you'll travel to the labs. There's some food and drinks in the cooler. If you need anything, press the intercom. Now try to get some rest."

I get to work surveying the snacks. It gives me something to do other than stare at Mira or dodge my eyes all around the passenger compartment in an effort not to stare at Mira. Meanwhile, the hover lifts off the ground and glides out of the loading dock.

"Check this out!" Cole rolls down the rear window as the hover slides from the garage and onto the road. The buildings rise up hundreds of stories. Our hover is like a tiny fly skimming through the grass, making its way to the sandbox.

After we've been driving for a while, Owen tells us to close the windows. "We've reached the city limits. We don't want the dust from the scorch zone getting in the car."

We settle into our seats. I pass out some carob-coated fruit balls that I found in the cooler. I ate so many of them during our last tour that I steered clear over the summer. But, yeah, they're still delicious.

Our hover runs parallel to the tracks as we enter the scorch zone. Trains fly by in a blur. The full cars haul loads of packaged foods and goods to the distribution centers of Americana East. The empty cars travel back for their next load. Aside from the rails, all I can see is vast, empty land. As we travel on, we pass skeletons of building foundations rising from the ground like bony hands pushing up from the grave.

I don't know how long we've been driving, but it's late, past midnight. Mira is curled up on the bench with her back to me, probably asleep. Cole messes around on his tablet with his headphones on. I'm sure he's playing *Evolution* in 2-D. I could join if I wanted.

Instead, I watch wisps of Mira's long braid blow in the current of the hover's air circulation system until my eyes grow heavy and I fall asleep.

When I wake, we've nearly crossed the farm plots. Green stretches behind us as far as I can see, but the color comes to a full stop directly in front of us at the gates to a city. Behind the city, humongous mountains rise from the Earth.

"I had no idea there was a city here," I say.

"That's not a city," Cole says. "It's a military base."

The window separating the front compartment lowers. "Almost there," Owens says. "You kids will transfer to a helicopter to take you to the labs."

The hovercar stops in front of a building with the Earth Force insignia hanging above the entrance and the flag of each continent flying from poles mounted to the facade. Owens ushers us out of the hover and instructs us to grab our duffels. He escorts us through the building and up to the roof, where a helicopter is waiting.

I pause for a second to look around at the military base, the vibrant farm plots beyond, and then the scorch zones stretching as far as I can see. Behind us, the mountains rise.

Owen gives my back a gentle nudge. Time to get going.

"Safe travels, kids," he says once he's helped us into the copter. "Thank you for your service to the planet."

· *EF* ·

Mira taps on the window as the helicopter closes in on a small collection of buildings built on a mountain ledge. That must be Waters's labs. The helicopter banks and starts its descent.

A two-meter wall surrounds the compound. A lone figure hops along the edge—tall, black hair, copper skin—one wrong step will send him toppling over. There's no mistaking who it is.

A smile tugs at my cheeks. "There's Marco!"

He must spot us as well, because he leaps off the wall and dashes for the helicopter pad. As soon as we land, I open the door, crouch low to avoid the rotor, and run.

Marco grabs my shoulder and pulls me in for a hug. "Ace! I thought you'd never show!"

I nod at the wall where he balanced a moment before. "Your leg must have healed." The last time we saw Marco, he was in a wheelchair after being injured in the battle on the Paleo Planet.

"Eh . . . mostly. It's still shaky at times, but I don't let it hold me up."

MONICA TESLER

"Clearly not," Cole says, coming up behind me.

"Wiki!" Marco says. "Don't be a stranger!" He wraps his arms around Cole, who stays rigid as a board. He's not a hugger.

"And Miss Mira!" Marco says. "Come here, Queenie!"

Surprisingly Mira lets Marco fold her up in a hug. He keeps it gentle and brief.

Gedney hobbles out from a side door. "Hurry, hurry, everyone inside! Lunch is waiting!"

"Hi, Gedney!" I can't believe how good it is to see our assistant pod leader. I race over and give him a hug, careful not to knock him off balance.

"So good to see you, Bounders!" Gedney pats Cole on the head and Mira on the shoulder before waving us all inside. "Grab those bags! Hurry now!"

"He's still all about the rush, huh?" I ask Marco.

"You know Geds. That's just how he is." Marco grabs Mira's bag and heads for the labs.

"Is Lucy here yet?" I ask.

"They had storms in West that delayed her ride," Marco says. "She's supposed to be here any minute."

"Are you coming in or not?" Waters's voice booms from the door. "You're moving so slowly I fear you may give Gedney a heart attack."

I know I missed our pod leader, Waters, but it's not until I hear his voice that I have a sense of how much. My feet rush toward him before my brain even sends the direction to move.

When I reach him, I stare at my shoes, oddly embarrassed and tongue-tied.

His hand clamps down on my shoulder. "It's good to see you, Mr. Adams."

I lift my eyes to his. "You, too, Mr. Waters."

We carry our bags into the building, and Marco leads us to a small bunk room, where we ditch our stuff. An adjoining door takes us to an identical room, where Marco sets down Mira's bag. Next, he shows us the bathrooms and the pantry and the library. Along the way, we pass a few lab employees wearing white coats like Gedney. All of them smile and say something like, "Welcome to the lab, Cole," or "Glad you're staying with us, Jasper," which is a little bit creepy but mostly just friendly.

"I believe your fifth wheel has arrived," one of the lab workers says to us as we head for the kitchen.

We spin back toward the door and rush to the helicopter pad. By the time we get there, a small girl with brown skin and intricate braids tied in orange and yellow ribbons is standing there with her bags, hands on her hips.

"Lucy!" I shout, dashing across the deck.

I stop short because she's giving me the evil eye.

"Take your time coming to say hello, why don't you?" she says.

MONICA TESLER

"Huh?" I can't always figure Lucy out, but apparently, I earn a few points for endearing cluelessness.

She lifts her hands from her hips. "Oh, come here, you silly boy!"

I wrap my arms around her. Lucy seems even smaller than before. I must have grown.

"How was your summer?" she asks.

"Great." I stand there grinning until her glare comes back.

"Oh, *my* summer, you ask? Well, where do I start?" she says and then manages to hug Marco, Cole, and Mira, distribute her bags for us to carry, and lead us into the labs without pausing her monologue. "As soon as we got back, I heard *The New West*—you know, that web show—was looking for beach scene extras. So me and the girls hit up the auditions, and we made it! Did you see it? I'm the one in the pink bathing suit with the purple and orange polka dots. You'll know it's me because I have matching ribbons in my hair."

She pauses for maybe a second, but when we show zero understanding of what she's talking about, she keeps going.

". . . so anyway, I met this new agent who reps Carlita Danton and Letch Bryson. You've heard of them, right? They're all the rage in West, and climbing the charts on the web rankings. So the agent asked me to come in for a meeting, but of course he suggested next week, and I'm here. Or, well, actually, I'll be in space, I assume, so that was a no-go. But when I told him why I couldn't meet, he was super intrigued. He doesn't rep any Bounders, *yet*. He was thinking maybe he could pitch me to a reality show or possibly the talk circuit. Of course, it would all have to be scheduled around our tours of duty, and—"

"Sorry to interrupt—actually, I'm not sorry; interrupting is the only way to say something with you—but I'm starving and the kitchen is this way!" Marco scoops Lucy off the ground and carries her in the direction of what I guess must be the kitchen.

She erupts in giggles. "Put me down, you slimy Youli lover!"

"Just as soon as I get my tofu dog," Marco says.

"Tofu dogs?" I ask. "You've got to be kidding me."

"I *am* kidding, actually," Marco says, returning Lucy to her feet. "You never shut up about how much you hated those things last tour."

"That's because they're disgusting."

"I kind of like them," Cole says as we walk into the kitchen.

"No tofu dogs today," Waters says. He sits at the head of the table with Gedney by his side. "Welcome, Lucy. It's great to have the gang all assembled."

He rises and gives Lucy a big hug, then gestures for the rest of us to grab a seat.

Once we devour a huge tray of tacos and veggie quesadillas and get the *So great to see you* and *How was your summer?* talk out of the way, or actually, once Waters tells Lucy we need to move on to other topics, Waters first looks at Gedney, then sets his serious gaze on all of us. Hopefully that means it's time for answers. Why aren't we on a passenger craft bound for the space station like all the other Bounders? I suppose my secret wish that we'd be just like everybody else this tour has already gone up in smoke.

Waters clears his throat. "Thanks for coming."

Did we have a choice?

"It *is* great to see all of you," he continues, "and, selfishly, I'm happy for the chance to reconnect as a pod without all the distraction of the Academy. There is, however, a practical reason why you're here and not there. It boils down to this: Gedney and I have been working on a new technology that has been fast-tracked by Earth Force. We need to finish preliminary testing before heading to space. We also need some test subjects. Since the timing coincided with the first week of your tour, when pods are supposed to come together for refresher training, we were able to reroute your travels here."

"Let me guess," Marco says. "We're your test subjects?"

WATERS PUSHES BACK HIS PLATE AND
folds his hands neatly on the table. "Yes, Mr. Romero. You
kids are the test subjects."

New technology? And we're the test subjects? I'm not sure
how I feel about that. "What exactly are we testing, Mr. Waters?"

"More on that later," he says.

"Excuse me for offering an unpopular opinion," Lucy says,
"although in all honesty I'm sure my opinion is the popular
one. Don't get me wrong, I *love* my pod mates, but I have
lots of other friends at the Academy, Mr. Waters, and missing
out on the first few days is a real disappointment. What will
everyone think? They'll probably guess I'm sick. Or dead."

"I'm fairly sure they'll figure out you're not dead once they notice our entire pod is missing," Cole says.

"Don't take her seriously, Wiki," Marco says. "She's the Drama Queen, remember?"

Lucy flashes her most innocent face at Waters. "I'm just saying the first few days are mega important for catching up on the goings-on."

"Lucy, your feelings are noted, but we had no choice. The order came from the admiral."

And it looks like that's the final word.

"While we're talking about Earth Force, Mr. Waters," Marco starts, "I missed some stuff at the end of last tour while cooped up in the med room with my broken leg, so maybe you can fill me in now. The Youli . . . Who are they anyway? And why are we fighting them?"

Way to cut to the chase, Marco.

Waters and Gedney exchange a glance. Gedney nods.

"The Youli are a highly advanced alien race," Waters says. "Our conflict with them is largely a territory and policy dispute."

Huh?

"You must know by now that there are strict constraints on how much I can say about this," Waters continues. "Someday you'll learn more, but keep this in mind: not everything is as black and white as Earth Force . . ."

"Jon," Gedney interrupts. "The time. We must continue with the testing."

"Right, then." Waters rises from the table. "Gedney and I are back to the labs, kids. We'll be working into the night. Tomorrow we'll meet as a pod, but the rest of today is yours. I've asked our cook to prepare a picnic for your supper. I highly recommend a hike into the mountains. I doubt you get to enjoy much of Earth's natural beauty where you're from."

Waters and Gedney leave the kitchen together. Once they're gone, I replay Waters's words in my mind. Something seems wrong.

"What do you think he was going to say about Earth Force?" I whisper to my pod mates. "And what about the testing? Doesn't all this feel strange?" I know that's like the world's vaguest question, but I'm not sure how to put what I'm feeling into words.

"Strange?" Marco asks. "As in do you think it's strange that Earth Force transported a group of kids halfway across the continent to test secret technology before shipping them out to space for more training? Our whole life is strange, Ace!"

Cole shrugs. "I suppose it's within the range of expected variables."

"Really?" I ask. Just yesterday he was pacing in my bedroom

about having to leave a day early, and now he thinks this is expected?

"Don't worry, Jasper," Lucy says. "Waters just feels bad about keeping us from our other friends. Speaking of which, if we have to miss the beginning of the tour, we might as well have as much fun as possible. Let's get going on that hike! I have the perfect outfit!"

Lucy drags Mira back to the girls' bedroom, and Marco and Cole take off for our bunks to change out of our uncomfortable dress formals.

I sit at the table, puzzling out what everyone said. They're probably right. We're all adjusting to being back together. Everything will be fine.

· ⧖ ·

We follow Marco through the forest until rocks dot the landscape and the trees fade. I scamper up the last stretch and turn around. We're nowhere near the top of the mountain, but we're definitely high. The ridge stretches for kilometers in either direction. Below, I can just make out Waters's labs between the trees.

I plop down at the foot of a boulder. Marco is stretched out on top, pretending to snooze. A minute later, Cole and Mira arrive.

Lucy finally hauls herself across the rock face, dragging her feet with full drama. "I'm so hot." She rests her hands on her thighs and breathes heavily in her diamond-stitched pink coat with faux-fur collar. Matching pink ribbons flutter in the breeze.

"Why don't you take that coat off?" Marco asks.

"This coat is high-fashion alpine wear! New this season! It was made for the mountains."

"In the *snow*!" Marco says. "For *skiing*! Or at least retro-pretend-you're-going-skiing. I don't think anyone skis any-more. My point is, it's hot, *take your coat off*!" He straightens his short-sleeved Amazonas futbol jersey as if to emphasize that he should get the blue ribbon in the alpine-wear category.

Lucy scrunches up her eyes and glares at Marco. Without acknowledging his obvious victory, she shrugs off her coat and compresses the poufy thing into her backpack. She slumps onto a rock. "Who's carrying the food?"

Marco hops down and tosses everybody a sesame and jelly sandwich, and I'm happy to pass out the apples weighing down my pack.

As we finish our sandwiches, Lucy asks about our birthdays. "Who's the oldest? Who gets to be a teenager first?"

"I'm already thirteen," Cole says. "My birthday was ten days ago."

"How did we not know this?" Lucy asks, scooting right into Cole's space.

"Right before you came to my house?" I ask. "Why didn't

you say something? My mom would have thrown you a party and everything."

"I think you answered your own question, Jasper." Cole crosses to the other side of the boulder, away from Lucy.

"Oh, come on," Lucy says. "Everyone loves a party! Let's have one tonight!"

"No," Cole says.

"I'm with Wiki," Marco says. "No party for me, either."

"When's your birthday?" Lucy asks.

"No comment." Marco picks up a handful of small stones and hurls them down the rocky ridge.

"Fine. But just in case you're wondering, mine is October twelfth, and I love parties!"

"Big shocker," I say.

Marco climbs back on the boulder. "Okay, pod, since we managed to ditch the adults, there are things we need to talk about before we blast off. Sure, Earth Force has huge plans for us. But what are our plans? If we're going to fight the Youli, I say we do it on our own terms."

I laugh. "That's easy to say."

"And impossible to do," Cole says. "How did you get here? Their cars. Their copters. Their spaceships. Their technology."

"Their war," Marco says. "Not ours."

"Now, wait a minute," Lucy says. "I don't exactly agree

with that. It's our war, too. The Youli attacked us on the Paleo Planet. They flung you into a herd of wildeboars, Marco."

"That's just because they wanted us to leave," I say.

Mira lifts her head and locks eyes with mine. If there was ever a question whether Mira heard the aliens' message, that doubt was just erased.

"What do you mean, Ace?" Marco asks. "Why are you two looking at each other like that?"

"It's nothing . . . I mean, maybe I should have told you sooner, but—"

Cole narrows his eyes. "Told us what?"

Great. The last time Cole was mad at me for keeping secrets, he didn't talk to me for almost a week. That is not the way to kick off our second tour.

"Well," I start, "how do I say this . . ." I glance at Mira, as if maybe she'll choose this exact moment to start talking. Yeah, right. This explanation is up to me. Turning back to Marco, I take a deep breath. "Remember how I told you guys that I thought Mira communicated with the alien in the cell block and none of you believed me? Well, I'm pretty sure it's true, because on the Paleo Planet, the Youli gave *me* a message."

"What?" Lucy shouts.

"Keep it down, Drama Queen," Marco says.

"Stop calling me that!"

"Fine, Miss Melodrama." Marco turns to me. "Seriously, J, I can't believe you didn't tell us this."

"When was I supposed to tell you? You were hurt, remember? And then the tour was over and—"

"But how did they give you a message?" Lucy asks in a whisper-yell.

"I know this will sound strange, but the message just appeared in my brain. I guess it's their way of communication."

"You're saying the Youli communicated with you brain to brain? And you're just telling us this today?" Now Marco's shouting, too.

"Oh my god!" Lucy says. "That is just too freaky! I can't deal with this. I can't let those aliens into my brain! And I can't believe they were in *your* brain! And Mira's, too? Is that right, sweetie? How come you—"

"Shut up! All of you just shut up!" Cole jumps to his feet. His hands are balled into fists, and he looks like he might explode. "What was the message?"

"Oh," I say. Of course Cole would focus on what really matters: the facts. *"Leave."*

"Leave?" Lucy asks.

"What do you mean *leave?*" Marco asks.

"Just that. *Leave.* I told Waters about it, and he said it made sense. He said the Youli aren't happy that we've been interfering with the native humanoid population on the Paleo Planet, and they probably want us to leave—stop the tourism initiative, cease mining operations, leave the humanoids alone, just leave."

"Why would the Youli care about the humanoids?" Cole asks.

"You told Waters and not us?" Lucy asks.

"They're concerned about the humanoids, so they throw flaming light balls at them?" Marco asks. "How does that make sense?"

Mira shakes her head and stands. She walks along the ridgeline, away from our group.

"What's with her?" Lucy asks.

"I'm not sure. She probably knows more than me—more than anyone, really. Waters says there's a lot we don't know about the Youli. He also said the battle lines are a bit blurred."

"See!" Marco says. "That proves it! It's just like he started to say at lunch. Not everything is as black and white as they want us to believe. We can't just go along blindly following orders. We need to stay alert. We've only scratched the surface of the Earth Force secrets. And I, for one, am not signing on to be their pawn."

"I think your parents signed you up a long time ago," I say, brushing bread crumbs from my pants and pushing myself up to my feet. "We should go back. We don't want to be heading down in the dark."

"I'll get Mira," Lucy says.

When the girls return, Marco hops up. "First things first, we need a pact and a plan. As for the pact, it's all about the pod now. Right?"

When we agree, he continues, "That means no more secrets, Mr. Hush Hush!" Marco points at me as he talks. "If you tell something to Waters, you tell it to the pod! And as for the plan, we need to do some digging. We have to uncover as much as we can about what Earth Force is really up to. Information is power."

"I don't know how much power our pod is going to wield over Earth Force," I say. "But sure."

"Don't undersell us, Ace. We're their secret weapon, remember?"

"That's true," Cole says. "They need our cooperation, so we do have some power."

"It's settled, then," Marco says. "Hands to the center."

He shoves his hand straight into the middle of our group. I place my palm on top, and the rest of the pod stacks their hands over mine.

"It's all about the pod!" Marco shouts.

"It's all about the pod!" we echo, and our voices ring out across the valley below.

After we break, Mira places a thick, flat rock on the ridge. She gathers more rocks, and together we stack them, building a cairn. No one talks as we work, but we all know the message. Our strength comes from our pod. Our pod is our power.

· E_F ·

By the time we make it down from the ridge and out of the forest, the sun has nearly slipped beneath the horizon. When we reach the labs, Marco buzzes security, and the gate swings open. Cole and Lucy follow Marco into the compound. I glance around for Mira, expecting her to be right behind me. Instead, she's waltzing across a field of wildflowers that borders the labs. Just as she's about to fade into the dusk, she glances back at me and smiles.

"You coming?" Cole asks, holding the lab door open for me.

"In a minute—you go ahead."

I wait until the door closes, and then jog across the wildflowers. I can barely see three meters in front of me. It's like the night sky sucked up the last light from the end of day and drowned the world in its darkness. Finding Mira in this field is a lost cause, unless she wants to be found.

I'm about to give up when something brushes my ankle.

My eyes focus, and I can just make out an arm stretching out of the grass.

Mira is there, lying on the ground. She twirls her fingers in the air. I place my palm in hers and kneel. When she shows no sign of sitting up, I stretch out long beside her, careful not to let go of her hand. I don't want to come up with an excuse for grabbing it again.

We lie still for a long time, breathing the sweet smell of violets and listening to insects scuttle between blades of grass. Above us, the night wields its glitter paintbrush. Before long, the sky is filled with a million pinpricks of light.

I squeeze her hand. *Hi, Mira.* I was such a moron when I first saw her in the hovercar, but now we've kind of settled in, and I'm happy for a quiet moment to connect.

I wish a whole string of words like *Oh, Jasper, I'm happy to see you!* or *I missed you so much this summer!* would magically appear in my brain, but the only things in my mind are my own fantasies. My disappointment only lasts a moment, though, because Mira squeezes back.

When she tightens her fingers around my hand, I'm filled with a tingly warmth like a cross between a cup of hot chocolate and that weird sensation you get when your leg falls asleep, but in a good way.

I don't know what to expect tomorrow—who knows what will happen with the tech testing or the second tour—but this moment is close to perfect.

WHEN MIRA AND I ENTER THE LAB
building around midnight, most of the lights are out. I don't
want to wake anyone, so I don't bother flipping any switches
as we open the door and slowly make our way down the dark
hall toward the bunk rooms.

When someone speaks my name, Mira flinches, and I
nearly jump out of my skin.

"Who's there?" I whisper.

A tiny light turns on. It's attached to the end of a stylus.
And the stylus is in Waters's hand. "Relax," he says. "I've been
waiting for you."

A dozen thoughts rush through my brain. Are we in

trouble? Is he mad that I was alone with Mira? Were we out too late?

"This way," he says. He leads us down a small staircase and through a heavy metal door armed with a security system. With the only light the tip of his stylus, I can hardly see a thing.

My heart races. I'm not sure why I'm so nervous, but I feel like something huge is about to happen. And I'm not too sure it's something good. Right now, Waters is a man with a mission. I tighten my grip on Mira's hand. I wish I knew what she was thinking.

"Here we are." Waters stops in front of another metal door with a security panel. He punches in a code and the door latch disengages. He walks into the room and turns on the light.

Bright lights illuminate what can only be the heart of Waters's and Gedney's laboratory. The place is huge. There are rows of monitors in freestanding carrels or mounted to the walls. Large glass enclosures house petri dishes and samples. Diagrams are posted along one wall, all labeled and color-coded. The center diagrams show anatomical pictures of a Youli, both from the outside and the inside.

I head in that direction, eager to get a closer look. I'm nearly at the diagram when Mira grabs my arm. She's standing in front of a glass specimen box I somehow missed as I traipsed across the lab. In the box, a Youli hand and forearm are suspended on a clear pedestal. Tiny sensors and wires are attached to the skin.

That must be the hand they used to make the gloves. My fingers run along my own forearms, and goose bumps blossom beneath my touch. I've known the gloves came from alien technology for a while, I just never fully processed what that meant until now, when I'm face-to-face with an alien hand.

A second box is filled with other Youli body parts. And a third contains something that's neither human nor Youli. If I had to guess, it looks like a reptilian arm. A robotic limb rests beside it.

"Over here," Waters calls from the other side of the lab.

We follow his voice to a desk in the corner that's walled off from the main lab. A corduroy blazer rests on the chair back. A leather blotter is barely visible beneath a mound of ragged-edged paper, fancy pens, and empty mugs. This must be Waters's personal work space.

Behind the desk is a table with a mounted screen hooked up to a microscope. A pair of bounding gloves lies on the table. They look exactly like our gloves, except they're covered with hundreds of minisensors like the Youli hand in the glass case. A clear compartment about half a meter square sits on the other side of the microscope. The only thing in the compartment, suspended in the exact center without wires or gears to keep it in place, is a sphere approximately the size of a golf ball.

Waters steps up to the compartment and activates a mini-crane mechanism that sits on top. Like the impossible prize grabber at the fair we go to each summer, the crane swings out into the compartment and opens its tiny claw. Controlling the claw with a touch screen, Waters slowly lowers the metal fingers until it clamps down on the sphere. With a flick of a finger, Waters raises the crane, and the little sphere, out of the box and into his waiting hand.

He laughs. "We go to such great lengths to keep this orb safe and then I just coil it in my palm. Good thing Gedney isn't here. He'd be mortified."

"What is it?" I ask.

"We're getting there," he says. "But a few words first. Typically I'm the last person to lecture about confidentiality, but I have to change things up today. What I'm about to share with you has to stay between us. And I mean between the three of us. I suppose you can talk to Gedney, too. He's bound to discover what I've done, not that he'll be too happy about it. So give it a day or two, and then you can assume that Gedney knows. But that's it. The four of us have to keep this in the deepest of vaults."

A chill runs across my skin. What is this all about?

He keeps saying *us* and *we*, but he's really instructing *me* not to talk. Mira's not going to tell anybody, and he's the one issuing the gag order. So, yeah, he can dress this up all nice like we have some three-way secret, or maybe four-way if you count Gedney, but the reality is he's making sure Jasper Adams keeps quiet about whatever's in his hand.

What could be so secret that he hasn't told Gedney? He even implied that Gedney would disapprove. This doesn't feel right. I glance back at the door, thinking that maybe I should make a run for it.

But then what? I'm in Waters's labs in the middle of the Rocky Mountains. It's not like I could execute an escape plan. Plus, this is Waters. If there's one adult in all the world who I trust, it's him. He wouldn't put us in danger.

Would he?

I glance from Waters to the orb to the glove with all the sensors on his desk. "Does this have to do with the gloves?"

"In a manner of speaking." He pulls a pair of tweezers from his front pocket. Then he presses his finger into the top of the orb, and it pops open. With a steady hand, he inserts the tweezers into the sphere and extracts a shiny green square no bigger than the head of a nail.

"What is that?" I ask.

Waters sets the sphere down on a metal stand next to the microscope. He flips on a super intense light, and holds the green square underneath. The iridescent material glistens like it's made of water.

"Gedney told me you guessed where the glove technology came from," Waters says to me. "What I'm holding here is different tech, but the origins are the same."

"You mean you stole it from the Youli?"

"I wouldn't use the word *steal*," he says. "*I* certainly didn't steal it. The materials came into Earth Force's possession earlier this year, and we took advantage of those resources."

"Wait a second, are you talking about the Youli prisoner at the space station?"

Waters straightens, and for a moment his relaxed, professorial manner is replaced by something commanding. "No more questions. Like I said, this is highly confidential. You know too much already."

I take a step back, and so does Mira.

Waters seems to catch his own behavior. He relaxes his shoulders and lowers onto the spinning chair behind his desk. He swivels around to face us and smiles.

Now I'm suspicious. It's like he's campaigning for something and we're his targets.

"Let me get to the point," he says. "Both of you have communicated with the Youli—isn't that right, Jasper?"

Heat rises to my cheeks as I steal a glance at Mira. I hope she's not mad I shared that with Waters. I nod.

"And I suspect it's not the first time you've experienced brain-based communication, at least in its basic forms, am I right?"

"What do you mean, 'brain-based communication'?" I ask.

"Well, take your sister, Addy. Do you ever know what she's going to say before she says it? Or have you ever communicated to her without words, maybe to keep your parents in the dark? Or have you even simply walked into a room and immediately sensed the energy—joy, anger, boredom? Our years of testing reveal that both you and Mira are highly advanced in this way. Lots of Bounders are, but the two of you test particularly high. The fact that the Youli communicated with you only serves to confirm it."

He's right, of course. That happens all the time with Addy. It's just how things have always been. When Mira touched my brain, it had felt so personal, so private, I'd never connected the dots that it was basically the same thing as my bond with Addy.

Does Waters know about me and Mira?

"Have the two of you ever communicated brain to brain?" he asks in a trying-to-act-casual tone.

He's guessed. But he doesn't know for sure.

Mira slips her hand in mine. I don't say a word.

"I'll take that as a yes," he says. "I may not be very empathic, but I'm not too shabby at nonverbal communication." He stands and lifts the tweezers so the tiny green square is right in front of us. "These patches expedite the growth of new neural pathways in the brain, particularly those aimed at communication. I'll just shave a bit of hair at the base of your neck, place the patch, and we'll be good to go. Once the patch is planted, your ability to engage in brain-to-brain communication should improve dramatically. The effect should be immediate, and will only continue to expand as the neural pathways multiply."

"I don't understand," I say. "You want Mira and me to wear these patches?"

"Yes. The two of you are by far the best candidates, even without your . . . connection. But I won't pretend that doesn't make it all the better."

My cheeks burn again. What does he mean, our "connection"? I shake it off and try to stay focused. "But what exactly is that patch? It looks just like Youli skin. Wait a second, *is* that Youli skin?"

"Not precisely. They're more like technologically enhanced Youli skin cells."

My stomach stirs, and my sesame and jelly sandwich threatens to resurface. I can't believe he wants to implant Youli cells in my brain stem. That can't be good. "Is it safe?"

"Absolutely."

"Have you tested it?"

"No. But none of the Bounders have had any trouble with the gloves' neural interface. This shouldn't be different."

Shouldn't be. How come I don't find that reassuring at all? "Why are you asking us to do this? Why is it so important?"

"There are many things I can't tell you, but let me say this: intragalactic relations are far more vast and complicated than you can possibly imagine."

Intragalactic relations? What is he talking about? Is he suggesting there are other aliens we don't know about? "What do you mean? There's us and the Tunnelers; we have a treaty. And then there are the Youli, who, apparently, we're fighting. What else is there?"

Waters runs his fingers through his hair and shakes his head. He must have thought he'd have no problem pushing this on us. "You know what Earth Force wants you to know. Or, actually, you kids know a bit more, but it's still just the tip of the iceberg."

If only Mira could help out. It's just me and Waters, and he can talk me in circles. It never mattered before, because I trusted him. Now I'm not so sure. "I don't understand. Why can't you tell us what's going on? How can you ask us to do this without explaining what's at stake?"

"What's at stake?" Waters asks. "There is more at stake than you can possibly imagine. In a few weeks, a summit . . . no, you don't need to know that. Let me keep it simple: we need to be able to communicate with the Youli if we are to achieve peace."

As soon as the word *peace* leave his lips, Mira steps forward. She turns her back to Waters and lifts her hair.

Peace? Waters is hoping to end the war? He wants to talk peace with the Youli and use Mira and me as interpreters, brain-to-brain go-betweens?

And Mira's ready to sign up for the job?

"Excellent," Waters says. Before I can process everything that's happening, he shaves a spot on Mira's head and applies the patch. "Sit down for a few minutes, Mira. Give the patch a chance to bind with you. Ready, Jasper?"

"Ummm . . . not really. I'm not a huge fan of having alien technology implanted in my brain. And why can't I tell my friends? Aren't they going to know something's up? You already told them there was a new technology you needed us to test."

"That's different. We'll talk about the pod testing tomorrow. The patches are only for you and Mira. Your pod mates don't need to know about them. They *can't* know."

I take another step back. Mira sits on the floor. Her head is tipped, and her eyes are closed. Is she okay?

I'm about to kneel and check on Mira, when Waters puts his arm around my shoulder and steers us to the other side of his work space. "I wouldn't ask unless this was really important, Jasper." He bends down so his eyes are level with mine. Then he whispers, "You'll be able to reach her."

Mira. This all comes down to Mira. We may be the key to peace in his mind, or even intragalactic relations, whatever that means, but Mira is the key to me. And he has me unlocked. There never was any real doubt that I'd do this. I'd never pass up the chance to communicate with Mira, and Waters knows it.

He shouldn't have said that. He shouldn't have invoked Mira to get me to do this. He crossed a line. He may not be one of the bad guys, but he's not one of the good guys either.

My throat tightens, and tears threaten to spill out of my eyes. How can he ask us to do this? How can *he* ask us to do this? I've come to expect this from Earth Force. But not Waters. Please, not Waters.

Marco was right this afternoon. It's all about the pod now. Maybe I'll sign on for the patch, maybe I don't have a choice, but I'm not doing it blindly. I swallow hard and squeeze back the tears. I'll take his bait, but I won't let him think he outsmarted me.

Waters stands in front of me, holding the orb with the Youli skin patches inside. I lift my eyes and look him square in the face. I want him to know that I understand the exchange, that I know he's manipulating me, that the choice I'm making is mine: I'll wear the patch in order to communicate with Mira.

He won't even look at me. His gaze is fixed on the clear sphere in his palm. He picks up the tweezers and extracts another patch. "What'll it be, Jasper?"

I take a deep breath so I'm sure my voice won't crack. "Let's get this over with."

I turn around so he has easy access to my head.

To my brain.

The clippers buzz the back of my scalp. Next, I feel a tickle, then a prickle, then a bit of pressure as Waters fits the patch.

Then I don't feel anything at all. With the gloves, I didn't feel anything at first either. But I just had Youli skin cells implanted in my brain stem—shouldn't I feel something?

Nada. Zip. Zilch.

Big, fat zero.

"Give it a few minutes," Waters says.

"What's it supposed to feel like?"

"I have no idea."

"Well, that's comforting."

I sink down next to Mira so our shoulders touch. I try to sense my neural connection like I do with my gloves, but there's nothing there. I even try my silly Mira mind talk. *Hello? Anyone there? This is Jasper calling. Mira, you hear me? Breaker, breaker one-nine, over?*

Maybe Waters lied. Maybe this patch has nothing to do with brain-to-brain communication. Maybe he's actually trying to control our minds. That could be it. Seriously. I don't trust him anymore. Why should I believe anything he says?

But I can't think about that. There's too much to think about already. Not to mention I'm exhausted. I barely slept last night in the hover as we drove from Americana East. Was that only last night? So much has happened since then.

"Anything?" Waters asks.

I shake my head.

Then Mira slides her hand along the ground and laces her pinkie with mine. As her finger presses against my skin, I feel her words in my brain.

Don't tell him anything.

It takes every ounce of control not to jump out of my skin. If I freak out, Waters will know we've made the connection. I focus on keeping my breath even and acting as disappointed as possible.

What comes next from Mira are pictures, impressions, feelings. The sky above us in the field. Wonderment. Our duet in the music room. Joy. The press of her cheek against my shoulder when I survived the jump off the Youli ship. Relief.

I feel her making words in her mind. She's struggling, like

words are not the way she likes to communicate. Then, she says with exquisite sharpness:

It's just you and me now, yes?

I close my eyes and think as hard as I've ever thought before.

Yes, Mira, a thousand times yes. It's you and me. Always.

THE NEXT MORNING, OUR POD MEETS UP
with Gedney, who leads us down the stairs and into the laboratory where Waters is waiting. I don't say anything about having been down here last night. And, of course, Mira doesn't either. I haven't tried to brain talk with her yet today. I'm waiting for her to make the first move. Plus, I don't want my pod mates to suspect anything. I already feel guilty for keeping the secret.

Cole starts in with questions about everything in the lab, but Waters brushes him off. "We'll have time for that later. Follow me." He drags Cole away from the glass case with the Youli hand and heads to another door at the back of the laboratory guarded by a standard eye-scanner security panel. "You know the drill. Step right up, lean in for the scan."

"What's behind door number one?" Marco asks.

When we've all been scanned, Waters enters a numeric code that unbolts the door, then stands back to let us enter. "See for yourself."

The room is dark, almost entirely devoid of light. A slight air current brushes my skin.

"The Ezone," Cole says as we all walk inside.

"Basically, yes," Waters says. "This is the original Ezone, or officially, the Beta Entanglement Zone."

"So the BEzone?" Marco asks.

Waters laughs. "BEzone, huh? Sounds about right. And you're due for some practice."

Gedney distributes our gloves, and we spend the morning practicing ports and basic bounding around the compound. After a short break for lunch, we meet Waters and Gedney back in the BEzone. In the center of the room, they've set up a table, and on the table rests a black briefcase.

"On to new technology!" Waters says. "Let's bound right in."

Bound right in? Ugh. That joke is so last tour.

"Gather round, don't be shy," Gedney says. "Now this is just a prototype. It wasn't supposed to be out of beta-testing mode for a few more months. All we hear for years and years is *ready the gloves, ready the gloves*. But now the gloves are ready, and they rush us on to this. Hurry, hurry, hurry. Always in such a—"

"Let's spare them the Earth Force politics," Waters says. "Show them."

Gedney opens the briefcase. On the top is a touch screen. I'm not sure what's on the bottom. It looks like a squishy black pad.

"This is a BPS—Bound Positioning System," Gedney says. "It's portable, capable of being carried directly into battle—or, ummm, capable of being carried anywhere really."

"Carried into *battle*?" Lucy says. "Now, wait a second—"

"That's just one potential use," Waters says, glaring at Gedney. "And not at all our focus today."

"Yes, but what does it do?" Cole asks.

"That's a most excellent question," Gedney says. "The BPS allows you to bound anywhere so long as we know the coordinates. Until now, your bounds have been limited to sites within visual contact or where you've previously activated your gloves." He presses a button and the BPS screen lights up. "Now, once we enter the coordinates, all you have to do is press your gloved palms on the BPS sensors, and you'll be able to open a port and bound to the coordinates."

Bound anywhere in the galaxy from coordinates? That is amazing!

"I know you're the mad scientist and all," Marco says, "but that sounds a little too good to be true."

Maybe it is too good to be true. They haven't tested it. That's why we're here. The whole reason we were rerouted to the labs for the start of our second tour sits in that black briefcase.

"We're your guinea pigs?" Lucy asks. "Uh-uh. I'm not doing it. I didn't sign on for this. What if the BPS doesn't work? We'll be lost in space!"

"I've built in a fail-safe," Gedney says. "If the bound doesn't succeed, the BPS should be able to pull you back."

"*Should* be able to?" I ask. "That's not entirely comforting."

Mira gently brushes my arm. A picture of her placing her hands on the sensors fills my brain.

No way. I do not want her going first.

"No!" I shout. The others look at me, probably waiting for me to add some more words to my veto. Oops. I shouldn't have said that out loud.

Yes, comes her reply. I'm filled with feelings of trust hovering around an image of Gedney as Mira steps forward and presents her gloved palms.

"See!" Waters says. "There you have it, kids! A believer!"

Gedney smiles warmly. "Thank you, Mira." He transfers data from his handheld to the BPS touch screen. "You're not going far. Just to another room within the labs. One of our lab assistants is waiting there for you."

Mira lays her hands on the sensors. She closes her eyes, and a second later her body jerks. My brain reacts. It's a strange sensation, sort of like sorting candies by color. Jumbled input falls into place.

Mira steps away from the table and opens her port. Seconds later, she bounds.

I expect to feel something, anything, inside my mind, but I don't. Mira could be anywhere—or nowhere—but my brain can't find her. I hold my breath.

"Mira made it," the lab assistant says over Waters's com pin.

Thank goodness. I'm about to volunteer to go next, but Marco beats me to it. He hardly waits for Gedney to reset the system before he presses his palms into the BPS.

I let Cole go after Marco, because I can tell he needs to get it over with. Then Lucy elbows her way in front. Before I know it, it's just me, Water, and Gedney gathered around the BPS.

My gloved hands hover above the sensors, but I can't bring myself to press down. Why is it okay to use kids to test dangerous technology? Two days in a row I'm the test subject of the most classified technology on Earth. It's *not* okay, and I want Waters to know it.

I lift my right hand and rub the back of my head. "New technology, huh?"

Waters is going to be furious, but I don't care. He said Gedney would figure it out eventually.

Gedney stares at me with a perplexed look on his face. I keep my hand on the back of my neck and meet his gaze with a grin. His expression shifts as the truth slowly dawns on him. First he questions, then he processes, then he spins on Waters.

"Jon! Tell me you didn't do this!"

Waters shoots me a nasty look. I smile back.

"You know it had to be done," he says to Gedney.

"Those patches were not ready! We have no idea what they can do! And we are completely unaware of the side effects!"

"Well, we'll find out soon," Waters says.

"Over my dead and decaying corpse!" Gedney shouts.

Maybe I should be a bit freaked about side effects, but this is awesome! I have never seen Gedney so mad!

"I will take that patch off his head this very day!" he continues.

"You won't," Waters says. "And you might ask Jasper if that's what he wants. I think he's already experienced some of the more positive side effects of the patch."

The perplexed look returns for a second, only to be cast aside as Gedney throws his hands in the air. "Mira, too? You didn't!"

"I had to," Water says with a sad smile.

Gedney braces himself against the table. He shakes his head. "Has she communicated?"

When Waters doesn't answer, Gedney turns to me. "Jasper? Has she?"

"No," I lie, remembering Mira's words from last night: *It's just you and me now.*

I place my hands on the sensors, build my port, and bound.

· *EF* ·

We spend the afternoon bounding to BPS coordinates. By the time dinner rolls around, we must have bounded to every room in the entire lab complex, including storage closets, the garbage bay, and even the bathrooms. Couldn't they have picked some better destinations? If we can bound anywhere in the known universe, why do we have to see where Gedney poops?

One thing is for sure: bounding makes me hungry. And when I'm hungry, I'm not capable of thinking about anything else, which tonight is a good thing. Even though we're dining with Waters, Gedney, and all the lab assistants, I'm able to push out of my mind all thoughts of the secret brain patch and their technology testing ethics and just eat. Pizza. Lots and lots of pizza. I lose count after seven slices.

After dinner, all of us head back to the boys' bunk room to play cards. When I make a particularly dumb move in the game, something tickles the edge of my brain, almost like static electricity. I shake my head, but it's there again, a gentle buzz, a little tickle. It feels like a laugh without any noise.

Mira stares at her cards with a colossal grin on her face.

Is she laughing at me?

My brain buzzes again. Now that I know what it is, a smile

spreads across my face. Maybe I shouldn't be so pumped that Mira is laughing at me, but I can't shake the excitement of our connection.

Lucy looks from me, to Mira, to me again. Then she smirks. "Jasper, you and Mira were out pretty late last night."

Great. The Jasper–Mira rumors are starting up again, and we haven't even met up with the other cadets. How am I supposed to stop the stories without breaking my promise to Waters that we'll keep the patches secret? And how can I keep everything from my pod mates in the first place? We're supposed to have a pact.

Wait a second . . . Waters only said we couldn't talk about the brain patches. Maybe there's a way to cut off the Jasper–Mira talk and clue them in on Waters without breaking my confidentiality agreement.

"Actually, I'm glad you reminded me," I say. "Mira and I were out late because we were talking with Waters. He didn't tell us much, but I think we have a head start on our Earth Force information mission."

"Ace! You've been holding back! Give us the goods!" Marco says.

No! Mira's thoughts flicker in my brain.

I send her a brain message that I'm not going to mention the patches, but I don't know if she gets it. I'm trying to be discreet, and I'm not too good at brain talk yet.

"Well, like I said, there's not much to tell." I shuffle the cards and start to deal. "But he did say that intragalactic relations are far more complicated than we can imagine. And he let one word slip."

Cole leans forward. "What word?"

"*Summit.*"

"Summit?" Lucy says. "You mean like *mountaintop*? What does that have to do with anything?"

Cole hops to his feet. "*Summit* can also mean *meeting*. Maybe there's an important meeting coming up! You're sure there wasn't anything else?"

No! No! No!

Got it, Mira. I keep my eyes on the cards, not wanting to look my pod mates in the eyes as I lie. "No, nothing else."

"Well, that's a start," Marco says. "We have to find out everything we can about this summit. Keep digging and share everything we learn. It's all about the pod now."

Marco's words work wonders for my guilt complex. If my pod mates ever find out about the brain patches, they'll know I made a conscious choice not to tell them.

When I had the chance, I chose Waters over my pod.

· *EF* ·

The next few days are basically the same—bound, eat, sleep—with a few minutes of free time before bed to hang out. Marco, Cole, and I talk a bit about the summit Waters mentioned and what it might mean. We talk about the Youli war and how we think the admiral plans to use the Bounders in battle. But we mostly chat about other stuff: our favorite levels in *Evolution*, how awesome it would be if Regis didn't show up at the EarthBound Academy this tour, bets about how many meals of tofu dogs they'll feed us at the space station.

Gedney tweaks the BPS. We improve our bounding skills. Waters alternates between being super friendly and being completely distant. Lucy says he's stressed about having to roll out the BPS under the tight timetable. Marco thinks he's tired of jumping through hoops for the admiral. Cole says he hasn't noticed Waters's split personalities.

I've tried to ask Mira about it, but I haven't had much luck. Sometimes she'll respond, but it's usually more of a feeling or an impression than an actual sentence. Other times, she'll act like she hasn't heard me. Maybe she hasn't. Or maybe she's just not used to communicating.

It's not like we have that much quality time together. Waters works us all day. And as soon as we break, Mira usually takes off. She's always needed alone time.

So when Waters or Gedney asks me about the brain patch, I don't feel bad saying that Mira hasn't communicated. She keeps pretty quiet. And since that's what we're all used to, it's pretty easy not to think about the little piece of Youli implanted in my neck. It's also pretty easy not to think about the huge secret I'm keeping from my pod mates.

What's on everyone's minds is this: When are we shipping out to the space station? Despite many attempts to get information out of Waters, most initiated by Lucy, he's refused to say a word. Finally, when we finish training on our fourth day at the labs, Waters announces that we'll be leaving in the morning.

"Yippee!" Lucy squeals. "I can't believe it! We're finally going to see our friends! And the other teachers! And our pod rooms! And the Ezone! I mean, the BEzone is great and all, but the Ezone is where we truly became Bounders!"

"Actually, there's been another change in plans," Waters says. "You won't be spending your tour at the space station."

Huh? We're not going to the space station?

"What do you mean?" Cole's voice breaks, and he jumps to his feet.

"Take a seat, Mr. Thompson. You'll be with the other cadets. In fact, you'll meet up with them tomorrow. They're already at your destination. Gedney and I will join you there in a few days, just as soon as we put the finishing touches on the BPS."

"No more secrets, Mr. Waters," Marco says. "Where are we going?"

"Tell them, Gedney," Waters continues.

"The EarthBound Academy will be training cadets on Gulaga this tour," Gedney says.

"Wait a minute . . . where?" I ask.

"The Tunneler home planet," Waters says. "The admiral decided the best way to train you is to simulate missionlike conditions on an alien planet. They've structured a pod competition on the frozen, rocky surface of Gulaga that will challenge your skills in teamwork, strategy, and, frankly, survival. Most of the cadets are already there. Shortly after you arrive, the Tundra Trials will begin. Now get packed. You leave first thing in the morning."

6

SLAMMED!

Stuffed!

Tofu-Puffed!

My lungs leap at the next breath, and I pull the sweet, cool air into my chest.

The best thing I can say about the ride in the bounding ship is that we made it. I'm glad Earth Force isn't training me to be a conventional pilot. Sure, I get the creepy crawlies when I bound with my gloves, but that's a lot better than all the puffing and stuffing. Plus, I can never ride in a ship without thinking of the Incident at Bounding Base 51 and the lost aeronauts.

"Welcome to the Earth Force Gulagan Space Dock," a voice blasts over the internal speakers.

The *tick tick tick* of the spider crawlers mean the hatch is opening. As we unbuckle our harnesses, our pilot tells us we have thirty minutes to catch the descent, and that our luggage will be brought down on a later ride.

Catch the descent? That means we have half an hour before the next space elevator trip from the docking platform to the planet's surface. I have to admit, I'm pretty freaked about the space elevator. I've seen it on the webs, and we watched a vid about it on Cole's tablet last night once we knew we were headed to Gulaga, but something about it gives me the creeps. It's like a giant finger pointing into space. I can't help thinking how easy it would be to snap it in two.

As I climb out of the bounding ship, there's no mistaking that we're very far from Earth. It's not the building materials, or the ships, or the equipment that look particularly alien. It's the company. Aside from a few human Earth Force officers, the flight deck is crowded with Tunnelers. Dozens of Tunnelers scurry about, hunched forward with their long snouts angled toward the ground. Some of them have Earth Force uniforms, like the Tunnelers at the space station, but most of them wear brown sacks. Okay, I'm sure they're not actual sacks, but they look like big burlap bags flipped upside down with holes for the Tunnelers' furry heads and arms. I'm no fashionista like Lucy, but I would never step outside my apartment wearing something that ugly.

I climb down the scaffolding and get lost in the crowd of fur. They busy about the flight deck, shuffling around with their signature hunch, talking in their guttural grunts, checking readings, performing maintenance.

A growl sounds at the back of my head: *Kleek. Arrrgh. Garragh. Korreek.*

I spin around and come face-to-face with a sack-wearing Tunneler.

Her voice box translates: "Please come with me for your descent to the planet." She waves her arms, herding us off the flight deck.

Cole wastes no time hitting her up for information. "What is the maximum velocity of the elevator?"

"I don't want to know," I say before her voice box kicks in. I jog ahead to walk with Marco and Mira in the front of our group.

Inside, the space dock is a cross between the small bounding bases we've visited and the huge space station where the EarthBound Academy was headquartered last tour. Outside is a different story. Instead of having a bunch of smaller buildings connected by a tube system, the dock is all housed in one giant building that's anchored to Gulaga by the space elevator shaft.

Our Tunneler escort hurries us through the halls. With

every turn, we pick up more people—Tunnelers and humans—everyone rushing to the space elevator. We move with the crowd until our escort stops short. She lines us up against the wall and waves us into a huddle.

"We are about to enter the elevator bay," she says through her voice box. "For some, this can cause feelings of vertigo or general sensory overload. I am warning you in advance. Take time to adjust upon entering."

Sensory overload? Was that warning directed at me personally? It sure feels like it. I can barely stand the florescent lights and reflective chrome in the space station. How am I going to tolerate something known to cause sensory overload? I'm not even sure what vertigo is, but I bet I'm candidate number one.

The Tunneler presses on, but I let the others pass. As the doors slide open, I brace.

When I catch a glimpse of the elevator bay, I grab the doorframe and hang on for dear life because one more step and I'll fall through the cosmos.

Calm down, Jasper. Deep breaths. I squeeze my eyes closed and gulp air. Slow. Steady. Just like Mom taught you. Air in. Air out. Repeat.

Tunnelers stream through the door, grumbling and bumping my shoulder.

You're okay. You're not going to tumble through space. All

those people went through that door, and they're just fine. You can do this.

I soften my eyelids to a squint. The elevator bay is a huge octagonal room made of clear plastic. Stepping into the room is like stepping into space itself.

Lucy is beside me, another victim of sensory overload. She clasps my hand. "On the count of three?"

I nod. When we reach three, I take a tiny step. My stomach drops to my feet. I feel like I'm falling. I step back and grab the wall.

Grunts rise up behind me. There's a bottleneck at the door, and Lucy and I are making it worse. I may not speak Gulagan, but I know they're yelling at us. A few shouts in English make it crystal clear.

"Keep moving!"

"I've got to catch this! Go!"

"What the . . . ?"

I need to move, only nothing's moving. I can't even get my lungs to move right, and any second now that's going to cause a mighty big problem.

Come on.

Mira? I search the elevator bay and spot her across the room.

You can do it.

Geez. I'd rather not have an audience inside my head for my sensory meltdown. Talk about embarrassing. But also possibly helpful? I feel a bit braver and a little less queasy. Maybe Mira zapped me with a special brain enhancer, the courage variety pack, the sensory overload antidote. All I know is I'm making jokes (if only in my mind), and I no longer feel like I'm reeling through space.

I gingerly step farther into the room. I will myself not to look down, but I last only a second before dropping my gaze to the clear plastic floor. Hundreds of kilometers below me is Gulaga. Seeing the planet grounds me, probably like seeing the actual ground from my building's elevator at home.

Long, winding crevices crisscross the planet's rocky plains. Where the elevator reaches the surface, a blotch of green dots the brown ground like a spot of spilled paint. That must be the aboveground leaf system for the subterranean tuber gardens. Almost all the Tunnelers on the planet live within fifty kilometers of those gardens in the metropolis of Gulagaven. The rest of the planet is too cold to support plant or animal life, although there are lots of legends about the creatures that prowl the darkest tundra of Gulaga.

Lucy, now a pace behind me, grabs my arm. "Doesn't this remind you of our first time in the Ezone? I couldn't get my bearings, and we got tangled up and tumbled to the floor. Eventually you pulled it together and helped me up. This is just like that, right?"

Lucy is freaked. Okay, we're both freaked. But maybe if I

focus more on helping her than on hyperventilating, it will benefit both of us.

"Right, Jasper?" she asks again, through gasps of breath. "Right?"

"It's kind of like the Ezone," I say as I link my arm with hers and bring us one step at a time farther into the giant elevator bay. "It's really disorienting, that's for sure. But it's also incredibly cool." Another few steps take us solidly inside. "Don't you think?"

Four hallways lead to the elevator bay at right angles, like the directional signals of a compass. The shaft is in the center of the room surrounded by banks of monitors and other equipment. The rest of the bay circles the shaft like a donut constructed of clear plastic, so no matter where we look, we see open space or the planet beneath us.

Lucy hasn't answered my question. The fact that she isn't talking is completely un-Lucylike and a very bad sign. I spin to face her, taking both her hands in mine. "Hey! Just think what all your friends at home will say when you tell them about this! What about that agent? I bet he'll definitely want to represent you once he hears you've ridden on the Gulagan space elevator."

Her eyes are glassy and unfocused. "I just can't do it. Maybe you can, but I can't. We'll be expected to bound to places like this! What if I miss, Jasper? What if I don't open my port in the right place and I end up out there?!" She waves her hands at the floor, the walls, the entire windowed elevator bay revealing the eternity of space.

Leave it to Lucy to find room for drama even in her moment of panic. But it's clear to me now. For Lucy, this isn't about the space elevator. This is one of those big-picture Bounder moments. The kind when suddenly the enormity of your duty to wield dangerous technology, to fight in an alien war, to protect your planet, comes rushing at you without warning. I know because I've had those moments.

Unfortunately, I'm not the best at pep talks, especially when I'm nearly on the ledge myself.

A Tunneler from across the room runs over, waving her arms in much the same way Lucy was just waving hers. She's wearing one of the sacks, but she's tied a big rope around the middle. And the Earth Force insignia is sewn on the center of her chest. She's hunched over like all the Tunnelers, but even if she stood straight, she wouldn't be much taller than my waist.

Ka. Ka. Ka.

Voice box: "Oh! Oh! Oh!"

Lucy and I look at the Tunneler, then at each other, then at the Tunneler. Bewilderment must be written on both of our faces.

Ka. Ka. Gareek. Keek. Keek. Arrrrgh.

"Oh! Oh! Something must have gotten lost in translation."

The voice box can barely keep up with the Tunneler's pace. "Are you not excited? I know I am. I can hardly believe I get to ride the space elevator! It's my first time. Or, I mean, my second time. My first time was when I rode here this morning to wait for you. And I am so honored to meet you! And I hardly know what to say!"

Whoa. I think I just met Tunneler Lucy.

"Oh! Oh! Excuse my bad manners!" The Tunneler steps back and does a funky kind of curtsy. "My name is Neeka. My father is Commander Krag of Earth Force. And *I* am one of the junior ambassadors selected to be your guide. Welcome to Gulaga!"

Neeka's body trembles with excitement, and all of her Gulagan grunts are about an octave higher than the other Tunnelers' voices.

"Hi," I say. "I'm Jasper, and this is Lucy."

"You're a junior ambassador?" Lucy sounds distinctly less anxious.

"Oh! Oh! Yes! It was very competitive. I had to go through five rounds of auditions. It probably helped that my father is an Earth Force officer, but that was only a plus factor. I still had to make it through all the callbacks on my own."

"Auditions?" Lucy asks, linking her arm around Neeka's furry one. "Tell me more! I'd love to compare notes."

And just like that, Lucy makes a complete recovery. The two of them scurry off across the elevator bay, leaving me alone.

I join Cole and Marco at the control panels where one of the Tunnelers is monitoring the progression of the cab from the planet's surface. A timer counts down its arrival. Just over eight minutes. Shortly after, we'll make our descent.

"We have a Tunneler guide," I tell them.

"We know, News Flash," Marco says. "She brought us here, remember?"

"Not her. See the Tunneler with the belt talking to Lucy?" I nod at the window where Neeka and Lucy are still standing arm in arm. "Her name is Neeka, and she says she's our junior ambassador."

"What's a junior ambassador?" Cole asks.

"No clue, but she seems young, maybe our age. And check this out, she's like the Tunneler version of Lucy."

"Creepy," Marco says.

"Chatty," I say.

"That sounds entirely strange and unpleasant," Cole says.

Since we arrived, the bay has filled. There are dozens of Tunnelers milling about. Most of them carry small packs strapped to their backs. Since they're so hunched over, the packs kind of make them look like furry turtles.

Along the far wall, carts piled high with boxes and machinery stand ready to be rolled into the elevator cab. One of the carts has huge green bins with the word WASTE marked along the sides in white block letters.

"What are those?" I ask Cole and Marco, nodding my head in the direction of the green bins.

"Trash," Cole says. "Even though most waste is recycled here at the dock, they must have some byproduct that needs to be removed."

"We're riding with trash?" Marco says. "That's disgusting."

"And it's not even regular trash," I say. "It's trash made from trash."

"First-class trash," Marco says.

"Trash that refuses to be repurposed," Cole says.

"The very essence of trash, itself," Marco says.

"I bet it stinks," I say.

Just then a low alarm sounds and red lights along the circumference of the bay start to blink. A mechanical voice announces that the cab will be arriving in two minutes.

Officers clear the area between the shaft door and the nearest hallway entrance. When the cab glides into the bay, Tunnelers push the line of carts onto the cab. Passengers queue behind them.

"Let's go!" Marco says. Cole and I tail after him to the back of the boarding line.

Carts and belongings are stowed in a center cargo compartment. The perimeter is for passengers. The crowd rushes in, filling the space. There are elevated rows of seats that circle the cargo compartment, but up against the window is standing

78

room only. The girls have already boarded. Lucy stands at the window with Neeka on one side and Mira on the other. We head in that direction.

I slide in next to Mira. Cole and Marco stand beside me.

Lucy and Neeka are talking so intently, neither seems to notice our arrival.

Marco taps Lucy on the shoulder. "Introductions?"

Ka! Kreek. Arrgh. Garrgareek.

"Oh! Allow me. I'm Neeka, your junior ambassador. I simply can not contain how happy and excited I am to escort you through Gulagaven! You are in for a most delightful and wondrous time. Oh! Silly me! I forgot my courtesy. I did not ask your name. But there is no need. I know you must be Marco Romero. Oh! Oh! You are ever so tall!"

"Ummm . . . yep, that's me." Marco points to me and Cole. "Jasper Adams, Cole Thompson. Now carry on with your girl talk."

Marco turns his back on Neeka and shakes his head. "You weren't kidding, J-Bird. She's like Lucy with a computerized voice and old folks' vocabulary. Although I'm glad to hear we're in for a delightful and wondrous time."

"Thanks for sparing us more talk," Cole says.

"Of course," Marco says. "I'm ready to ride!"

"Make sure to hold on, Cole says. "I've read it moves fast."

An automated speaker announces that we're moments

away from departure, and that any carry-on items should be secured in the storage areas. Beneath us, the planet looks like a giant walnut, and we're a tall toothpick piercing its surface.

"Here goes," I whisper as I bump Mira's shoulder. I grip the safety rail in front of me with my right hand.

Mira drops her left hand from the bar and slyly links her little finger around mine. I don't even need the brain connection to know she's excited. We both are. I coil my pinkie tightly around hers.

Three beeps sound in the cab. We drop a few meters, then the cab slowly turns, unwinding itself from its own safety guard, like the twisting of a bottle cap.

I brace in anticipation and squeeze Mira's finger.

"Wait for it," Cole says, bouncing on his toes. "Wait for it."

The cab stops turning, and for a moment it feels like we're suspended in space with nothing at all to keep us anchored.

Then we plummet.

The gravity stabilizers in the floor fight with the laws of science that want to keep us stationary. I grab the rail with both hands, but still feel the pull. My feet push against the tops of my shoes. Even the skin on my face stretches toward my scalp. Meanwhile, we race through space, barreling toward the planet's surface.

This is awesome!

"Woo-hoo!" I shout, joining the hoots and hollers of my pod mates.

After we've been riding for several minutes, Cole leans over. "Remember your sister wanted me to hack that elevator joyride?"

Geez, that seems like forever ago. Was it only last week?

"This is a million times better!" I say. "I can't wait to tell Addy!"

As we rush toward the planet's surface—the great brown ball growing bigger and bigger beneath us—I think about my sister. I can't believe how long it's been since she popped into my brain. I must have intentionally shut her out. I don't want to think of how mad she was the day I left. I don't want to think about all the secrets I've kept from her, too. And I definitely don't want to think about her coming to the Academy in the spring. Sure, she'll love the gloves and the blast packs, and she'll probably rule the girls' dorm by the end of her first week, but I don't want her to have to learn the truth. As much as this is awesome—and I know most of the kids on Earth would trade places with me in a millisecond for a ride on this elevator—it can't cover up what's waiting for us on the ground.

That's where our real military training will begin. In the tunnels and on the cold surface of Gulaga, far away from our cozy homes, Earth Force plans to mold us into soldiers.

7

THE CAB SLOWS AS WE APPROACH THE
occludium shield. The gauzy silver haze floats just above the
atmosphere. When we cross through, the cab shutters, but
it's the air, not the occludium, that causes the disturbance.
For objects like the space elevator, occludium is just a veil
to pass through. If we were trying to bound, that would be
a different story.

With every second, we get closer to the surface of Gulaga.
The elevator shaft is built into the foundation of the planet's
main settlement, Gulagaven. It's the only place on the planet
where modern, Tunneler-made structures appear on the surface. Still, there isn't much to see. From above, Gulagaven

looks about as big as the Earth Force aeroport off the coast of Americana East. Even though I know the diameter of the subterranean metropolis stretches far beyond the surface structures, and Gulagaven descends several kilometers into the belly of the planet, it doesn't look like much of a city from here. In fact, except for the small radius around the elevator shaft, all I can see in any direction are rocky plains of packed dirt.

Next to the shaft is a small base and aeroport for traditional aircraft and hovers. There are no bounding ships, of course. All of the quantum ports were relocated to the space dock when the occludium shield was installed. Exhaust vents extend out of the ground, discharging the stale air from the tunnels and sucking in a fresh supply. Tiny egg cars like the ones we saw on the Paleo Planet are parked in a row near the paved channels leading to the occludium mines.

The leaf systems we saw from above stretch across the cold and rocky surface. Now that we're getting closer, they don't look much like leaves. They're thick and furry, and each one is almost as big as a hover. They're supported by scaffolding and protected by a clear shield that probably provides some warmth while still allowing access to the limited light.

As we finish our descent, I'm more aware of what's *not* on the surface. For starters, there's not much that looks like Earth. This definitely isn't the Paleo Planet. But what's even more noticeable is that there's not a single Tunneler anywhere.

"How come no one's out and about?" I ask.

"Out and about?" Neeka asks. "Right now no one's out because it's after curfew. And no one just hangs out on the surface. If you're aboveground, it's for a reason . . . unless you're one of the Wackies who live on the tundra."

"Wackies?" Marco asks.

"Oh! Oh! Never mind. That definitely was on the list of things junior ambassadors are absolutely not supposed to talk about. Just pretend I never even said the word Wackies, okay? Nope, you didn't hear about Wackies from me. Even though I have no idea why it matters if we mention that some crazy old Tunnelers insist on living on their own, outside of Gulagaven. I told them I didn't see why it would matter. But they insisted. Absolutely no mention of the Wackies."

"Who told you not to tell us?" I ask.

"They're a breakaway group?" Cole asks.

"Cool," Marco says. "You have rebels."

"Oh! Oh! I never said anything about rebels. I just said . . ."

"Neeka!" Lucy says. "Quiet! Don't let these boys bait you into telling them this stuff. Maybe you should try to be a little less like me and a bit more like Mira."

Mira gives a quick glance at Neeka and smiles.

Neeka shakes with the effort of not talking, but she manages. For about a second.

"Fine," Marco says. "Forget the Wackies. What's up with the curfew?"

Neeka lets out an enormous breath of relief. "It's a strict rule. Following the afternoon bell, no one is allowed on the surface. The temperatures drop too low for anyone to be out safely."

As we talk, the cab travels the rest of the distance to the surface. Then, for several meters, the walls of the vertical tunnel are all that's visible out the window. The slick surface looks like garden-variety mud.

"What's up with the walls?" Marco asks. "Are they wet?"

"Oh! No! Ha! Ha!" Neeka says. "That's not water, it's an adhesive. It makes the walls stronger."

"So, like, sticky mud?" I ask.

"Not mud," Lucy says, rolling her eyes. "An adhesive. Kind of like clear nail polish, right, Neeka? You know, top coat? That's what it looks like to me, anyway."

"Maybe," Neeka says. "I'm not sure what nail polish is."

"OMG!" Lucy says. "You don't know about nail polish? Well, then I'll have to . . ."

Lucy is off and chatting a mile a minute. She has Neeka's paw in her hand and is suggesting colors that will bring out the auburn undertones in Neeka's fur. I'd say I feel sorry for Neeka, but she looks like she's loving it. In all the universe, Lucy has found her true soul mate.

I tune out the girl talk and tune in to my surroundings. The cab enters a metal chamber and slows to a stop. Mechanical arms extend from the sides of the chamber and secure to the cab. The lift mechanism disengages from above. The mechanical arms drop the cab into a grooved channel, and we rotate the remaining meters of our descent, like the unscrewing of a bottle top.

We spin into an elevator bay very similar to the one we left behind at the space dock, although the walls are made of that adhesive mud rather than clear plastic. Earth Force officers—both humans and Tunnelers—busy about the bay, checking gauges and computer readings. One monitor shows the space dock. Another shows the entire elevator shaft stretching up from Gulaga. We came a long way.

"Oh! Oh! I am so excited to show you around!" Neeka says.

Neeka's excitement is contagious. I'm super fired up to see Gulagaven, and I'm psyched to have a Tunneler tour guide, even if it comes with way more girl talk than I typically tolerate.

"What is your job as a junior ambassador, anyway?" Cole asks.

"Oh! A junior ambassador is paired with each EarthBound Academy pod. We are supposed to escort you through Gulagaven, assist in adjustment to life in the tunnels, answer any questions, and make sure you keep out of all restricted areas. Did I just say that last part out loud? Oops! Oh! No! Father will be most upset!"

"Her father is an Earth Force officer," Lucy says.

"Restricted areas, huh?" Marco shoots me a mischievous grin.

Poor Neeka. She doesn't know who she's dealing with.

"Why don't they call it Gulaga Force?" I ask.

Neeka tips her snout in a way that reminds me of shrugging.

"Is there a separate Gulaga Force?" Lucy asks.

"No, just Earth Force."

"What about your Gulagan government?" Cole asks. "I thought you were governed by a parliament."

"It's just Earth Force now," Neeka says.

"You don't even have your own government?" Marco says.

"Oh! Oh! You boys are baiting me again. This kind of talk is definitely on the restricted list. As my father would say, you're starting to sound just like the Wackies! Come on! We're unloading! Let's go!"

Neeka and Lucy head for the door with Cole and Marco on their heels. Mira and I follow a few paces behind. Neeka seemed to blow off the fact that Gulaga doesn't have its own government, but it left me unsettled. Why would the Tunnelers allow Earth Force to govern? They don't even govern on Earth. Sure, the Force is pretty powerful, but Earth has actual elected leaders who are entirely independent. At least, that's what I've always thought. It's what I was taught to believe. Who knows what's really true anymore?

When we asked about the government, Neeka let it slip that we sound just like the Wackies. Is that why the Wackies left Gulagaven? Maybe they're not so wacky after all.

I shake my head, trying to toss those thoughts out of my brain. I don't want to be distracted while we explore. But the thoughts are pretty hard to shake. Mira links her arm with mine as we head for the elevator exit, and a strange feeling washes over me. Kinship? Whatever it is, I think Mira is having a hard time shaking the troubling thoughts about Gulagaven, too.

We follow the line of exiting passengers out of the bay and into a connected waiting room. The line falls apart, and there's a big crush of people near the door. Most of the Tunnelers aren't wearing voice boxes, but I know they're annoyed because of all the grunting and jostling.

"What's happening?" Lucy asks.

"Same thing that always happens when Earthlings visit Gulagaven for the first time," Neeka says. "Five new Earth Force officers were on the elevator, too. And from the looks of this foot traffic, I'd say they're the problem."

"What do you mean, Gula Gal?" Marco asks.

"This is a spectator delay," Neeka says. "And what's a Gula Gal?"

88

"Ignore him, sweetie," Lucy says, before turning to Marco. "Shut it, Tofu Face!"

I don't have to wait long to discover what Neeka was talking about. The crowd starts moving, and we're funneled out of the waiting room.

Three Tunnelers stand guard in front, directing the crowd left and right. The one in the center is an Earth Force officer and wears a voice box: "Proceed with caution. Gulagaven does not have guardrails. Please use extreme care at all times."

"What does he mean they don't have guardrails?" Marco pushes past us and leans between the guards. He throws his arms out to the sides and stops cold. "No joke! Proceed with bucket-loads of caution!"

Marco backpedals. I still can't see, but Marco's freak-out is a pretty good indication that I'd better follow directions. Neeka waves us on. We stay close to the wall and follow her down a short ramp to break free from the crowd.

"Whoa!" I flatten myself against the wall.

We're on the edge of Gulagaven, the buzzing, breathing, busy nucleus of Tunneler civilization.

And we are literally standing on the edge.

As in, we're perched on a narrow ledge with no guardrail, looking out over a deep central chasm that extends farther down than I can see, like a hollowed-out beehive. Tunnels branch away from the multilevel cavern, and bridges span across. Elaborate pulley systems anchor into the pit and haul supplies up and down. Tunnelers are everywhere, hustling along the walkways, crossing the bridges, swinging from elaborate rope systems.

The air smells like autumn leaves and moldy tomatoes. My stomach twists. I'm afraid to take a deep breath, or I might lose my lunch.

Our path spirals around the central core. Tunnelers pass in both directions, muttering grunts, maybe greetings. The adults are dressed in brown sacks, the Tunneler children aren't dressed at all. They walk so close to the edge, it's a miracle they don't fall. Why would they do that? And with their kids!

Mira grabs my hand. Her brain feels like fireworks.

Breathe.

I'm not sure whether she thinks it or I do, but we sync and slow our breath until we both are a bit calmer.

"This place is intense," I say.

"Enormous," Lucy says.

"Hollow," Cole says.

"Check out all the Tunnelers!" Marco says.

"There are thousands of them!" I say.

"Millions, to be exact," Cole says.

"How come they don't fall?" I ask. "Those bridges are so narrow, and they're so crowded. How do they make it across without—"

"Plunging to their deaths?" Marco finishes.

"We've been crossing these bridges since the day we could walk," Neeka says. "You'll get used to it. Let's go!"

I'll get used to it? Is she kidding? Half the kids at school thought my actual name was Klutz. Those bridges and me don't mix. It looks like I'll be taking the long way around in Gulagaven.

WE FOLLOW NEEKA ALONG THE WALK-
way, which is far too slippery to be safe. It looks like it's made
out of that same muddy adhesive stuff that we saw from the
elevator. In fact, this whole place is made from mud. It's like
we're inside a giant mud castle. I stay far away from the edge,
with one hand on the muddy wall at all times.

Every few meters, a round silver lamp is mounted to the
wall. The faint smell of metal means the lights must be pow-
ered by the occludium they mine here on Gulaga.

About a quarter of the way around the central pit, Neeka
turns left into one of the intersecting tunnels.

Ouch! My head collides with the ceiling.

"What's with the roof?" Marco calls.

"What do you mean?" Neeka asks.

"It's so low!" I shout from behind, rubbing my hand against the bump that's blossoming on my forehead.

"Oh?" she says. "I never noticed."

"Yeah, you wouldn't," Marco grumbles.

Neeka leads the way with almost half a meter to spare between her head and the ceiling. Lucy and Cole both have a few centimeters of clearance. Mira just fits at her full height. She grins, and I'm doused with that tingly, sparkly energy. She's laughing at me. It would be really annoying if it weren't brain to brain, which is still novel enough to earn a free pass.

"I hope all the tunnels aren't like this," I say to Marco, who falls back beside me in line. We're not moving as fast as the others since we're so hunched over.

"No joke," he says. "If we have to bend over like this all the time, we'll end the tour looking like Gedney."

At least we're no longer staring down a drop into the chasm. Having a low ceiling and walls on both sides may be claustrophobic, but it's much less risky.

After a few turns, we walk straight into a huge crowd of Tunnelers carrying packs on their backs like the ones we saw in the elevator bay. Half the Tunnelers push through from the other direction, and we're jostled about in a sea of fur.

Neeka guides us through the crowd until we emerge

in a huge, hollowed-out room with high ceilings—thank goodness—packed with Tunnelers. It's the noisiest place in the galaxy, I'm sure of it. There are thousands of Tunnelers bustling about, grunting and growling. Aside from Neeka, none of them are wearing voice boxes, but all of them have something to say.

"What is this place?" Lucy asks.

"It must be a market," Cole says.

"Oh! Oh! Yes! This is the busiest market in Gulagaven. We come here for snacks and sundries and all sorts of extras."

Stalls are set up around the perimeter of the room, and dozens more form aisles across the space. Tons of Tunnelers display their wares, and even more line up to buy. From what I can tell, every purchase requires long and loud negotiation.

"Can we look around?" Lucy asks. "Pretty please?"

"Only for a minute," Neeka says. "Then we need to get to the Bounder Burrow. They're expecting you."

The first stalls we pass sell an assortment of trinkets and jewelry. Now that I'm paying attention, I see that not all Tunnelers are wearing the exact same thing. Yes, the brown bag is the base for the outfit, but lots of Tunnelers wear belts like Neeka, or intricate metal pins, or piercings on their ears or snouts. Lucy stops to admire a ring covered with amber stones. When she tries it on, the merchant runs to her side and chatters away in Gulagan. Neeka gently removes the ring from Lucy's finger and returns it to the display case. Apparently, there's no time for haggling today. Plus, how would we pay?

"What kind of money do they use here?"

"Our money doesn't work like yours," Neeka says. "At least, that's what they told us during junior ambassador training. We barter for goods. Earn credits. It's hard to explain. I have a small allowance to use at the markets with you, but not today. Oh! We really must go!"

In the next stalls we pass, Tunnelers sit in high chairs while others buzz around them, snipping elaborate designs or stroking shades of crimson and purple and black dye into their fur.

"Look, Lucy," Marco says. "A Tunneler beauty salon! That's your kind of place."

"It sure is," she says as we turn into the next row. "And these stalls scream your name, Jasper!"

I barely hear what she says, because I'm too busy making sure I don't puke right in the middle of the market. Directly in front of me, a Tunneler is holding a huge basket of live, wriggly caterpillars. The guy next to him grabs a handful and tosses them into his mouth.

"Gross!" I shout. Obviously Lucy was joking. We've just entered the food aisle. "Please don't tell me this is what they'll be serving us."

"Oh! No!" Neeka says. "These are yummy snacks. All the

main meals are served communally. The Tunneler names don't translate well, but most of our meals consist of tuber, fungi, and forage."

Is she serious? I try to ask, but I can't move my mouth. I'm so sickened and stunned I can't even move my feet. Mira and Lucy coax me forward, down the row of so-called snacks. I can't bear to look, so I cover my eyes. The smells are enough to nauseate me—spoiled milk, slimy spinach, month-old lunch meat from the back of the fridge. When I take a peek, half the snacks appear to be moving, just like the caterpillars. Creepy crawlies inside my stomach? The stay on Gulaga is going to be rough.

The girls steer me out of the food aisle, and we make our way through the rest of the market. I push all thoughts of food from my brain. It's either that or succumb to death by diet right here and now.

Shortly beyond the market, we enter a chasm like the one near the space elevator. It's not as wide across, but it looks to be just as deep. And then there's that whole lack-of-railings thing. Yikes.

"We're almost at the Bounder Burrow," Neeka says. "It's in the Earth Sector, straight across and through a few turns. We'll just cross here." She takes a step toward the bridge that spans the chasm. Marco and Lucy are right behind her.

"No way," I say.

"What's the problem?" Neeka asks.

"I'm not crossing."

"Come on, J," Marco says.

"No," I say. "There must be another way across. If not, I'm happy to burrow right here."

"Just use your pack," Cole says. "That's my plan if I have a problem."

"That's genius, Wiki!" Marco says. "Let's fly across!"

Cole's idea is pretty awesome. Now, instead of being afraid of the bridge, I'm pretty psyched to try it. I unzip the corner pockets of my pack to release the hand grips. Then I dig in my pack for my gloves.

"Oh! No! That is not allowed," Neeka says. "We were told in junior ambassador training that cadets can only use their blast packs outside of the tunnel systems."

"Why?" Marco asks. "The whole purpose of our packs is efficient travel on other planets. I'd say this fits that description."

Neeka shakes her paws, and starts talking super fast. Her voice-translation box struggles to keep up. "Oh! Oh! No! No! You don't understand! We simply can't do that! That would absolutely not fall within the parameters of allowed supervised behavior that we learned in our junior ambassador training!"

"Well, then why don't we just bound across?" I suggest.

Neeka's natural voice jumps.

"Oh! Oh! No! No!" The voice box sounds like it's glitching, but it must just be translating Neeka's freak-out. "Oh! No! That is an absolutely horrible idea! Oh! No! Didn't anyone explain the rules to you? You can't use your gloves in Gulagaven! No! Bounding is absolutely prohibited anywhere on the surface of Gulaga unless within a training exercise! Oh! This is monitored! No! It would be detected! Oh! There would be alarms! No!"

"You're this freaked out about a few alarms?" Marco says.

"No! No! You don't understand! Oh! It's so much worse! There is an occludium scrambler! Oh! Your bound would fail! No! You could fail to materialize! No! No! I would be in— Oh! Oh! Oh!—so much trouble! Oh! No! So much trouble, that I would have to sacrifice my junior ambassador badge! Oh! Oh!"

Neeka is worked up into a total frenzy. Her voice climbs higher and higher, and she's shaking her stubby arms like she might take flight herself, without a pack.

I know she's freaking out, and I feel kind of bad about it, but I'm also trying hard not to laugh. I mean, it's funny. Even though her stress levels are shooting for the roof, the voice box keeps relaying everything in the one-note, no-emphasis robotic tone.

"Oh! Oh! Oh! Oh! Oh! No! No! No! No! No!"

A giant guffaw escapes my lips, which pulls the plug on

Marco's laugh containment, which then completely kills any self control I have left. We sink to the floor, holding our stomachs and shaking with laughter.

Lucy kicks me hard in the shoe. "Stop that! Both of you!" She rubs her hand across Neeka's back, and tries to talk over the constant stream of "Oh!" and "No!" "Come on, now, sweetie. No one's going to make you sacrifice your badge. There must be another way, right? We'll just find that."

She links her left hand with Neeka's paw, and grabs Mira's hand with her right. "Let's go, girls. If we're not with the boys, they can't get us in trouble." She leads Neeka and Mira down the spiraling ramp of the chasm.

"What about us?" Cole shouts after them.

"You're the genius!" she calls back. "I'll leave it to you to wrangle those two morons and find your way to the Bounder Burrow."

I'm still laughing. Sure, I realize I'm being ridiculously rude, but that voice box is just too funny. And it's even funnier the way Cole is looming over Marco and me with that mad look on his face.

"Can we go?" he asks.

Marco gasps for air in between laughs and buries his head between his legs. I cover my face with my hands and try to settle down.

"Seriously," Cole says. "What is so funny?"

Marco lifts his head. "Really, Wiki? You don't think that voice box is hysterical?"

"No. I really don't. How do you expect her to communicate with us? I have been working on my Gulagan, but it has a long way to go." Cole opens his mouth super wide and lets out a horrible shriek-grunt that sounds more like a dying cow than a Tunneler.

Marco and I break out in hysterics all over again.

"Oh, Fact Man, that was priceless." Marco snorts. "Do that again. Please!"

Cole turns beet red and starts down the ramp where the girls disappeared a few minutes ago. I jump to my feet and chase after him.

"Wait up!" I grab his arm and swallow what's left of my laugh attack.

"Why should I?" Cole asks.

"Come on, it was funny." When he doesn't smile, I add, "But the fact you're learning Gulagan is super cool."

"And very *you*, Genius," Marco adds from behind.

"Let's just find the Bounder Burrow," Cole says.

We wind around until we reach the other side of the chasm. From there, we follow the hallway Cole thinks he saw Neeka lead Lucy and Mira down when I was too busy laughing to pay attention.

Everything looks the same. The walls, floor, and ceiling are all made of that adhesive mud stuff. Different halls branch out from the one we follow. Small coves open on both sides. In the first coves we pass, it looks like Tunnelers are working—fixing machinery, sewing the brown material into clothes. One cove even looks like a preschool, with lots of Tunneler tots running about.

"I know this place is cool," Marco says after we've been walking for a while, "but don't forget why we're here. We need to keep our pod mission front and center: Discover what Earth Force has planned for the Bounders. Find out more about the summit."

"Right now I'd be happy just to find the Bounder Burrow," I say.

"I think Neeka might be a great source of info," he says. "She said her dad's an Earth Force officer, and she sure loves to talk!"

"I don't think she's going to give us classified information," Cole says.

"Not on purpose," Marco says. "But she's already slipped up a few times. Maybe if we mention the summit like we already know about it, she'll spill the beans."

"That's not the way to treat our junior ambassador," Cole says.

"Maybe not, but it's all about the pod now, remember?"

Marco's words twist like a knife in my gut. Why did I promise Waters I'd keep the brain patch confidential? I hate keeping secrets from my pod. And this is important! It could be the clue we need to find out what Earth Force is up to. Still . . . I gave Waters my word. I try to push the whole mess out of my head.

As we continue on, the Tunnelers recline on chairs and chat with friends. Maybe we passed from a work area into a relaxation area. But one thing stays the same. Everywhere we go, all eyes are on us. A chorus of grunts and snorts carry us down the hallway. And they don't sound too friendly.

"What are they saying?" I whisper to Cole.

"I have no idea," he says.

"I thought you said you spoke Gulagan," Marco says.

"I said I'm *learning* Gulagan," Cole says. "I have a long way to go."

"They sound mad," I say.

"They always sound that way," Marco says. "It's hard to make grunts sound happy."

That's true. Tunnelers always sound gruff, but something about their mannerisms says there's more to it. Something makes me feel like they're not happy *with us*.

We continue on.

The ceiling is so low.

My back aches.

Eventually we have to come upon the Bounder Burrow, right?

MONICA TESLER

"I'm starving," I say.

"Me, too," Marco says.

I pass out the protein bars I stashed back at the bounding base this morning. Sharing with my friends is the right thing to do, but I know I'll wish I had the bars when they try to force-feed me fungus later on.

We eat and walk.

And walk some more.

This looks like a residential area. That must mean we're close.

I hope we get there soon.

It can't be much farther.

I just wish they'd stop staring at us.

Sure, it sounds like they're saying mean things when we pass, but that's just because they always sound that way, like Marco said.

And we're the special visitors, right? We're Bounders, the future of Earth Force. That must carry some weight around here seeing as Gulaga is governed by Earth Force.

So why is this solid mass of nastiness growing in my stomach?

And why do I feel like the walls are closing in?

"Ouch!" Marco shouts behind me. "Is the ceiling getting even lower?"

I hadn't really noticed, but I'm definitely crouching more

than when we started down this hallway. When I look at the others, it's even easier to see. The ceiling is much lower. Even Cole is hunching.

"You still think we're headed in the right direction?" I ask Cole.

He doesn't say anything, but his steps slow.

"Hold up, Wiki," Marco says. "I'm just going to put this out there. . . . We're lost."

"WE MIGHT NOT BE LOST," COLE SAYS,
speeding up. "I'm sure I saw them take this tunnel. If we just go a bit farther—"

Marco grabs Cole's arm. "The girls could have turned down any of those hallways we passed. You need to face facts, Fact Man. We have no idea where they are or where we're going."

Marco's words are like a cup of cold water to the face. Everything comes into sharp focus, including the many Tunneler eyes bearing down on us at this very moment. There's no mistaking anymore. The grunts are hostile, and the stares are not of the *I'd love to get to know you* variety.

We need a plan. Now.

"What are we going to do?" I whisper.

Marco shrugs. "Wiki?"

"We need to ask directions. Someone around here must have a voice-translation box."

"Right," I say, although the last thing I want to do is walk into one of the small coves filled with Tunnelers and try to communicate. Since Cole hasn't moved a muscle since he made the suggestion, I'm guessing he feels about the same.

"Let's do it, then," Marco says. He takes five strides toward the nearest cove, glares over his shoulder at us, then keeps going.

We can't let him fly solo on this. I grab Cole's arm and drag him after Marco.

Even though the cove has no door, it's clear where the threshold is. The Tunnelers are in, and we're out. Three stone tables stretch the length of the room, with long benches pulled underneath. At least fifty Tunnelers huddle around the tables, drinking dark liquid from small bowls and blowing into pots that burn thick, dark smoke. Marco stands at the threshold for a solid count of ten, but none of the Tunnelers make any sign of acknowledgement.

"Hi, there!" Marco shouts across the threshold.

No reaction. If I had to guess, I'd say they were ignoring him.

"Here goes nothing," Marco says and steps across the threshold.

Instantly the Tunnelers leap to their feet and shriek like Neeka did earlier, but this time it's not funny at all. They charge the threshold, shrieking and hissing and baring their teeth.

Marco jumps back with his palms in the air. "Whoa, whoa, chill. I didn't mean to make you so mad. See, my friends and I are lost. We just need to ask directions. . . ."

The Tunnelers rush right to the threshold and keep up their shriek attack. I want to run away, but that wouldn't make it better. We'd still be lost, and we might have fifty angry Tunnelers on our tail.

"Hey!" Marco shouts. "Cool it! We just need directions! Don't any of you have voice boxes?"

None of the Tunnelers seem to understand anything Marco's saying. Some of them stop shrieking, but all of their lips are still curled, and their pointy teeth look pretty sharp.

Cole steps in front of Marco. "Kerr—accck. Grrrr—nok, Earth Force!"

The Tunnelers grunt among themselves and exchange curious glances.

"Kerr—acck. Grrr—nok, Earth Force!" Cole tries again.

"What are you saying to them?" I ask.

"*We are officers of Earth Force.* Or, actually, it's probably more like *we top people.*"

"We top people?" Marco asks. "Great. They're probably shrieking because of how ridiculous you sound."

"And you should work on your accent," I say.

"I don't see either of you coming up with a better idea," Cole says.

An older-looking Tunneler with a black streak in his hair and a deep scar across his face splits the crowd and steps across the threshold. He heads down the tunnel the way we came.

I lift my eyebrows at Marco and whisper, "What do we do?"

Marco shrugs.

The older Tunneler stops, slips something around his neck, and turns around. He grunts quietly, and then a hyper-robotic voice says, "Are you coming or not?"

"He's wearing a voice box," I say.

"It's the original beta model," Cole says.

"You heard him," Marco calls as he runs after the Tunneler. "Let's go!"

Cole and I catch up with Marco. The old Tunneler is moving so fast, we have to jog to keep up. How can he move that fast all stooped over?

"Hey! Thanks!" Marco says. "I didn't know what we were going to do back there."

The Tunneler quietly grunts. "Keep your voice down," booms the old voice box. "Holy Hovercraft, why don't they have a volume setting on these things?"

Holy hovercraft? I whisper to Cole and Marco.

"I heard that," the Tunneler says. "And that's not what I

said. They don't have an English translation for it. Some joker programmed the box to translate Tunneler expletives into the most annoying human colloquialisms imaginable."

"But yet it actually translates an insane phrase like 'the most annoying human colloquialisms imaginable,'" Marco says.

"Go figure, wise guy," the Tunneler says.

"So do you mean I'm a smart dude or were you using the annoying human colloquialism *wise guy*?"

I elbow Marco and mouth, *Shut up*. I'd rather him quit being a wise guy than us stay lost.

Cole jogs alongside the Tunneler. "Hello, or should I say, Argotok? My name is Cole. And these are my friends Jasper and Marco. We just arrived this afternoon on the space elevator. I fear we're lost."

"Your fears are right, Earth Boy. A few more meters in the wrong direction, and you may never have made it back."

Well, that's comforting.

"Your luck—not mine—put you in my path," he continues. "I'll take you to the Earth Sector and be on my way."

The Tunneler dips his head and speeds up again. I get the feeling that he doesn't want anyone to notice him. He really is running low on luck. It's hard not to get noticed when you're escorting three human kids along the back channels of Gulagaven.

We chase after him through several twists and turns. We

never would have made it to the Bounder Burrow on our own.

"Why do you have that old voice-translation box?" Cole asks.

"None of your business."

"I didn't think they were still in circulation."

"They're not."

"Then why do you have one?"

"Can't you take a hint, Earth Boy?" The Tunneler slows down. "Are you Waters's kids?"

"How do you know that?" I ask.

"I heard you were coming today. If I didn't have a hunch who you were, you'd still be back there hovering at the entrance of our members-only drinking establishment."

"Drinking establishment?" Marco ask. "That was a Tunneler bar?"

"Let's not get off track," Cole says. "How exactly do you know Waters?"

The Tunneler ignores Cole's question and turns around. "You'll find your Bounder friends around the next bend. I've brought you far enough."

"Wait!" Cole shouts. "Who are you? How do you know Waters?"

Just then, up ahead, a Gulagan Earth Force officer turns the corner. He takes one look at us and starts yelling. I'm sure he's shouting at Cole, Marco, and me until his voice box starts translating.

"Hey! What are you doing here, Barrick? You're not allowed in Gulagaven, old man. You're going—"

I'm not sure what else he says, because he turns off his voice box. He runs full speed and nearly knocks me over. That's when I realize the old Tunneler, who I guess is named Barrick, is no longer around. He must have bolted as soon as the officer started shouting.

"Whoa," Marco says. "That was unexpected."

"Where did he go?"

"He took off in the direction of the market, I think," Cole says.

"We never even got to say thanks."

"Adams! Thompson! Romero!" a familiar voice calls. "Where have you been? We have search parties out for you."

When I spin back around, Earth Force Officer James Ridders is marching toward us.

"You should have been at the burrow over an hour ago," Ridders continues. "Explain yourself."

"It's a pretty basic explanation, sir," Marco says. "We got lost."

Ridders shakes his head. He opens his mouth to speak a few times, then eventually says, "Fine. But let this be a warning. You'll get no preferential treatment from me. You're here to do your duty, just like the rest of us. See to it that you stay in line."

"Yes, sir," we say in unison.

"The burrow is around the corner. It's close coed quarters. No nonsense."

Coed quarters? As in we'll be sleeping in the same room as the girls? That will be . . . different.

"And, gentlemen," Ridders says with a nod, "welcome back to the EarthBound Academy."

We swing around the corner, and I immediately recognize where we are. Across the chasm and up one level is the hallway leading to the market. Geez. How did we miss this? If we'd only kept walking instead of taking that turn, we never would have gotten lost.

A few more steps take us to the Bounder Burrow. Before I have a chance to look around, Lucy barrels across the room and slams into me, wrapping her arms around my back. "Oh, thank goodness! Why did you separate from us? We thought you were lost!" From the way she's clinging to me, you'd think we hadn't seen each other since last tour, as opposed to having spent the last week together at Waters's labs.

"We *were* lost," Cole says. He stands straight as a board when Lucy hugs him.

"Where's my hug?" Marco asks.

"You don't need one," she says. "There are a lot of people here waiting to hug *you*."

Sure enough, while Lucy hugged and lectured us, a small crowd gathered around. When she finally steps aside, a field of familiar faces, all clad in indigo and orange, stands in front of me.

A round boy with orange hair and freckles elbows his way to the front. "Hi, Jasper!"

"Ryan!" I grab his fist and bump his shoulder with my own, the same move I've watched Marco do a hundred times. "You bring your rocks this tour?"

"Nah," he says. "I opted for my *Evolution* figure collection." He aims this last remark at Cole beside me. "Want to see?"

"Let's go," Cole says.

"Maybe later," I say, but Cole and Ryan are already dashing off.

I stick with Marco and try to hang in for the wave after wave of Bounders coming to say hello. He takes it in stride, but I'm a little freaked by it all. Something is definitely different this time around. Sure, we all know one another, so it's not like our first days at the space station. But that's not all that's different. A couple of cadets kid about the Paleo Planet and my dive off the Youli spaceship. Except they're not really kidding. I can tell they're impressed, even a bit in awe of me.

Everything's compounded by our pod arriving late to the tour and the rumors about the new technology.

We're shrouded in mystery, and I kind of like it.

". . . he still makes me nervous," Meggi is saying when I tune back in. I feel kind of bad—Meggi is Lucy's friend, and she's always been nice to me—but she was probably saying the same stuff as everybody else. *How was your summer? You didn't miss much at the space station. Did you hear Maximilian Sheek took Florine's job as head of Bounder Affairs?* And when she says he makes her nervous, I'm pretty sure she's talking about Marco.

"Oh, Marco is harmless," I say. "And that stuff from last tour is old news."

"Not really," she says. "All anyone wants to talk about is the Youli battle on the Paleo Planet, and your pod is the all-star team who just so happened to arrive fashionably late to our second tour." She lowers her voice to a whisper. "Is it true about Waters? Did he invent a new weapon?"

"What? No!" Does she know about the brain patch? I rub the back of my neck, then realize I'm being the opposite of discreet and quickly lower my arm and clench my hands at my back.

Meggi looks at me quizzically.

Wait a second. If there are rumors about Waters and a new invention, they're probably about the BPS. "I mean, we're not supposed to talk about it."

MONICA TESLER

"I won't tell anyone," she whispers. "I promise."

"It's not that, it's just—"

Ka. Ka. Gorneen Konteer Arrr. Neeka elbows her way through the crowd. "Oh! Oh! Thank the stars above! I thought I was going to be in so much trouble. Oh! Even now, if Father finds out that I let you boys go off on your own . . . Oh! I don't even want to think about what will happen. He might make me give up the junior ambassadorship!"

"Don't worry, Neeka. We'll tell your father it was all our fault."

"Oh! Thank you!" Neeka says. "Now come with me. I need to show you your hovel."

"Our what?"

Neeka does something funny with her eye—Is she winking at me?—then links one arm in mine and the other in Marco's and pulls us away from the other cadets. I wave to Meggi and mouth, *Sorry.*

Once we leave the crowd, I can actually see the burrow. It reminds me of a cave. It's a large, hollowed-out indentation with a half-dome ceiling and the standard mud walls, like the cove where we found Barrick, only three times as big. Looking closer, I notice a bunch of smaller holes lining the edges of the burrow. Those must be the hovels. Yep, a rack of bunks stacked three high lines both walls of each hovel we pass. And from the looks of the occupants, the boys have one side of the burrow, and the girls have the other.

When we pass Ryan's hovel, Neeka waves Cole along with us. "I'm sorry," she says. "Since you didn't arrive with the others, you got last choice for bunks."

We collect our duffels, dump our blast packs at the charging station, and head to the hovels. Neeka slows to a stop just before the last one in the row.

"This looks like a good location," I say. "Near the back, lots of privacy."

"I don't know for sure," Neeka says, turning the volume down on her voice box, "but I think no one wanted to share space with the boys who claimed these bunks first."

My stomach churns. Who haven't I seen yet?

Regis.

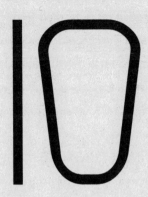

"THIS IS GOING TO BE FUN." MARCO STEPS
into the hovel.

I cross the last few feet so I can see inside. Sure enough, Regis, Hakim, and Randall stare back from their bunks.

"Get out," Regis says from the top bunk. "I already told them we won't share with you."

"Looks like you're out of options, Hotshot," Marco says. "You had twenty-four hours to find other bunk mates. You didn't."

"And it looks like we'll have to pay for it," I say.

"What's that, Jasper?" Regis asks, hopping down from the bunk. "You're away from the Academy for a few months and think you can come back here with an attitude?"

"*I'm* the one with the attitude? Why do you think no one wants to bunk with you?"

Hakim and Randall jump to their feet.

"Is that how you see it?" Randall says, jerking his face and fists forward, trying to make me flinch. Hakim puffs his chest and gives me the stink eye.

"Forget it," I say. "If we have to bunk with you, let's make the best of it."

"We'll start with this," Regis says. "The left side is ours. The right side is yours. Don't cross the center line." He struts out of the hovel, gesturing for his groupies to follow.

When they're gone, I take a deep breath. My exhale comes out in a stutter. Why do I still let him bother me?

"How did this happen?" Cole asks. "Why do we have to bunk with them?"

I don't have time to reply before Ridders shouts, "Lights out." Neeka grunts a quick good night and scurries away. We divvy up the right-side bunks in the hovel—Marco on the bottom, Cole in the middle, and me on the top. I have the most headroom, which is why I claimed the top bunk, but I'll be staring at Regis all night.

As of now, though, there's no sign of Regis. Are they going to miss head count? Ridders will slaughter them.

We change out of our uniforms and shove our duffels under the bottom bunk.

At the last second, the dimwits slip in. Randall rattles my bunk before jumping into his own. All three of them burst out laughing.

Ridders shows up at the foot of our hovel with his tablet in hand. "Quiet!"

Something tickles my foot. Then my thigh.

"Count off," Ridders commands. "Left to right, top to bottom."

Maybe the blanket's just scratchy.

"One!" Regis shouts.

There it is again. A tickle.

"Two!" yells Hakim.

A prickle. Both legs.

"Three!" shouts Randall.

My boxers. My belly.

"Ahhh!" I shoot up in bed and throw off the blanket. "Get them off!" I thrash and kick and shriek. "They're crawling all over me!"

"What is going on?" Ridders demands. He shines a flashlight at my bunk.

Dozens of creepy-crawly caterpillars scurry across my bed.

I leap off my bunk, screaming, and brush the critters from my body.

By now, Marco and Cole are both out of bed and trying to help.

Cole plucks a particularly fat caterpillar from my hair. "These are the kind they were selling as snacks in the market."

Great, now I feel creeped out *and* sick to my stomach.

"Romero!" Ridders shouts. "Get those insects out of his bed!"

Marco strips the sheets and shakes them out. Meanwhile, one of the plebes must have called for assistance, because a Tunneler arrives with a broom and sweeps the crawlers out of the hovel.

With Cole's help, I check my body at least ten times. It looks like I've rid myself of every last bug, but I can't shake the feeling that something's crawling on me. Every few seconds, I shudder.

Once my bed is back in order, Ridders fixes me with a stern stare. "You caused enough racket to wake all of Gulagaven, Jasper. Perhaps you didn't hear me earlier. I have zero tolerance for your pod's antics. Am I clear?"

"Yes, sir." I want to protest—he saw the bugs; he knows why I freaked—but I keep my mouth shut.

"No more noise! All of you!" Ridders says to our hovel.

As soon as Ridders moves on to the girls' side of the burrow, Regis whispers in a mocking voice, "You caused enough racket to wake all of Gulagaven, Jasper." He and his minions explode with laughter.

"Hope you liked the welcome gift," Randall says.

That's right. Randall rattled my bunk just before Ridders showed up. "You planted those things?"

They crack up again.

"We thought you might want a midnight snack," Hakim says.

"Don't forget you started this, Brute Brain!" Marco says. "We'll get you when you least expect it."

"Is that a threat, Romero?" Regis asks.

"No. It's a promise."

The nearing footsteps of a plebe walking a final patrol lap quiet us. Soon, the only sounds in the burrow are the hum of snores. I try to sleep, but I can't. Whenever I close my eyes, I feel like the muddy walls are collapsing, like I'm buried alive.

And I still feel like bugs are crawling all over me.

My entire body is tense, like I'm waiting for the next attack. Who needs to worry about the Youli when you're sleeping two meters away from Regis?

· E_F ·

"Hey, Lazy Boy! Get up!" Marco's voice slips into my brain as I sleep, but it's not enough to wake me.

His fingers creep along the bottom of my feet. "I think there's something in your bed!"

I jerk up. "Get it off me!"

"That worked well," he says.

"Cut it out," I say. "I had back-to-back nightmares about those bugs. I barely slept."

"And we barely have any time before breakfast," he says. "Let's go!"

The opposite bunks are empty. Regis and friends must have already left. "Cole?"

"He went to talk with Ryan. I left, too, but I'm nice enough to come back for you. Not to mention, we can't cut any more corners with Ridders, remember?"

"Yeah, yeah, yeah. Go easy on me. I was attacked by a horde of caterpillars last night."

"About that . . . I have a few ideas for revenge. I'll fill you in later. Now get dressed."

I scramble into what I hope are my dailies (where's Cole when I need him?) and run out of the hovel. I'm just in time. The plebes are lining us up to march out of the burrow.

Then it hits me. We're going to breakfast, and what did Neeka say? Tubers, fungi, and forage? I'm pretty sure it's going to be disgusting.

I race to catch up with Lucy and her friends. "Hey!"

"Hey yourself, sleepy head," she says.

"What's the real deal with the food?" I'm sure Lucy knows. She has a way of finding out information about almost anything.

"Why? Afraid they'll make you eat tofu dogs?"

MONICA TESLER

"You were in the market yesterday. I'm afraid it's going to be a lot worse than tofu."

"It is," Lucy's friend, Annette, says in the standard monotone I remember from last tour. I haven't seen Annette since arriving at Gulagaven. Something's different. She's taller. Or maybe her hair is shorter. Or longer. I'm not sure, but I can't stop looking.

"Hello?" Lucy says. "Earth to Jasper? What planet are you on? Aren't you even going to ask any questions?"

"Oh yeah." That was weird. I'm not usually distractible when it comes to food.

"So?" Lucy has stopped walking and has her hands on her hips.

"So what?"

"Ask your questions!"

"Stop teasing him," Meggi says, linking her arm with mine. "Walk with me, Jasper."

As Meggi waves the other girls ahead, they erupt in giggles. Great. I'm the joker of the Bounders again.

"Don't mind them," she says. "And don't think about the food. You'll go to the cantina. You'll eat. You'll be fine."

We walk out of the burrow and turn left down the hallway, heading the opposite direction of how we arrived yesterday. Everything looks the same, but different. The walls are still made of the muddy stuff, but the ceiling is higher. I can walk comfortably without any fear of bopping my head. My claustrophobia hasn't been waved away with a magic wand, but it's not as bad as it was in the narrow tunnels where we met Barrick. Everyone we pass is wearing Earth Force uniforms. There's not a single Tunneler anywhere.

"What is this place? How come there aren't any Tunnelers?" I ask Meggi.

"This is the Earth Sector. The Force had it custom built. It's not home, but it feels a lot less alien than most of Gulaga. They just expanded to add the Bounder Burrow. They wanted the EarthBound Academy to feel just like its original home."

"What was in our burrow before?"

"Just a regular old burrow, I suppose. The Tunnelers who lived there were relocated."

"They gave up their home for us?"

"I wouldn't say that," Meggi says. "It was just where they slept. I bet they didn't like being so close to the Earth Sector anyway."

Maybe not, but still. It makes me uncomfortable that we took someone's burrow. I don't think about it long, though, because we've arrived at the cantina. The nauseating smells stop me at the door.

"See?" Meggi says. "Just like the space station."

"Kind of." Really there's no mistaking this is Gulaga.

Muddy walls? Check. No windows? Check. Disgusting food? Check. But in some ways, Meggi's right. They must have imported the tables from the same place as the space station. I'd know that funky orange color anywhere. The cafeteria line looks exactly like the one at the station, too. And disgusting food is not really a distinguishing factor.

"Let's eat." Meggi leads me to the line where we pick up familiar plastic trays and wait our turn.

At the first station, a plebe lobs a purple blob onto my plate that smells an awful lot like overcooked potatoes.

I scrunch up my nose and turn away. "What is that?"

"It's not bad," Meggi says. "It tastes kind of like yam, but a little more earthy."

Does she really think that sounds appetizing?

The next plebe slices a thick slab of something black and slimy and slides it next to the purple blob on my tray.

"Some cadets think that tastes like a mushroom," Meggi says, "but it's a tad too chewy for me."

Another promising review.

The last station yields a scoop of thick brownish-green mush that smells like cooked collard greens soaked in vinegar.

"Let me guess, that's forage," I say. "What even is forage?"

"Did you see those big leaves above the surface when you came down on the space elevator?"

I nod.

"Forage," she says. "You may want to plug your nose while you eat it."

"Yum." I take my tray and look out over the sea of indigo uniforms gathered around the orange tables. Marco waves me over. I thank Meggi and head in that direction.

When I set my tray down, I see that Marco is halfway done with his breakfast.

"Not gonna lie to you, J," Marco says. "Just get it over with."

I stare at my plate and try to convince myself to dig in. After all, it could be worse. I didn't spot any creepy crawlies in the food. There's nothing that's actually alive on my plate.

My hand shakes as I lift my fork with a bite of the purple tuber. As soon as I place it in my mouth, I want to spit it out. It literally tastes like eating dirt. Maybe this is what they made the muddy walls from. The tuber is so versatile it's both an adhesive wall coating and a food source.

The mushroom is worse. I can't even spear it with my fork. It keeps sliding all around my tray. When I finally slice a small chunk and get it in my mouth, I nearly puke. It slips around my mouth, making it hard to chomp on. When I get it between my teeth, I can't even chew it. It's like gnawing on a vaguely mushroom-flavored rubber ball coated in slime.

This is not going well, and I haven't even tried the worst-looking food on the tray.

Marco watches my attempt at eating with a crooked smile.

"Do you find this amusing?" I ask.

"Just eat it," he says. "You need the energy."

I take a deep breath then slowly exhale. Let's get this over with. I scoop some forage onto my spoon and shove it in my mouth.

Oh. My. Nastiness.

I can't describe what's in my mouth. It's like eating the stringy part of celery rolled into a massive ball. All I can picture are those huge furry leaves. It's like that fur is tickling the roof of my mouth.

I gag and slam my lips closed to stop from puking.

I gag again.

Up come the tuber and the fungus.

I should swallow them back down. I don't want to throw up.

But that would mean swallowing the furry celery ball.

I won't do it.

I just can't do it.

I'm going to . . .

I leap from the table and bolt across the cantina, pressing my hands firmly against my mouth. I skid to the garbage can, grab the rim, and vomit everything in my belly into the trash.

My knees are week as I stagger out of the cantina and into the narrow hallway of the Earth Sector. Geez. The walls feel like they're closing in around me, and the ceilings here are higher than almost anywhere in Gulagaven.

With the double-punch combo of food and claustro-phobia, I'm not sure how I'm going to make it this tour. Add in our ultra-awful bunkmates and the supersize serving of guilt I can't shake thanks to Waters and his stupid brain patch, and this is shaping up to be a rough tour.

I don't know how long I've been slumped on the ground with my head between my knees when my pod mates finally find me. They're all charged up and chattering.

"There you are!" Lucy says. "Let's go! We don't want to be late!"

The hall spins as I slowly stand. "Late for what?"

Marco swings an arm around Lucy. "Gossip Gal heard the admiral arrived at the space dock this morning."

Lucy slaps Marco's arm. "Don't call me that, especially if you expect me to hook you up with info."

"The admiral's here to kick off the competition," Cole tells me.

"What competition?" I grab the wall to steady myself.

"That's the problem with puking at breakfast, Ace," Marco says. "You miss all the news."

"Just shut up and tell me," I say. Thankfully my equilib-rium is starting to level off.

"The word is," Lucy says, gesturing for us to lean closer, "the Tundra Trials are about to begin!"

I'M ABOUT TO ASK IF THEY LEARNED ANY-
thing more about the Tundra Trials when Ridders blows his
whistle. Once we're lined up outside the cantina, he marches
us out of the Earth Sector and down the tunnel headed for
the closest chasm. I say a silent prayer that we stay on the path
rather than veer for the bridge.

That would be just my luck—tripping on a bridge and
plunging to my death in front of the entire EarthBound
Academy.

Fortunately, Ridders winds us the long way around. I
brush my fingers against the muddy wall to be sure I'm not
accidentally creeping closer to the edge.

As we make our way through Gulaga, hundreds of pairs of Tunneler eyes follow us. Just like yesterday, their grunts sound like accusations. Maybe it's what Marco said—grunting just sounds mad. Maybe not.

Up ahead, Ridders stops in front of a pair of enormous, intricately carved stone doors guarded by a cadre of Earth Force officers. And it's a good thing, from the looks of it. A crowd of Tunnelers is gathered in front of the wall of officers. And this time, there's no mistaking that they're angry. They grunt and shove against the officers who hold them back.

The sound of a voice box mingles with the guttural noises: "That is our sacred space! How dare you!"

Then the command of a nearby officer: "Find the offender and seize that box!"

"Did you hear that?" Cole whispers. "They called this their sacred space."

"Maybe that's why it has such fancy doors," I say.

The doors depict highly detailed scenes. In the first square, the Tunnelers are underground, crouching in a burrow. In the next, a flying object appears in the sky. The narrative continues: the Tunnelers emerge from below; they bow on the ground; an object descends from the stars; someone steps out of a ship onto the planet's surface. I can't be sure, but it looks like a human.

"Is that a spaceship?" I ask. "Is this scene depicting first contact?"

"It sure looks like it," Cole says. "But that doesn't make much sense. If the Tunnelers were so excited about our arrival that they carved it on their sacred doors, then why are they so upset now with us entering them?"

As if to emphasize Cole's point, a Tunneler hurls an object at the doors. It hits with a large *crack* and bursts apart. Yellow goop drips drops down the door, roughly tracing the path of the human visitor descending to the Tunneler surface.

"Cool!" Ryan says. "They must have eggs! Maybe we'll have some for breakfast later this week."

I'm about to tell Ryan that his comment was kind of offensive, but then I realize I'd gladly eat eggs if they served them. Finding food I'll eat here is hard enough; there's no need to make it worse just on principle.

The officers carve a path through the protestors. Two plebes grab the door handles and haul them open. Eager to escape the angry Tunnelers and their projectile eggs, everyone with the orange EF insignia on their chest rushes the room.

"Whoa," I say as we step into the huge chamber. It kind of looks like the inside of the Roman Colosseum, if you stretched the top so that it was tall and thin. "What is this place?"

"I think it's their hall of Parliament," Cole says.

"You mean their government?" Ryan asks.

"Yes," Cole says. "But not anymore."

That's right. Neeka told us that the Tunnelers no longer have their own government. It's just Earth Force.

Ridders corrals the Bounders off to one side. He points to carrels along the wall, kind of like the hovels where we sleep. He instructs us to grab our pod mates and find a carrel.

Up here.

Mira? She takes me by surprise. It's been radio silence since we arrived. I feel kind of guilty, but she hasn't really been on my mind. I've been getting lost in Gulagaven, catching up with the other Bounders, dealing with Regis and the caterpillars. But as soon as I sense her, I know two things: I miss her more than I'd like to admit, and we've never really been apart.

I turn my head to scan the carrels, but I already know exactly where to look. I zero in on the middle row, center carrel. A second passes before Mira steps from the shadow of the carrel and fans her fingers in a could-be wave.

"Up there!" I grab Cole and head for the ramp. We pick up Marco along the way. Lucy tries to wave us down to another row, but I ignore her. I slide into the carrel next to Mira.

Hi! I form the word in my brain and think of her. She doesn't reply, but she lays her fingers next to mine on the bench.

"Smart choice," Marco says, inspecting our carrel. "If those Tunnelers ever succeed at busting down the doors, we have an easy escape route." His hand is on the handle of a side door

I hadn't noticed when I first entered the carrel. It leads to a narrow hallway that exits the chamber from the rear.

Down below, Ridders marches to the center of the chamber. When he reaches a podium on the raised stage, every plebe in the chamber snaps to attention. It takes a few seconds for the Bounders to catch on, but soon we swing our hands into salutes.

The podium is so low it must have been built for Tunnelers. Ridders hunches over the microphone. "Attention, cadets and fellow officers: welcome to Gulaga. We are honored that our Tunneler friends have offered to host the EarthBound Academy here on their planet for the second tour of duty. I trust you are adjusting to your accommodations. Training will get under way today. Now for some administrative announcements."

He pulls a piece of paper from his shirt pocket and continues. He instructs us which bathrooms to use and where we can obtain basic sundries and toiletry items. He reminds us to stay out of certain tunnels unless escorted by a Tunneler officer or junior ambassador. He reviews the timeline for the tour of duty and explains that the EarthBound Academy was moved to Gulaga for the second tour to focus on field training.

Next, he announces an important staffing change. Like I heard last night in the burrow, Maximilian Sheek has replaced Florine Statton as the Director of Bounder Affairs. Florine, apparently, is focusing on her new EFAN gawk show, *In the Flo with Florine Statton*, and won't be coming to the EarthBound Academy this tour.

I don't catch all of what Ridders says, thanks to a hunger-induced zone-out, but when I tune back in, he's reading straight from the piece of paper, practically choking on the words. ". . . I am so pleased to introduce a legend in his own time, Maximilian Sheek."

I bet Sheek wrote that introduction himself.

Sheek enters from the hallway next to our carrel. His hair is all poufed up in its signature style. He walks right to the edge of the row, stops, and poses. He turns his chin from side to side like he's so used to catching a camera angle that he does it automatically even when there's no lens in sight.

The chamber erupts in applause, and the cheers don't let up as Sheek takes his merry time making his way to the podium. When he finally arrives, he poses again, then leans low over the microphone, somehow still managing to look stylish.

"Thank you for your elegant words," he says. "I am so incredibly humbled, *Captain* Ridders." He raises his arms to the crowd. "Did you hear that, cadets? Ridders has been promoted to captain! Let's share some applause with him!" Sheek claps, and the crowd cheers along as he does that cheek-to-the-camera move again.

MONICA TESLER

"Ooh!" Lucy whispers. "Do you think Ridders will be featured in the annual aeronaut calendar?"

I roll my eyes. Only Lucy could morph into a mega-fangirl that fast.

"Now that he's a full-fledged aeronaut," Sheek continues, "and I am oh so stretched in my new role, Captain Ridders will be taking over my pod. Of course, he'll still have access to my wisdom and know-how in a mentorship capacity."

Mira slips inside my brain. *Yuck.*

I laugh out loud, which, fortunately, no one notices since everyone's clapping.

Double yuck.

"How do you like Gulaga? Isn't this absolutely, indubitably fantastic?!" Sheek says, alternating his pose with every clause.

More cheers. At this point, I'm not even sure what we're cheering for.

"I am so deeply honored to take up the reins left behind by the incomparable Florine Statton as the new Director of Bounder Affairs. Now, without further ado, I am pleased to announce that the Tundra Trials begin today!"

Now I'm cheering along with the masses. I still only know what Waters told us about the Tundra Trials, but I bet they're going to be epic.

It seems Sheek doesn't know much about the Tundra Trials

either, because he returns the podium to Ridders for a full explanation.

"You're right to be excited," Ridders says. "But make no mistake, you have much work ahead of you. The Tundra Trials are a grueling pod-against-pod astrocache competition across the surface of Gulaga."

Ridders activates a projection screen, and a visual of the planet's surface appears in the air above him. He presses a button, and dozens of Earth Force insignias appear on the landscape. The projection turns, and more targets come into view across the planet. "Caches are placed strategically at different geographic locations on the surface. You will need to use your skills in navigation, teamwork, blast-pack flight, and bounding to find as many caches and collect as many tokens as possible over the weeks ahead."

Ridders deactivates the projection. "The point of the Trials is to simulate real-life situations in your training and prioritize the pod over the person. We expect you to hone your skills and your cunning, as you will need both to be successful Earth Force officers. The Trials will commence this morning and will be overseen by Commander Krag, the highest-ranking Gulagan officer in Earth Force. The commander will explain the rules of the Tundra Trials once you reach the surface."

Lucy elbows me and whispers, "Commander Krag is Neeka's dad!"

A plebe approaches the podium. Ridders covers the microphone with his hand. "Excellent timing," he says after talking with the plebe. "Stand and salute your admiral!"

So the rumors were right. We leap to our feet, whipping our hands against our foreheads.

As I watch for the intricate doors to open, an honor guard marches by our carrel. The admiral must be using the back door.

The guards escort a small figure clad in the Earth Force uniform. As they descend the ramp and approach the podium, their ranks part. Admiral Eames steps to the microphone. It's the perfect height.

Maybe I was wrong. Maybe it was built for *her*.

She gestures for us to quiet down. "Greetings, fellow officers, cadets of the EarthBound Academy, and esteemed guests. Welcome to the Earth Force sovereign nation of Gulaga. Cadets, today your training begins in earnest. Make no mistake, the progress you make at the Academy will translate into victories in battle. Your duties are to your planet, and your planet needs you."

Sheek, standing at her right elbow, bursts into applause, our cue to do the same.

"You have looked into the face of the Youli," the admiral says somberly. "You have seen their rotten core through their hollow eyes. Those eyes are searching for you across the galaxies. They will hunt you down and try to extinguish you."

Whoa. That seems a bit extreme. Hunting down and extinguishing us sounds quite a bit different from the Youli urging us to *leave* the Paleo Planet.

"They seek to exterminate all of humanity and claim Earth as their own," she continues.

Marco bumps my shoulder. "Exterminate us and claim Earth?" he whispers. "That's not what I imagined when Waters mentioned a territory and policy dispute."

The admiral leans forward. "The hour could not be more grave. Focus on your training, master your skills. You will be called upon to use them imminently. The time is now to seize your birthright."

When the admiral stops talking, the chamber is silent. Then a lone voice rises up. "Birthright! Bounders fight!"

Cole and I exchange glances. Whoever decided to shout in this moment of military decorum is definitely going to be in big trouble.

But then another voice joins the chant, and another, and another.

"Birthright! Bounders fight!"

"Birthright! Bounders fight!"

"Birthright! Bounders fight!"

Soon almost everyone in the chamber has joined the chant,

pumping their fists in the air with each word. At the podium, Admiral Eames slowly lifts her hands overhead. The volume in the chamber swells.

I don't know what to do. This feels all wrong. There's so much we don't know. There's so much we do know that's not right. Like how they bred us to be soldiers, how they've lied about the Youli, how they've tested alien technology on kids. Mira is agitated and nervous. She grabs my hand.

On either side of me, Cole and Lucy chant. I guess they'd rather blend in than stand out on principle.

Marco shakes his head. "Not doing it."

The admiral stares up at our carrel. We must be the only cadets not chanting.

I'm so torn. I don't want to feel like the odd man out anymore. But I know too much to see things in black and white.

Mira squeezes my left hand. *Stay strong.*

"Birthright! Bounders fight!"

"Birthright! Bounders fight!"

"Birthright! Bounders fight!"

I lift my fist in the air, but I don't say the words.

THE ADMIRAL RETURNS THE PODIUM TO
Ridders and exits through the hall next to our carrel. When she passes by, she nods at us. I'm not sure if it's a *Welcome back* nod or a *You'd better shape up* nod. Either way, she makes me nervous.

Ridders wraps up the briefing and invites in the twenty-six junior ambassadors, one assigned to each pod. We have an hour to get to the surface for the start of the Tundra Trials, and our ambassadors are charged with bringing us there. If there's one thing I learned yesterday, it's to not leave Neeka when we need to navigate the twists and turns of Gulagaven.

All the junior ambassadors are wearing the same custom

Earth Force brown bags, which Lucy calls *frocks*. I'm not sure how we'll spot Neeka in the crowd.

I don't worry long, because as soon as we step foot on the chamber floor, Neeka nearly knocks Lucy down with a hug. She's tied orange and blue ribbons around the left shoulder strap of her frock. I don't need to guess where those ribbons came from.

"Oh! Oh! I'm so happy to see you this morning! I was so devastated yesterday when the boys got lost, and Father had some hard words for me last night, and I promised that today things would be different and we would all stay together. You hear that, boys? I said we'd all stay together. And that means no wandering off on your own or exploring off-limits tunnels or befriending any Wackies. Got it?"

"We didn't wander off on our own," Cole says. "You left us."

"How were we supposed to know that tunnel was off-limits?" I ask.

"Befriending Wackies?" Marco says. "I wouldn't exactly say we befriended him, but do you mean Barrick is a Wacky?"

I hadn't thought about Barrick since we made it to the burrow yesterday, but if Neeka's saying he's a Wacky, that may call for some follow-up questions.

"Oh! No! I most definitely did not say that. We are not allowed to talk about Wackies. That is on the prohibited list for sure. Father would be very disappointed."

Lucy links her arm with Neeka. "Remember what I said yesterday, sweetie? These boys will trick you into saying anything. Now, same plan as yesterday: girls up front, boys in the back. But this time, you boys need to stay in line." She delivers these last words with her hands on her hips, glaring at us.

Marco salutes. "Yes, ma'am."

She slaps him on the arm. "Cut that out."

We follow Neeka out of the chamber and through the winding tunnels of Gulagaven. At first, we're with most of the other cadets in a huge herd. But soon the crowd thins, and it's just our pod, gradually making our way to the surface, listening to Neeka and Lucy drone on and on. Marco puts his hands out to slow me and Cole.

"What?" Cole says as the girls pull ahead.

"Quiet, Wiki," Marco says. "Just hang back."

"We don't want to get lost again," I say, urging us forward. "Plus, Lucy will flip if we get separated."

"We won't. I just want to give them a little space so they can't hear our every word."

The girls pull ahead. They don't seem to notice that we've fallen behind. From what I can tell, Neeka and Lucy are engaged in a game of competitive talking.

"What's up?" I ask Marco.

"Did you hear what Neeka said about Barrick? That he's a Wacky?"

"That's not what she said," Cole says.

"It's what she *implied*," he says.

"Maybe," I say. "But what are we going to do with that information? Barrick bolted the second he got a chance. We'll probably never see him again."

"We need to find him," Marco says.

"Maybe Waters knows where he is," Cole says.

"That's right, Brainiac!" Marco says. "Barrick said he knew Waters! What do you think about that juicy nugget? A Wacky who knows Waters who happens to rescue us? What are the odds? It's fate, and we need to find him."

"It has nothing to do with fate and everything to do with him spotting three cadets out of their element and reluctantly stepping in to help," I say. "Although I admit it's weird he knows Waters." Somehow Waters seems to be at the center of everything. I wish I knew why. Maybe if I told my pod mates about the brain patch, we could come up with an explanation. Of course, they'd be so mad at me for keeping secrets, they may never talk to me again.

"I want to find Barrick, too," Cole says. "I want to get a look at that first-generation voice-translation box."

"Let's try to get some more info out of Neeka," Marco says. "She may know about the summit, and she definitely knows about the Wackies."

"Fine," I say. "And we can watch for signs of the Wackies

out on the tundra during the Trials. But let's not get derailed with this. I don't want to be on anyone's radar this tour, and we're already on Ridders's watch list. As far as I'm concerned—"

I almost crash right into Lucy, who's planted herself in our path with Neeka and Mira by her sides.

"Are you trying to get Neeka in trouble, and our whole pod right along with her?" she asks.

"Huh?"

"Don't you play all space cadet with me, Jasper Adams! We turn around and you're so far back we can barely spot you. From now on, you're my buddy. I'm going to keep track of you if I have to hold your hand for the rest of the tour." Lucy swipes my hand up in her own. Neeka loops her paw around Marco's elbow. That leaves Mira and Cole to walk side by side in the back of our buddy train.

We fall in line and take the long way up to the surface. Fortunately, Neeka honors my request not to cross any bridges. As we make our way through the last stretch of tunnel to the surface, the air gets colder by the second. Our breath puffs in chilly clouds as we walk. There aren't any side tunnels with burrows or bars or even work spaces. The higher levels of Gulagaven are truly inhospitable. It makes me fear what's waiting on the surface.

"Almost there." Neeka rubs her fur and hurries along.

If she's cold in a fur coat, you'd better believe it's freezing.

"Any chance we could get some hot chocolate? Or at least some winter gear?" Marco asks. "I'm turning into a Popsicle."

"As a matter of fact," Neeka says, pointing ahead to a large door with a thick metal knocker, "the outfitter is the first stop of the final ascent." When we reach the door, Neeka twists the knocker and pulls.

We follow Neeka inside. The walls of the room are covered with a thick, fuzzy coating which I'm guessing is for insulation because it's quite a bit warmer. Thank goodness. I can barely feel my toes. The room is filled with Tunnelers and Bounders. Most of the cadets made it here before us. They must have crossed a few bridges.

Long benches stretch across the room. They're packed with cadets piling on layer after layer of protective weather gear. The Bounders who are furthest along look like giant puffer fish. That's what we have to wear? How are we going to walk? Or fly? Or bound, for Earth's sake?

Neeka waves us over to a counter manned by a couple of Tunnelers. She asks our shoe size and passes that information along. The Tunnelers head to the back and reemerge minutes later with a gear bin for each of us.

I take my bin and find a spot near the wall. Unfortunately, I'm directly across from Regis. I didn't recognize him beneath all those layers.

As soon as I sit down, he's on me. "How was your first night, Jasper?"

I figure not responding is the best approach, but I forget that Marco is sitting beside me.

"How's your sad, pathetic life, Regis?" he asks.

"Am I talking to you, Romero?"

"I sure hope not."

Thankfully I'm saved by Captain Edgar Han, Regis's pod leader, who I also didn't recognize at first under all the gear. "Regis, Randall, Hakim, let's go. We're having a pod meeting before the Trials start. Wear your bounding gloves. They'll keep your hands warm. And you're going to need them."

"Pod meeting?" Cole whispers as Mira, Lucy, and Neeka grab the seats left behind by Regis and crew. "That's completely unfair! Our pod leader isn't even here!"

"Oh! You're in for a treat!" Neeka says. "Father told me this morning. Since your pod leader hasn't arrived on Gulaga yet, the most famous aeronaut in the world is going to be your substitute—"

Oh no. "Not—"

"Maximilian Sheek!" Neeka is obviously expecting us to jump up and down, or at least cheer or something, when she tells us that Sheek is going to be our substitute pod leader. When she sees our downcast expressions, she slumps, too. "Whatever is the matter? I thought you'd be delighted!"

"Sheek is nothing but a liability," Lucy says. "The only thing awesome about him is his hair."

"But I thought—"

"You and the whole world, sweetie," Lucy says. "Sometimes we know too much for our own good."

As if he heard his name whispered among the masses, Sheek makes his grand entrance. He's decked head to toe in custom-made winter fashion, of course. His outfit reminds me of the coat Lucy wore on our mountain hike, although ten times fancier.

"There you are, honorary podettes!" He waltzes over to us. "Chop! Chop! I'm holding a strategy session in two minutes!" He pauses—and poses—for the whole room to take in his greatness before waltzing out of the outfitter.

"Strategy for what?" Marco asks. "How to be a complete fraud?"

"Oh! Oh! Quiet!" Neeka says. "That kind of talk will have you banished!"

"What?" Lucy, Marco, and I say at the same time.

"Oh! Oops!" Neeka waves and tiptoes up the aisle. "You're all set right? I'll be back to pick you up after the Trials. Good luck!"

"Wait a minute!" Lucy says. "What did you mean 'banished'?"

Neeka twists her head around to check if anyone overheard us, and then scurries from the room.

"Did you see her turn her head?" Cole asks. "The Tunneler turn radius is remarkable. Their neck muscles are very loose."

"Neck muscles?" Marco says. "Neeka drops a banishment bomb, and you're talking neck muscles? What's with you, Wiki?"

"Do you think that's what happened to the Wackies?" I ask. "They were banished?"

Lucy opens her eyes super wide, shakes her head in tiny jerks, and keeps quiet. If Lucy's not talking, there's a problem. I slowly pivot my own head around to find Sheek looming over me.

"Let's not concern ourselves with trivial topics," he says. "Instead, let's focus on the fact that I asked you to rendezvous with me outside for our strategy session." He crouches down, somehow still managing to look like a web star, and whispers, "The last thing I want to do is babysit you insolent twerps. You will do what I say and you will do it now, or the admiral will know of your insubordination." He stands back up to his full height and announces to the room with a twirl of his hand, "That's right, the other pods will be racing for second place today."

Lucy, Marco, and Mira follow Sheek out of the room. Cole stays back and helps me lace up my boots, then we dash out together. We don't want to get on the wrong side of Sheek. He may be a coward, but he's got mega pull in Earth Force.

We exit the outfitter center into a small waiting room filled with other cadets and Tunnelers. An intercom makes an announcement in Gulagan, followed by its English translation: "One minute until the doors will open. You will have thirty seconds to enter the first antechamber."

"What's the antechamber?" I ask.

"We'll find out," Cole says.

The doors slide open and the crowd funnels through. Thirty seconds later, the doors close. The room we're in looks a lot like the room we left, only smaller and colder. A Tunneler officer directs us through a clear tube that sucks the extra air out of our gear so we look a bit less like snowmen. Now there's a chance we'll be able to maneuver our blast packs, but we still look pretty silly.

Another intercom ushers us through a second anteroom. Finally it warns that the anterior gate is opening. We'll have thirty seconds to exit onto the surface ramp. "Don face masks now," the announcement concludes.

Cole and I pull on our clear masks and lift our hoods. Scanning the room filled with other cadets, I realize it will be hard to tell who's who on the surface.

When the doors slide open, we're hit with a blast of arctic air so cold I instantly know where my skin is exposed. I adjust my face mask to cover the patch of cheek I'd missed. The intercom beeps, signaling the doors are about to close. Cadets push from behind. Cole grabs my sleeve, and we jog up the ramp, guided by the dim natural light.

It's awesome to be outside, cold or not. Once we clear the ramp, I stop and tip my head to the star shining down on Gulaga.

The ramp dumped us onto the tarmac of the small aeroport we saw yesterday from the space elevator. Beyond the aeroport, the elevator shaft stretches up into the sky. From the space dock, we could see the entire length of the elevator, straight to the planet's surface. But from down below, we can't see through the atmosphere, so it looks like the elevator shaft goes on forever. It reminds me of "Jack and the Beanstalk."

It's easy to spot our pod, because it's easy to spot Sheek. In addition to Marco, Mira, and Lucy, he's managed to attract a small crowd of Tunnelers to regale with his tales.

When Cole and I arrive, Sheek is telling some fantastical story—probably made up—about how he was the first aeronaut to map P-92. He talks and talks. Around us, Bounders meet with their pod leaders. Soon, cadets start to converge in the center of the aeroport where a group of Tunnelers are already assembled.

Great. We're going to have no strategy and no energy after being bored to death by Sheek.

MONICA TESLER

"He may be the world's most annoying, narcissistic person," Lucy whispers, "but he has a great sense of style! Do you think he'll let me wear my new alpine coat on the tundra?"

I don't answer. Lucy's fashion concerns are the least of our worries right now.

Marco raises his hand. When Sheek doesn't acknowledge him, he interrupts. "About that strategy session . . ."

At first, I think Sheek is going to flip out, but apparently, he decides to make a show of his commitment to guide us. He smiles at the crowd. "Perfect timing, cadet. I was just getting to that. Why, when I was leading an expedition on Planet Thirty-seven . . ."

All the other pods look organized and poised for competition, with some kind of symbol for pod identification and unification. Han's pod has purple armbands. The cadets in Suarez's pod have red stars painted on the tops of their helmets. Ridders's cadets wear green neck warmers—easy to spot and an extra layer of warmth.

When I tune back in to Sheek's tips, here is the kernel of wisdom that awaits me:

". . . so my primary pointers are work as a team, take breaks, and never, ever underestimate style." With that choice nugget, Sheek reaches into his coat and whips out a stack of decals. They're enormous close-up photos of Sheek's face, the head shot they use for *Chic with Sheek*. "Just stick these beauties on your helmets and you'll be ready for the Trials!"

"You want us to wear those?" I ask, hoping Sheek will detect the reservation in my voice and reconsider.

"Absolutely. You must have a mark for your pod as a sign of unity." Sheek withdraws a pen from another pocket. "I will even do you the honor of autographing them."

As Lucy slaps Sheek's face on our helmets and he signs, one of the Tunnelers runs over to tell us we need to join the group. The Tundra Trials are about to begin.

I can't believe this. We won't even get a chance to talk about our pod strategy because we're stuck here listening to Sheek's drivel and plastering these ridiculous stickers on our helmets.

We are in Tundra Trial trouble.

As we join the other cadets, an older Tunneler steps to the center. His grunt is deep and grizzly as he speaks into his voice box. "Good morning, cadets. I am Commander Krag."

Neeka's Dad! Lucy mouths to me.

"We are about to kick off the course competition," he continues. "Here is how things will run. Each of you will receive an astrocache compass that contains downloads of topographical maps and the cache list. Your objective: travel to each location on the list in whichever order you choose; locate the Earth Force flag and retrieve the cache; scan iden-tification for each pod member and take a token; return the flag and cache to exactly where you found them. There are one hundred caches in total."

"Sounds kind of easy," Marco whispers.

"This may sound easy," Commander Krag says, like he read Marco's mind, "but I assure you it is not. You can use anything at your disposal: bounding gloves, blast packs, intellect, deceit. There is only one rule: you must be back through the doors by sixteen hundred hours each day. No exceptions." He gestures to the anterior gate, which now looks a lot more threatening than it did on the way through.

"One more thing," the commander says. "There are twenty-six pods, but only twenty-five tokens at each location. The first pod to find each cache and collect every token is the winner. So use your time wisely. We expect the competition to be brutal and rigorous, and last for several weeks. If no one completes the cache course, the pod with the most tokens at the end of the tour will be declared the victor."

Wow. That's intense. There will be tons of strategy involved. And everyone in the pod will have to pitch in.

I glance at my pod mates. Cole hops on his toes. Lucy smiles. Mira stares across the tundra. Marco looks at me and nods. We've got this.

"My officers are passing out the astrocache compasses now," Commander Krag continues. "Wait for my signal to activate them."

Marco grabs the compass marked for our pod. It looks like a large watch. The Earth Force insignia glows orange on the screen.

Commander Krag lifts a thick metal rod from the ground near his feet. Next to him, a silver disk the size of a small table hangs from a tall metal stand. The commander raises the rod and slams it against the disk. A low gong reverberates across the land.

"Let the Tundra Trials begin!"

"THIS WAY!" MARCO YELLS AND RUNS
for the other side of the tarmac while the gong still hums.

We have no choice but to chase him.

"What on earth, Marco?" Lucy says. "Why'd you run?"

He holds up his hand, telling us to wait.

"Seriously?" she spouts. "Give me that!" She grabs the
compass from his hand.

"You could have broken it, Lucy!" Marco shouts.

"You're the one who ran off with it!" she yells back.

"Yeah, so we could talk strategy without having to worry
about anyone overhearing us!" Marco says, trying to snatch
the compass back.

At the podium, Commander Krag beats the gong as each pod departs. At least a dozen gongs reverberate across the tundra. As each moment passes, we fall farther behind.

Lucy spins away from Marco. "Well, you could have said something!"

Cole throws his hands up. "This is a terrible way to start!"

Mira steps between Marco and Lucy. They're so startled, they actually stop moving and yelling. Mira pries the compass from Lucy's fingers and hands it to me.

You. Her gentle word slips into my brain.

"What do you want me to do with it?"

You. Now everyone's staring at me.

"Yeah, you made that clear already."

You.

"Why me? Why does it always have to be me?" I didn't sign up to be the decision maker. We have too many volunteers for that job already.

"What is going on?" Cole says.

"I can't believe this!" Lucy says. "Should we just give up now?"

"Seriously, Ace," Marco says. "Are you just going to stand there?"

You.

Fine, Mira. Fine.

I dodge Marco's run at the compass, buying a few seconds to think things through.

"Okay," I say. "This is how it's going to work. We all have jobs. Cole, you're in charge of overall strategy. Lucy, there'll be a major social dynamic to this game. That's your area of expertise. Mira and I will partner up and cover any issues with the gloves, and we'll work with Cole to determine the best routes and travel methods. We have a major advantage over the other pods. We know they'll be rolling out the BPS later this tour, and we know how to use it."

"What about me?" Marco asks.

"You'll handle special assignments."

"What does that mean? It sounds like you just don't know what to do with me."

"That's not it at all," I say. "There'll definitely be some dicey moments that require nerve and creativity."

Marco grins and rubs his hands together. "My specialty."

"Exactly," I say. "So, to kick things off, I'm giving the compass to Cole, our strategy master."

Cole seems a bit surprised to be handed the astrocache compass, but he quickly morphs into the *Evolution of Combat* expert strategist. He straps the compass on his wrist and activates the screen. "Excellent. I can plug in our routes and plot our course directly from the device. We should identify the closest cache locations and hit those first. Once Waters and Gedney arrive with the BPS, it will be easier to travel to the caches that are farther away."

"Shouldn't we just start with the first cache on the list?" Lucy asks.

"No," Cole says. "I expect lots of pods will do that, so the race to that site will be crowded and competitive."

"But what if all the tokens are snatched up?" I ask. "You heard what Commander Krag said about each cache being one token short."

"It's a strategic gamble," Cole says. "We have to assume at least some of the pods will come at this from a similar strategy as us and not start with Cache 1. My biggest concern is that we have no sense of distance and travel time. Even so, the first location looks far on this map. There are much closer targets."

"Sounds logical, Wiki. So where are we headed?"

"Here." Cole points at the map pulled up on the astrocache compass screen. "Cache 42."

"But that one looks closer," I say, pointing to a different target.

"Yes, but look at the topography. I can't tell what that is on the map, but it looks like a ravine or a mountain range."

"Do we have time to get there and back?" Lucy asks.

"We should," Cole says. "We'll fly there and bound back."

"Okay," I say. "Your plan it is. Let's go."

We consult the map, get our bearings, and take off in our blast packs in the direction of Cache 42. The gong sounds as we go.

Within a few minutes, we leave behind Gulagaven and cross into the lonely, barren landscape of Gulaga. The surface of the planet looks like a never-ending sea of rocks and frozen mud. The light from their star is bright enough to guide us where we're going, but it feels like dusk.

When we first set out, some of the other pods are visible in the distance. Lots head north in the direction of the first cache, but a few fly west like us, and some scatter in other directions.

We take breaks every twenty minutes to rest and consult the map. We're not used to covering long distances with our blast packs, and we're definitely not used to flying with all these extra layers. My legs hang heavy beneath me, and my shoulders are already sore from my pack straps. Not to mention my belly aches with hunger. The last bit of food I managed to keep down was the protein bar I had yesterday when we were lost in the tunnels.

"Everyone remembered to charge their packs last night, right?" Cole says during our next break. "We don't want to run out when we're hundreds of kilometers away from Gulagaven."

"How do we know how much is left?" I ask.

Lucy strips off her pack and unzips the motor compartment on the back. "See this gauge? It looks like I've already burned through a quarter of the charge."

I check my pack. I've used a quarter, too. "If our packs run out of juice and we can't make it back by curfew, it's game over."

"Better add *blast pack charge* to our list of strategy points, Wiki," Marco says. "Maybe we can trick Regis's pod into flying for a cache out of charging range."

"That's cruel," Lucy says.

"Hey, Neeka's dad said deceit was fair game," I say.

"Well, we'd better be on guard for those clowns trying to trick *us*," she says.

After we travel for what seems like an eternity, but is really closer to two hours, we land near a cropping of large boulders. When my feet hit the ground, I trip, landing face-first in the mud. When I sit up, the world spins. I slip out of my pack and lean back against a boulder.

I'll be fine. I just need to rest for a few minutes.

And maybe eat.

But I can't eat. There's no way I can stomach Tunneler food, not when I'm already nauseous. Plus, we're nowhere near the cantina. We're supposed to be gone all day, and I didn't even think about packing something. Some leader I turned out to be. With me at the helm, we'll starve.

"Surprise!" Lucy says, pulling a bag out of her blast pack. "Who's hungry?"

"Where'd you get that?" I ask.

"From Neeka." She hands small wrapped packages to each

of us. "The kitchen prepared lunch for all the pods. Mira, you have the water, right?"

Mira opens her pack and pulls out a thermos.

No one but me seems surprised that Lucy was carrying the lunch. Were they keeping this from me after what happened at breakfast? Did they plan an intervention? A lunch ambush?

"What's going on?" I ask.

"Food is fuel, Ace," Marco says. "We need you to be fueled up to kick it in the competition."

Whatever the Tunnelers packed is going to be disgusting. I sit on the ground and bow my head to my knees.

Mira kneels beside me and strokes the back of my head where the hair has grown over the Youli patch.

I want to be mad, but Marco's right. We're in a competition. We need our strength. My picky eating shouldn't be a factor. I'm embarrassed as it is.

I grab my lunch package, pull back the wrapper, and stare at the lump of brown in my lap. "What is it?"

"BERF," Lucy says.

"Barf?" Oh my god. This day could not get worse.

"Not barf," Cole says. "BERF. It stands for Bacteria-Enriched and Refined Fungus."

"Oh, great," I say. "That sounds so much better than barf." Not really.

The big, brown, brick of BERF stares up at me. It looks

kind of like a brownie. If I just pretend it's a brownie, maybe I can get through this.

I lift the brown hunk to my mouth, but before I take a bite, the smell weasels its way into my nose. Moldy bread mixed with sweaty armpits.

I gag and turn my head.

Mira rests her hand at the base of my neck. *You can do this.* Her touch infuses me with strength.

Mira is the strongest person I know. She's so strong, she has strength to spare.

Think of all she's had to deal with to be part of our pod. Last tour, she could hardly make it through lunch with us. She barely flew in the relays. She couldn't stay in bed at night.

She had to get through all of that. And she did. She doesn't always like it, and it's not always easy, but she does it anyway.

And that's what I need to do.

I need to start eating even though I don't like it and it's not easy.

I need to eat anyway.

I plug my nose with one hand and bring the BERF to my mouth with the other. As I chomp down, my tongue curls around the thick, chalky mush. My stomach seizes and my throat constricts, but I refuse to give up. I chew, swallow, and press my fingers to my lips to keep it down.

Repeat. Repeat. Repeat.

I eat as fast as I can with as little thought as possible. Finally—shockingly—only one bite remains. I chew, swallow, and hold out my hand. "Mira! Water! Now!"

She hands me the thermos, and I gulp the cold water, clearing away the remains of BERF.

I feel light-headed and giddy.

"I did it," I say, half to myself.

"We're so proud of you!" Lucy throws her arms around me.

Cole nods.

Marco slaps me a high five. "To BERF!" he shouts.

"To BERF!" we echo back.

When everyone's finished eating, we gather up our trash and consult the map. According to Cole, we should reach our first target in roughly an hour. I can already feel a new surge of energy coursing through me. We are going to dominate the Tundra Trials!

Game on!

As we cruise across the barren tundra in our blast packs, the landscape below slowly changes. The plains give way to sloping hills. The ground is cut by narrow crevices. The clusters of boulders grow sharper and more frequent until we reach a steep decline littered with tall, jagged rocks.

Cole lowers down at the edge of the slope, and the rest of us follow. Now that we're on the ground, the rocks seem gigantic.

"The map shows the cache coordinates as roughly halfway down the hill," Cole says. "Does anyone see anything?"

We stand in a row, scanning the slope, nobody spotting anything but rocks.

"It could be anywhere," I say. "Stuffed beneath a boulder. Shoved in a crevice. I think we'll have to split up and cover some ground."

"Those rocks don't look particularly stable," Lucy says.

"From the pattern of the debris," Cole says, "I'm guessing there was a landslide, and not too long ago."

"That's comforting, Wiki," Marco says. "Sometimes keeping your knowledge to yourself may be the best policy."

"It's almost fourteen hundred hours," I say. "We've got to be in Gulagaven by sixteen hundred, and I don't want to go back empty-handed."

"Let's get on with it, then," Lucy says. "But be careful!"

We split up and search the slope, but it's slow going. We don't even know exactly what we're looking for.

Not to mention, every time I touch down, a slew of rocks slides down the hill, threatening to take me down with them.

I check the time. We need to bound back soon.

I'm half-ready to give up when Lucy shouts that she's found the cache.

Then she screams.

LUCY'S SCREAM FADES INTO THE RATTLE

of tumbling rocks. My footing gives, and I lift off in my pack. A second later, a giant boulder rolls over the place where I'd been standing.

"Lucy!" I call. "Lucy!"

I fly higher, so I can scan the slope. Cole is far to the side, flying for the center. Marco and Mira are both beneath me. All of them are airborne, so they should be able to steer clear of the landslide.

All of them except Lucy. I still haven't spotted her.

"Lucy!"

Finally I spy a hint of indigo in the middle of a cluster

of boulders. There's no way those rocks will stay stable for long.

I zoom in that direction. "Lucy!"

She's crouched beneath a boulder, tugging at a piece of orange cloth.

"Get out of there!" I shout.

"I can't! It's the cache."

The boulder she's under looks pretty well planted, but the ones beside her are starting to slide. If she doesn't get out of there now, the boulder will shift, and she'll be crushed.

I zip around to the other side and hover next to her. "Let me try!" I lower myself to the slope.

As soon as my feet touch, the ground gives way and the boulder pitches forward. "Lucy!" I reach out with my gloves to hold the boulder in place, but other rocks are coming fast. Lucy ducks out of the way. I release my hold on the boulder, and it slams the ground where she was seconds before.

"Follow the cache!" Lucy shouts, lifting off in her pack. "Don't lose sight of it!"

The indigo box with the orange flag tumbles down the slope. Lucy and I fly just above the landslide, tracing the path of the cache. It picks up speed and more rocks with every turn. I try to grab control of its atoms, but it's no use—there's too much in the way.

Finally the cache reaches the bottom of the slope in a pile

of rocks and debris. Hundreds more rocks pile on top. When the air is still and the landslide has passed, we wave our pod mates to the bottom of the slope.

"Everyone okay?" I ask. When they nod, I say, "Let's start digging."

It takes twenty minutes for us to dig out the cache, even while using our gloves to move the heavier rocks. Thank goodness Lucy and I saw more or less where it landed, or we would be leaving without a token.

"Got it!" She uncovers the orange flag and casts off another layer of rocks to reach what it's anchored to: an indigo box with the orange Earth Force insignia stamped on the front.

Lucy examines the box. She runs her hands along the outside. "How do we open it?"

I take the cache from Lucy. It's about the size of a lunch box. It weighs about as much as the houseplant mom makes me carry to the sink to be watered. I shake it. There's definitely something inside. I turn the box over. The Earth Force logo is stamped on every side, but there's no sign of a latch or a button or anything else that might open it.

Marco grabs the box and inspects it. He's just as clueless as I am. "Maybe if we throw it on the ground." He raises his hands over head.

Just as he starts to bring them down, Mira frantically waves her arms in his trajectory. She gestures for him to hand it to her.

Mira sits the box down gently on the top of the rock pile. She places a gloved hand on either side. Her fingers swell with light, and then the box pops open.

"You need your gloves to open the box," I say. "Genius!"

"It's a good thing we have you, Mira," Lucy says.

"Seriously," Cole says. "That's a huge strategic advantage. How long do you think it will take the other pods to get their boxes open?"

"Yeah, yeah, yay for Mira," Marco says. "What's in the box?"

I pick up the cache and pull out a tablet. When I turn it on, a message flashes on the screen:

Congratulations!

You have found Cache 42 of 100.

Every pod member must provide a retina scan.

The screen advances, and indicates I should lean in for an eye scan. Once completed, the words *Jasper Adams, Waters Pod* appear on the screen.

"Easy so far," Lucy says, looking over my shoulder.

We pass the tablet around until everyone's been logged. Once the tablet acknowledges that our pod has completed the scans, these words appear: *If a token remains, scan it and take it with you.*

"Fair enough," I say, pulling a token—a small coin with the Earth Force insignia on one side and the number 42 on the other—from the cache box. Once I scan it, the screen reads *Token 1 of 25, Waters Pod.*

I almost slip the token in my pocket. Bad idea. "Who wants to be the token keeper? That is not part of my skill set."

Lucy grabs the token from my palm and zips it into her pack. "What next?" she asks.

Replace the cache exactly where you found it.

We look at each other, then up the hill. That's a bit easier said than done. Touching down on that slope is guaranteed to start a second landslide.

"We've got to follow directions, right?" Marco asks. "Leave it to me." He extends his hand, and I give him the cache box, all closed up and ready for the next pod. He wedges it under his arm.

We take off in our packs and fly for the top of the hill. Midway to the peak, Marco drops the cache. It flutters to the ground with its orange flag waving.

On top of the slope, we open our ports and bound back to Gulagaven with a full half hour to spare before curfew.

As soon as I'm sure we all made it, I jog for the gates. Day one, our work is done. And I'm freezing!

· *EF* ·

The rest of the week flies by—literally, because we spend most of it flying across the barren landscape of Gulaga finding caches and collecting tokens. Everything is going pretty well, really. Our pod is working together. The food, while still as unbelievably horrible as day one, is no longer my nemesis. I'm able to force down (and keep down) enough to keep me fueled for the long days. We spend the evenings catching up with the other Bounders, chatting with Neeka and her friends, and sometimes even playing *Evolution*—the beta version, of course. Fortunately, Earth Force didn't wipe the game from our tablets in between tours.

Even the bunk situation has been okay. We're usually so tired by the time bed rolls around, that we don't have the energy to get into it with Regis. And it seems the feeling is mutual. Still, Marco spends many a flight across the rocky plains of Gulaga scheming how we'll get them back for their prank on me the first night. Lucy usually tells him to shut his Tofu Face and focus on the Tundra Trials.

There hasn't been a chance to focus on much else, really. Our grand Earth Force reconnaissance mission has gone absolutely nowhere, but there are still four weeks left of the tour. And, selfishly, the less we focus on Earth Force's secrets, the less guilt I feel about my own.

The strategy is starting to kick into high gear. Now we don't just fly to targets. We use a combination of flying and bounding. Often we can cut our travel time in half by leapfrogging between locations we've already visited. Every time we travel, Cole makes us stop strategically along the way and mark the spot in our mind so that we can bound there in the future. It's like creating a network of stepping-stones across the tundra.

Of course, what our pod knows and most of the Bounders don't is that soon we won't need to have been physically present in a location to bound there in the future. Soon, Waters and Gedney will arrive with the BPS, and we'll be able to bound anywhere as long as we have the coordinates. Knowing about the BPS in advance is an advantage, maybe even an unfair advantage, but we're keeping quiet.

When we secure a token from Cache 8, it's a bit of a shock. More than half of the tokens are gone. That means getting closed out of a token is becoming a real risk.

"Where to, Captain?" Marco asks Cole.

"Cache 12."

"But Cache 4 is much closer," Marco says.

"It's not," Cole says. "Look how close Cache 12 is to where we had lunch today."

"Okay. So we bound?" I ask.

"Let's do it," Marco says.

Mira seals the cache, and Lucy returns it to its hiding place. Once we're all assembled, Mira opens her port and bounds.

I tap into the brain connection, open a port to where we had lunch, and—*Bam*. My landing is awful. I hit the ground at a funny angle and twist my ankle on a rock.

"Graceful, Ace," Marco says. He must have arrived seconds before me.

There's a brief moment of panic when Cole doesn't show up, but he eventually bounds in. We're about to take off in the direction of Cache 12 when Mira points. *Others.*

"Look!" Lucy shouts. "There's another pod!"

"From their route, I'd say they just left Cache 12," Cole says. "What do we do?"

"Nothing," I say. "We should just go. Give them a high-five in the air as we pass if you want."

"Not so fast," Lucy says. "Remember Commander Krag said we could use anything at our disposal so long as we get in by curfew? I'm thinking an information exchange could be useful, especially if they just claimed a token at Cache 12."

"What do you mean?" Cole asks.

"Depending on who it is, we give them a heads-up about the landslide at Cache 42 and the dwindling token supply at Cache 8, and they give us some info on the caches they've hit."

"Maybe," I say. "It really depends on who it is."

"Leave it to me," she says. "You put me in charge of the social game, remember?"

We take off flying straight for the incoming cadets. Before long, Ryan's red hair is easy to spot through the clear face mask. "It's Ridders's pod."

"Perfect," Lucy says.

As we close in, Lucy zooms to the front of our group and then touches down. She waves her hands over head, signaling the other cadets to stop.

At first, it looks like they're going to cut wide and avoid us, but then Ryan changes course and heads in our direction. The rest of his pod follows, and soon we're standing face-to-face, pod to pod, in the middle of the Gulagan tundra.

"How are you guys?" Lucy asks in a voice that practically bubbles.

"This is a race," Annette says. "We're losing time. Why did we stop?"

"Now, that's not particularly friendly," Marco says. He turns to Meggi and flashes a smile. "Which cache are you coming from?"

"Don't tell him that!" Annette says.

"Oh, please," Lucy says, "since when are you such a secret keeper, Annette? We know you're heading back from Cache 12. Let's cut to the chase, shall we? We'll tell you the scoop about the caches we've hit, if you spill the beans about yours."

Annette and her pod mates exchange glances. Eventually she nods. Ryan spills the details on Cache 12, including the peculiar markings on the stones where they found the cache. True to her word, Lucy warns them about the rock slide at Cache 42 and the limited tokens at Cache 8.

"There are even fewer tokens at Cache 3," Meggi says. "We were there yesterday morning."

"Thanks for the scoop," Lucy says to the other pod. "Let's touch base tonight after dinner. We may be willing to consider an alliance." She smiles and takes off in her blast pack, leaving us to chase after her.

MARCO AND I CATCH LUCY IN THE AIR
after ten minutes of hard flying. "An alliance? Where did that
come from? You should have checked with us first!" I shout.

"Oh, please," she says as we drop to the ground. "I didn't
say we'd make an alliance. I said we'd *consider* one. That means
we can say no. I can't be expected to run everything by you in
advance. This was a good play."

"Fair enough," Marco says. "It was a gutsy move, Madam
Diplomat, but you pulled it off."

"Oh, thank you so much, Marco," Lucy says in a mocking
tone. "Anyway, you left me no choice. I had to rescue you
from your pathetic attempts at flirting."

"Why don't you ask your friend Meggi how pathetic my flirting is?"

"Trust me, she'll be hearing from me for sure."

"Shut up and fly," I say as Cole and Mira zoom past us.

We pick up a token at Cache 12 without any trouble and bound back to Gulagaven. There are no other Bounders in sight, and we have a whole hour to spare.

"Are you sure we shouldn't make a run for another target?" Lucy asks.

"Not today," Cole says. "We'd cut it too close to curfew. Plus, there's no cache we could collect without using our blast packs. I'm pretty low on charge."

The star dips on the horizon, and it's much harder to see than when we started out this morning. And as the light fades, the temperature drops.

"I'm freezing my butt off," Marco says.

"Me, too!" Lucy says.

"Well, there's no sense standing around out here," I say. "Let's go inside and warm up. We have two hours before dinner. Maybe we can find Neeka and hit the market."

"And map out our strategy for tomorrow," Cole says.

"Sounds like a plan," Lucy says.

Mira leads us down the ramp into the antechambers. As we move from one room to the next, we shed our layers. By the time we reach the last anteroom, we've stripped off our face masks and unzipped our heavy parkas.

"There you are, sweetie," Lucy says, giving Mira's braid a tug. "We spend so much time under cover of all this gear, it's nice to see your pretty face."

Mira smiles and shrugs off her coat.

We're about to enter the outfitter center when we hear voices beyond the door.

". . . just don't understand why I can't be present. I'm the face of Earth Force, after all."

Sheek. He's the last person I want to see right now. If we run into him, he may feel like he needs to grace us with another strategy session, and then our free time will be lost forever. I wave to the others to take a seat on the benches along the wall.

"Let's give it a minute," I whisper. "Maybe he'll leave."

Marco gives the thumbs-up sign, and the others nod their agreement. They don't want to run into Sheek any more than I do.

"With all due respect, Max, this doesn't have anything to do with you."

"Ridders," Lucy whispers.

"Call me *Sheek*. You may be a captain now, but I'm senior to you in every way but rank."

"What I was trying to say . . ." There's no hiding the irritation in Ridders's voice. "Is that the admiral wants to assure our guests that this exchange will be kept in the utmost confidence. If you were to attend the meeting— you being the face of Earth Force, as you say—they may get the wrong idea. They may think the cameras will start rolling at any second."

Guests?

Exchange?

Utmost confidence?

"Much as I hate to admit it, Ridders, you are talking sense. When people see me, they see a web star. And that means they're thinking publicity on a mega scale. I'll agree to keep my distance, but I expect to be kept informed. I need to know the second a military engagement is under way."

Military engagement?

"Of course, Captain. I'm sure the admiral will keep you abreast of all war operations. After all, you'll need to prepare the cadets."

My eyes almost bug out of my head. Lucy gasps, and then presses her hands to her lips to stop from making more noise. Mira shakes her wrists and backs away from the door.

"Do you think that means . . . ," Cole starts at full volume.

"Shhh!" Marco, Lucy, and I hush him together.

"Did you hear that?" Ridders says from the other side of the door.

"I didn't hear anything," Sheek says. "When is the summit?"

"We're not sure," Ridders says tentatively. "Sometime in the next few weeks. Now we must be cautious. There are eyes and ears everywhere. In fact, I have a sneaking suspicion . . ."

"He hears us!" Lucy whispers.

"We need to hide!" I say.

"Quick! In here!" Marco says, holding open a side door.

Without a second thought, we duck inside. The door latches shut at the same moment the sliding panels to the outfitter center swish open. Ridders must be checking the anteroom for eavesdroppers.

"That was close," Cole whispers. "Did you hear him? He was talking about the summit!"

I lift a finger to my lips. We still need to be super quiet, or Ridders is sure to hear us.

A minute passes. Then, we hear new sounds. The intercom announcing the second anteroom doors blares, followed by scuffling footsteps just outside our hiding place.

"Welcome back, cadets!" Ridders says. "Was it a successful day?"

"No offense, sir, but you lead another pod now," says one of the Bounders. I think it's Amari, this guy from Africa who is in Suarez's pod and a total wiz at *Evolution*. Sometimes I think he might be as good as Cole. "We're not going to tell you anything."

"Understood," Ridders says.

"What should we do now?" Lucy asks. "We can't just open the door. Ridders will know we were hiding."

"I guess we have to wait it out," I say.

The intercom sounds again, and another pod enters the anteroom.

"There goes our hour," Cole says.

"Over here," Marco calls. He stands between a row of laundry carts piled high with discarded cold-weather gear and what looks like a hole in the wall. The hole is about waist high and the size of a door tipped on its side.

We push aside the laundry carts and crowd next to Marco.

"What's with the hole?" I ask.

"Our way out," he says. "I think it's a laundry chute."

"You *think* it's a laundry chute?" Lucy asks. "What if it's *not* a laundry chute? Or what if it *is* and it dumps us directly into a giant Tunneler washing machine?"

"It doesn't," Marco says. "Look!" He shines his tablet down the chute, illuminating a huge pile of laundry at the bottom. "See? Soft landing."

"What do we do once we get down there?" I ask.

Marco shrugs. "We'll figure it out. The Tunnelers have to do the laundry, which means there has to be another way out. We'll find it. Remember, you put me in charge of special assignments, handling the unexpected. I'd say this qualifies."

"I'm not doing it," Cole says. "We've already been lost once. And we've been warned not to go off on our own again."

"Count me out, too," Lucy says. "In fact, I'm leaving. If Ridders has words about us being in the laundry closet, I'll just have to sweet-talk him."

Lucy crosses to the door and pulls the handle. The door doesn't budge. "Uh, guys? It's locked."

Cole rushes over and tries the handle. "She's right. Locked."

Lucy puts her hands on her hips. "Like I really needed you to confirm that."

Cole ignores her and searches the surrounding walls, presumably for something that can open the door. Eventually he shrugs. "This locks from the other side. We're trapped."

"Can't you hack it?" Marco asks.

"It's a dead bolt, Marco. I'm a computer genius, not a miracle worker."

"Don't know the difference, Brainiac."

"So we pound on the door," Lucy says.

"I've got another idea," Marco says. "The laundry chute!"

"We've already said no!" Lucy grumbles.

"So you'd rather pound on the door, obliterating any chance that we can play it cool with our exit, than take our chances with the laundry chute? That's like volunteering for a fresh round of trouble. How did I end up in a pod with you cowards?"

"I am not a coward!" Cole says.

"Neither am I, Tofu Face," Lucy says. "And fine, we'll take the chute, but if anything goes wrong, it's entirely on you."

Cole and Lucy reluctantly back away from the door. We discard our cold-weather gear in the laundry bins and hoist ourselves onto the chute. Mira is to my left and Lucy my right, with the other boys on the bookends.

"Hold hands?" Lucy says, squeezing my palm. We all link up.

They look to me for a signal.

"One, two, three, go!"

We scoot our butts and then we're sliding.

"Geronimo!" Marco shouts.

We shoot down the ramp like it's an old-fashioned playground slide. The ride is over in a second. We land with a *thud* on a pile of dirty parkas.

"Fun!" Lucy says. "Can we do it again?"

"That was a one-time ride, sister," Marco says.

"This laundry is disgusting," Cole says, sliding down the pile of soiled coats.

"And stinky!" I plug my nose. There's no doubt these parkas have been well worn. They reek of sweat and the dank stench of Gulagan mud.

We climb off the laundry pile and look around. We've landed in a large cavern. It's like the other places we've visited in Gulagaven, but a lot more primitive. The walls aren't smooth and glossy. Instead, it looks like someone took a shovel and dug a huge hole, and we're standing in it.

Next to the laundry pile, there's a long trough filled with purple fluid for soaking clothes. Wet garments are squeezed with an enormous press and then soaked again in a trough of water on the other side. Then there's a trip through another press into a giant earthen stove that must be for drying.

"They cook the coats," Marco says. "Funky."

"This place gives me the creeps," Lucy says. "Let's get out of here."

Three doors line the far wall of the laundry hole. We check each one. The first is locked, so that's a no go. The second two both open to empty tunnels.

"Which one?" Cole asks.

"Eenie-meenie-minie-moe," Lucy says.

"This one," Marco says.

"Based on?" I ask.

"Gut instinct. And the fact that there's a bag of trash sitting just outside the door. It must mean they use this tunnel." Marco doesn't wait for our agreement. He takes off down his chosen hallway, expecting us to follow. And we do.

"Oh my god! Did you hear Ridders?" Lucy says, as we trudge after Marco. "They're sending us to war!"

"Drama! Drama! Drama!" Marco says. "That's not exactly what he said."

"Well, it's obviously what he meant!" she says.

"Shhh!" I say. "Sound really carries in this tunnel, and we don't know who might be down here."

"This could be the clue we need to find out what Earth Force is up to," Cole says. "Sheek asked about the summit."

"I know!" I whisper-shout. "And we can talk about it later."

Cole starts to protest, but I wave my hand across my neck, making it clear he should shut up.

After walking down the hall for about five minutes—Marco and me all hunched over for head clearance—I begin to notice something. It starts gradual, and then builds and builds until I can't escape it. I thought the laundry hole was stinky, but this hall absolutely reeks!

"What on earth is that smell?" Lucy asks.

"I don't know," I say. "But I'm about to lose my lunch."

"You mean barf your BERF?" Marco asks. "Don't do that, Ace. I bet it would taste twice as gross on the way back up."

"That is the most disgusting thing I've ever heard," Lucy says.

"Not as disgusting as the actual act of barfing BERF, I bet," Marco says.

"Quiet," Cole says. "I heard something."

"I don't hear anything," I say.

Thud.

"Actually . . ."

Thud.

"I heard something, too!" Lucy says.

Thud. Thud. Thud.

We round a bend in the tunnel and nearly trip over the source of the sound. There's a huge pile of trash bags in our path.

Thud.

Another bag falls from the sky. There's a hole in the wall. A trash chute.

Thud.

The bag bursts open as it hits the ground. Rotten purple tubers poor out, along with a cloud of flies. My stomach heaves. The joke about me losing my lunch is about to become a reality.

"Oh, that is nasty!" Lucy says.

"No wonder it stinks," Marco says.

Thud. Thud. Thud.

The stench is almost too much to bear. And the pile is building at an alarmingly fast rate. We need to get by soon, or we might be forced to climb over a garbage mountain.

"What are they going to do with all this trash?" I ask.

"Don't know. Don't care," Marco says. "We've got to get out of this tunnel. Let's go."

We slide against the wall to avoid touching the trash pile. Once clear, we break into a jog.

Suddenly trash is falling from everywhere. Did we just not notice the trash chutes before? How come the Tunnelers are all dumping their trash now? There are even some of those huge green waste bins from the space dock lined against the tunnel wall.

"Look out!" I shout at Mira. She barely avoids a triple-bag bomb.

We dodge back and forth to avoid stepping on the trash bags in the tunnel or getting knocked out by a falling bag from above. It's like the world's nastiest video game. And we're not playing it, we're living it!

"This is the grossest thing ever!" Lucy whines. "If I'm not out of here soon, I think I'll die from disgust."

"Hey, Drama Queen, is that purple potato in your hair?"

Lucy freaks, screaming and swatting at her head.

"Just joking," Marco says.

"Marco Romero, I am going to murder you!" Lucy says. "I can't believe you took us this way!"

"*I* took you this way? The way I remember it, I was the only one with any ideas. If it were up to you, we'd still be back in that locked laundry closet."

"No, we wouldn't!" Lucy shouts. "We would have pounded on the door, and someone would have let us out!"

"Yeah, *out* just to be *in* a lot of trouble with Ridders!"

"Trouble is better than trash!"

A loud beep sounds in the tunnel, interrupting Lucy's and Marco's bickering. Three beeps follow, then a robotic announcement in Gulagan, followed by the English translation:

"Attention! Clear the trash tunnel. Clear the trash tunnel immediately. The worm will be released in one minute."

WE ALL STOP WALKING. AND TALKING.

And fighting. We stare at one another with clueless expressions on our faces.

"Did it say 'worm'?" Lucy asks.

I nod.

"What exactly does that mean?" Cole asks.

"No clue," Marco says. "But it can't be good."

"We need to get out of here," I say. "Let's fly."

"What about the scrambler?" Cole asks. "We can't use our gloves."

Yikes. We'll have to use the manual grips, the ones that nearly got me laughed out of the EarthBound Academy last tour. I fish the grips out of my pack pockets and swap out my glove grips.

"We're not supposed to use our packs inside Gulagaven no matter which grips we're using!" Lucy says.

"No one's going to know, because no one's down here!" Marco yells.

"Yeah, no one is stupid enough to be in the trash tunnel!" Lucy screams back.

"Are you calling me stupid?" Marco snaps.

"Shut up!" I shout. "This is an emergency!"

Just go. Mira lifts off in her blast pack and soars ahead in the tunnel.

I'm not going to stand around listening to Marco and Lucy fight either. I push off after Mira.

Fly straight, Jasper. That's all I have to do. No crazy maneuvers, just straight ahead.

As I close in on Mira, a second alarm sounds in the tunnel: *"Attention! Worm released. Trash clearance in progress."*

"Oh no!" Lucy cries behind me.

"I have a bad feeling about this!" Marco shouts.

My pack stutters and drops. I hit the ground hard on my right hip. Scrambling to my feet, I try to fly, but my pack won't budge.

Marco and Lucy zoom past.

"Hey!" Stupid straps. I can't even lift off.

Mira stops in midair and zooms back for me. Her brain bumps up against mine, questioning. Up ahead, Marco drops to the ground. "I suck with these straps, remember?" I say to Mira.

She shakes her head. *Battery.* She shrugs out of her pack and shoves it in my face, showing that the orange charging light is blinking.

I check the battery charge on my pack. It's not the straps. I'm out of juice.

A strange noise sounds in the tunnel, a peculiar combination of squishing and scratching. The noise grows louder every second. Then the walls of the tunnel start to shake.

Mira's eyes latch on to mine. *Run.*

We take off on foot through the tunnel. Marco and Cole are up ahead, checking their packs. Lucy hits the ground several meters in front of Cole. It looks like packs aren't an option for anyone.

"We've got to get out of here!" I shout as we overtake Marco. "Go!"

Marco catches us, and we speed ahead to Cole and Lucy. "It's coming! Run!"

A sound like wet sneakers on a tile floor swells behind us, louder every second.

"*Ohmygodohmygodohmygod,*" Lucy gasps as she sprints.

I'd tell her to shut up, but I don't want to waste my

breath. I need all the lung power I have to outrun whatever is behind us.

The squishing noise is so loud, it must be close. So close it could squash me. I chance a glance over my shoulder.

"Oh my god!" I shout. Fifty meters behind us, and closing the gap with every second, is the most enormous, disgusting creature I've ever seen. It looks like the world's biggest earthworm. It's the color of dirty bathwater and has thick wrinkles all over its body. As far as I can tell, it doesn't have eyes or ears or a nose, just the most gigantic mouth ever. And its mouth is open, stretched almost as wide as the tunnel itself, devouring everything in its path.

And the squishy noise? The worm is literally squeezing its way down the tunnel. There is no room above, beneath, or on the sides. The worm takes up the entire tunnel. Everything is funneled into its mouth.

The perfect trash removal system.

And we're about to be trash.

"Run!" I yell.

Squish!

Legs burning.

Squash!

Must run faster.

Lucy sprints at my side. Marco and Mira are in front.

Cole falls behind. "I can't . . . ," he shouts. "Help!"

I glance over my shoulder. Cole is just steps ahead of the giant worm's mouth.

"Stop!" I yell to the others. "We need to help Cole!"

"I can see the end of the tunnel!" Marco shouts.

"He needs help now!"

"What can we do?" Lucy says.

I spin around. Just as I do, Cole trips. That's it. He's trash.

Mira soars past me with the bit of battery she has left in her pack, heading straight for the worm.

But it's too late. Cole disappears into the worm's mouth.

"No!" I shout.

Mira flies in after him, right inside the worm.

Lucy screams and tugs at my arm.

The worm keeps coming.

"Run, Jasper!" Lucy shouts.

There's no sign of my friends.

"Haul it, J!" Marco yells.

Oh my god . . . are they dead?

A second later, Mira flies out of the worm's mouth, dragging Cole by the shoulders. A few meters in front of us, her pack gives out and they drop to the ground. Mira lands gracefully and starts running. Cole scrambles to his feet and stumbles forward.

The worm thrashes, and a horrible noise bellows from deep in his belly.

"Go!" I shout.

We race for the end of the tunnel. The worm closes the gap.

"High gear!" Marco yells. "We can make it!"

The tunnel narrows like a funnel. At the very end is a door. That's the best shot we've got.

The worm roars. Trash spews from his mouth, pelting us from behind as we race.

Marco slams against the door. He grabs the handle.

The door doesn't budge.

"Open it!" I shout.

Marco fights with the door as the rest of us close in. I have to duck more and more with each step.

When I reach the door, I shove Marco aside and yank the handle. It's no use. It's locked.

We're out of options.

I turn around.

The worm speeds toward us.

Now that there's nothing left to do but wait to be devoured, everything sharpens into focus. A thick, pink tongue fills the worm's mouth and waves side to side like a fat snake. Drool oozes from the corners of its cavernous mouth. Pieces of tuber and paper and maybe smeared poop cling to its skin.

Mira squeezes my hand. Lucy burrows her head against my shoulder.

This is it. At least I get to die with my friends.

A warm wind brushes my skin, and a vile stench pours over me. Wait a second . . . that's not wind. It's the worm's breath. That is so disgusting I laugh out loud. I am literally living my worst nightmare.

I brace myself. In seconds I'll be in that thing's body, dying a slow death of digestive juices and rotten Tunneler trash.

Hold on . . . is the worm slowing down? And why does he seem smaller?

Actually, it's not the worm that's smaller. The tunnel got smaller. That's right! The tunnel narrowed before we reached the door. Could it be . . .?

The worm is two meters in front of us, but he is not getting any closer.

Marco lets out a high-pitched laugh. "He's stuck!"

Lucy lifts her head from my shoulder. "For real? He can't reach us?"

"He can't squeeze through!" I yell.

We bounce up and down chanting, "Stuck! Stuck! Stuck!"

I sink to my knees. I can't believe it. I thought that was the end.

"Don't forget that we're stuck, too," Lucy says.

I can hardly think about that now. All I can manage to do is press my back against the wall and stare into the mouth of the nastiest creature I've ever encountered.

Marco being Marco, he crawls forward and pokes the

MONICA TESLER

worm's tongue. "You've got to feel this! It's like a basketball but warm and bumpy."

"Get away from there!" Lucy shouts.

Marco scrambles back just as the worm whips his tongue through the air.

"You really are stupid," she says.

An alarm sounds, followed by three beeps. "*Attention! Trash cycle complete. Worm recalled. Lockdown will conclude in three minutes.*"

Marco looks at me. I shrug. I'm not sure what's happening, but I let a glimmer of hope wiggle its way in.

Sure enough, the worm recoils back up the tunnel. Three minutes later, the distinct sound of a lock disengaging sounds at our backs. Marco tries the handle. The next thing we know, we're out of the trash tunnel and steps away from the Grand Tunneler Marketplace.

· *EF* ·

"Why is everyone looking at us funny?" Lucy asks as we walk down the trinket aisle at the market.

"Probably because we're not Tunnelers," I say.

"Yeah, but it's not just that," she says. "It's like they're recoiling from us. Like we carry a disease or something."

I kind of see what Lucy's saying. At first, I was so relieved not to be the trash worm's dinner that I really couldn't think about much else, but now it looks like our pod is walking in its own little bubble, like others get within a certain radius of us and then bounce off.

Brrrk. Arrrgh. Kadareek, comes a Tunneler voice from behind, followed by a fit of coughing.

"Excuse me," a voice box translates as two Tunnelers wearing Earth Force uniforms approach and then step back. "Who is your pod leader?" Then the box says, "No translation. No translation. No translation." I'm guessing that must be the coughing.

"Jon Waters is our pod leader," Lucy says. "But he's not on Gulaga yet."

"Who is your junior ambassador, then?" the second Tunneler asks. He puts a hand over his long snout as he talks.

"Neeka," she says.

"Neeka, as in Commander Krag's daughter?" the first Tunneler asks.

When we confirm, he shakes his head, like he's not surprised. What's that supposed to mean?

"Stay there," the first Tunneler commands.

They step even farther away from us, and everyone else in the market keeps their distance, too. The Tunnelers talk to each other and then the second one speaks into a com pin.

After more than a minute passes, the first one takes a tentative step back in our circle. "You'll need to follow us. And not too closely."

MONICA TESLER

It's not clear we're in trouble, but following them wasn't presented as an option. As we set off after the Tunneler officers, I check my watch. It seemed like we spent an eternity in the trash tunnel, but we still have more than half an hour before dinner.

"Are you taking us to Neeka?" I have to shout because the Tunneler is so far in front of us, and no matter how fast we walk to catch up, they walk just as fast to keep their distance.

"She will be alerted. We are taking you to your pod leader."

"But like we told you, Mr. Tunneler," Marco says, "Waters isn't here yet."

"Call me *sir*. Your information is outdated."

"Waters is here!" Lucy says for just our pod to hear. "Thanks goodness. Now we don't have to deal with any more Sheek strategy sessions. Maybe Gedney is here, too. When do you think they're going to roll out the BPS?"

Before any of us can answer, the two Tunnelers stop at a door several meters in front of us, around the corner from our burrow.

"What's in there, Sir Tunneler?" Marco shouts.

Sir Tunneler? Way to push the guy's buttons, Marco.

We catch up with the officers and crowd behind them at the door. When the first one turns—I'm guessing to yell at Marco for calling him names—he erupts in a coughing fit.

The voice box goes haywire again. "No translation. No translation. No translation."

We burst out laughing. In fact, I'm laughing so hard I almost miss what the other Tunneler says.

Breek. "The baths."

They push open the door and then take off so fast they're practically running.

I glance at Marco. He shrugs and steps inside. Following him in, we enter a space about the size of my living room back on Earth. Both sides of the room are lined with puffy, round seats that look like toadstools. At the end of the room, two old Tunnelers sit at a desk. They bark at each other when we walk in.

Leaning against the desk is Waters. He takes a stride in our direction and then jumps back. "They weren't kidding." Waters waves a hand in front of his face. "You stink!"

We should have guessed. Of course we smell as horrible as a pile of rotten trash, because we were just standing in a tunnel full of it. Not to mention we bathed in the bad breath of that monster worm. We've been stinking for so long, we can't smell it anymore.

But now we're busted. I glance at Marco, who gives an imperceptible shake of the head. I'm not sure what that means. Maybe it means *toe the line and say nothing*, but if Marco thinks that's going to fly with Waters, he's not thinking straight.

MONICA TESLER

And did he forget we have Cole with us?

"We ran into some unforeseen difficulty," I say.

"I'd say so," Waters says, scrunching up his nose. "What happened?"

"We . . . ," Cole starts.

"Oh, I'll tell him," Lucy says. "We got locked out, so we had to find another way back. And someone—I'm not going to name names, but it wasn't me—had this brilliant idea to take this laundry chute, which was all fine and dandy until we had to get out of there and we ended up in this never-ending tunnel. And when we'd been walking for what seemed like forever, all this trash started raining down, which was super disgusting, and then this buzzer sounded and this enormous worm with this humongous mouth almost ate us."

"Nice to see you haven't changed, Lucy." Waters crosses to the side of the room, far away from our stinky bunch, and sits down on a toadstool. As soon as his butt hits the seat, it sinks around him, morphing into a super comfy chair. "So you met the infamous Tunneler trash worm. I've heard about that thing. Frankly I thought it was a legend. Whoever heard of using a worm for garbage disposal?"

"Not us until about thirty minutes ago," I say.

"Well, let's get you cleaned up. I'd like to hear about your first week in the Tundra Trials, but it can wait until you no longer smell like a rotten banana left out to decay in the scorch zone. Tomorrow morning, we'll convene as a pod." He stands up and jogs to the exit, like he can't wait to escape the stench.

The door blasts open, and a panicking Neeka nearly knocks Waters down.

"Oh! Oh! What happened? What did I miss? Is everything okay? Father said there was a problem. Oh! Oh! Ewww! What is that smell?"

Lucy rolls her eyes. "We got locked in a tunnel and chased by the trash worm, but we got out, so everything's okay."

"Oh! Oh! Oh! No! Father will be so upset. How ever did you get in the trash tunnel?"

"Excuse me," Waters says. "Who are you?"

Neeka spins around. When she sees Waters, she stands up straight (or as straight as she can as a Tunneler) and smooths her uniform. "Oh! I'm Neeka. I'm their junior ambassador. Who are you?"

"I'm Jon Waters, their pod leader, which means I outrank you in the whole pecking-order thing." Waters smiles and adjusts his blazer. "You know, I never get to say that, and I kind of like it. Anyway, Junior Ambassador Neeka, make sure they get cleaned up! Bounders, I'll see you at the Trials."

17

NEEKA IS OBVIOUSLY FLUSTERED. EVEN though she had nothing to do with the trash-worm incident, she seems to think she's going to be in big trouble with her dad. She turns off her voice box and jabbers away at the two old Tunnelers behind the intake desk at the baths. One wears tinted glasses and the other has a lacy cloth on her head, and neither looks too happy to be dealing with our stinky crew.

The Tunnelers bark back at Neeka. The one with the head cloth rushes the girls through a curtain on one side of the desk and waves Marco, Cole, and me toward the other. When at first we don't budge, the other Tunneler practically chases us through the curtain. The room we enter is dimly lit and cramped. I can't even stand up without cracking my head on the ceiling. The old Tunneler follows us in. She removes her glasses, grunts at us in Gulagan, and gestures madly at her Tunneler frock. When we stare back with confused expressions, she grabs Marco by the shirt and starts unfastening buttons.

"All right, all right, cool it, Furry Friend," Marco says. "You want us to take our clothes off. Got it."

As we strip off our shirts, the Tunneler turns some knobs on the wall, and the room fills with steam. She grunts and pulls back a curtain revealing a shower with the water at full blast. She waves at us, points at the shower, and rushes from the room. I guess the shower is for us.

Once we finish soaping up and rinsing off, three enormous Tunnelers enter the shower carrying blankets. They wrap us up like burritos, heft us into their stocky arms, and carry us out of the shower to a small hovel where three tall tables are lined up. Placing us facedown on the tables with the blankets covering us, they slap our backs like they're playing the drums, then follow that up with about a hundred karate chops. It seems like it should hurt, but it actually feels pretty good.

When they're done with the back beating, they grunt and point at stacks of cloth lying on a shelf against the wall. Then they leave us alone, pulling a curtain across the hovel.

"Well, that was weird, fellas," Marco says, cinching the blanket around his waist and hopping off the table.

"Do you think the girls went through the same thing?" Cole asks.

"Probably," I say. "I don't know if I want to do it again, but I liked it, in a pummel-my-body-into-butter kind of way."

I wrap the blanket around me and grab a cloth bundle from the shelf. When I shake out the coarse, brown cloth, I see it's one of the Tunneler frocks.

"Ummm . . . Do they expect us to wear these?" I hold the frock against my body. It won't even reach my knees.

"These aren't Earth Force uniforms." Cole glares at the cloth bundle in his hands like it might cause a terrible disease.

"Thanks for the news flash, Genius," Marco says.

"Unless we're in our bunks, we're supposed to be in Earth Force uniforms at all times," Cole says.

"Yeah, well, last time I checked our dailies smelled like trash-eating worm," I say.

Despite looking like he might freak, Cole doesn't argue. It's either Tunneler garb or no clothes at all, so it's a straightforward choice.

We pull the coarse cloths over our heads.

The frocks don't look as bad as they do on the Tunnelers. They look worse. Tunnelers and humans aren't built the same. They have a huge hunch on their backside, so on us the front of the frock is too small and the back is way too big. It has the unfortunate effect of making us look like we're wearing diapers.

After we're dressed, we find the girls in a lounge near the waiting area. Lucy paces across the rug. Mira perches on a stool with her legs tucked inside her frock.

As we enter, Neeka scurries over. "Oh! You smell so fresh and clean! What a very big improvement!"

"Do we really have to wear these?" Lucy says, balling up the sides of her frock in her fists. "I can't be seen in public like this!"

"They are laundering your uniforms," Neeka says. "You should have them back before bedtime. But until then, they've loaned you Tunneler attire, which is a very nice alternative."

"What's the problem, Lucy?" Marco says. "Just tie some brown ribbons in your hair and tell them it's the latest fashion trend."

"Shut up, Marco! Honestly, if I have to tell you to be quiet one more time, I'm going to—"

"You're going to what, Pretty Face, talk me to death?"

"Enough!" I shout. "It's bad enough that we have to wear these to dinner without having to listen to you two fight about it."

"We're not . . . ," Lucy starts. "Well, I suppose we are fighting, but it's all Tofu Face's fault."

"Seriously?" Marco says. "You're really going to call me that?"

I sink down on a stool next to Mira. The sides mold around

me like a cradle, so I'm entirely supported. I stretch my legs out on the furry, purple rug. Above, the ceiling curves and the soft occludium light casts shadows.

Marco ignores Lucy and stretches out on the floor. "Hey, Neeksters, what is this rug made of?"

"Oh! It is so very comfortable, isn't it? It's from the top layer of an edible mold we grow in the sublayers. Very soft, like real fur. I must go now. I've left your blast packs charging in the waiting room. They'll be fine there. Hardly anyone comes here since Earth Force had the custom human baths built."

Edible mold? Gross. I lift my feet in the air.

"I'm going to forget she told me that," Marco says, climbing up on the bench.

When I close my eyes and ignore the itchy Tunneler frock against my skin and the moldy rug beneath my feet, I can almost believe I'm in Waters's pod room, cushioned by the million tiny beads of my favorite turquoise bean bag.

"You know what I miss?" I ask. "Our pod room. I'm thinking everyone would get along if we had a pod room. And I nominate this room right here."

The others mull over my idea, which is good, because it means we get a break from Marco–Lucy bickering.

"We could call it the Nest," I continue. "Doesn't this room remind you of a nest? It's so cozy and comfy. It's the right size; it's totally private—what do you say?"

"You know, Ace, when you're right, you're right," Marco says, kicking his legs up and lying back on the bench. "This place is pretty cool."

"We *do* need a place to talk strategy," Lucy says, sitting down on the other side of Mira. "Maybe we can invite Ridders's pod sometimes. That will help keep our alliance secret."

"*Potential* alliance," Cole corrects. "I'm fine with the idea. As long as I don't have to wear this frock every time we come here."

"It's settled, then," I say, sinking even farther into my seat. "The Nest is our temporary pod room."

"While we're talking about the pod," Lucy says, "since Waters is back, think we can lose the Sheek face from our helmets?"

"I don't see why not," Marco says. "You're the fashion expert. Any ideas what we should use instead?"

"I have lots of ideas! Chartreuse is a hot color this year, although fuchsia is always my fallback. I'm thinking alternating color bands along our helmets with sleeve ties to match."

"Pink and green stripes?" I ask. "No way."

"Fine," she says. "My backup idea is faux-fur collars. They're the absolute rage in winter wear. Remember that coat I wore back at the laboratory?"

"H-2-O-s-5," Cole says, pacing across the rug.

"What? Was that English, Wiki?" Marco asks.

"H_2Os_5," Cole repeats. "We should place it on a sticker right over Sheek's decal."

"Okay . . . ," I say. "Are you going to clue us in on what it means?"

Cole shakes his head. "Isn't it obvious? H2O is the symbol for water. H2Os5 means Waters's Five. Our pod."

"Waters's Five," Lucy says, mulling it over. "It's subtle, cryptic, completely original. I have to admit I like it."

"Our very own trademark," I say. "Sounds good to me."

"Clever, which I've come to expect from you, Wiki," Marco says. "Now we have more serious things to talk about, like those nuggets from Ridders and Sheek."

Cole finally takes a seat next to me, and the same expression he has when playing *Evolution* settles on his face. "I think two things are clear. There's going to be a meeting, and it has to do with a military engagement, which I assume means a strategic initiative in the war against the Youli."

"So they *are* sending us to war!" Lucy says, shooting a nasty look at Marco.

Marco shrugs and turns to me. "Does that sound like the same thing Waters was talking about, Jasper?"

"Maybe." I pull at the frock that rubs across my collarbone. "He called the meeting a summit, and he said something about us only knowing the tip of the iceberg about the galaxy."

"Is that all he said?" Marco asks. "You're sure he didn't give any details that might explain the summit?"

My breath catches, and I shift my gaze to the moldy rug. I should really tell them about the brain patch. I promised my pod mates that I'd put them first, that I wouldn't keep secrets. Maybe I should spill the dirt now. Why would it really matter if they knew? It could help us get to the bottom of what Earth Force is really up to.

No. Mira shifts in her seat and glides her hand over mine. She wants me to keep quiet.

It's not fair for you to read my mind without permission, I think. *But fine.*

"Hello? Earth to Jasper?" Lucy says.

"Sorry. I was just replaying the discussion in my mind. I can't remember anything else Waters said that might be important."

"Fair enough," Marco says. "We'll just have to keep our eyes and ears open. If Earth Force wants to use us for a military engagement, we need to find out why."

"Then I suppose we'd better brave the cantina." Lucy stands and straightens her frock. "We might as well get this fashion nightmare over with."

· *EF* ·

"Here he comes." Cole shifts in his seat and tugs at his frock.

It's not like I have eyes in the back of my head or anything, but I can see Regis coming. I can picture his smug face. His casual saunter. His nasty grin expanding by the second as he gets a good look at me and my Tunneler frock. I resist the urge to look and shove another bite of forage into my mouth. "Ignore him."

"Something tells me that's going to be a challenge," Lucy says.

Before we came to the cantina, she managed to roll and tuck the sleeves of the coarse Tunneler cloth so it doesn't look quite as bad. It certainly won't spare her from Regis's teasing, just as it hasn't spared us from all the laughs and stares and snide comments we've received since we grabbed our trays and got in line. The footsteps grow louder and then stop right behind my chair. My muscles tense, bracing for impact, even if it's only verbal impact.

"When I heard the rumor, I thought it was too good to be true," Regis's voice booms. "But you B-wads never fail to disappoint."

Don't respond. Don't respond. Don't respond. First, I think this to myself. Then Mira echoes the same command in my head. At least Marco's not here. He acted all mysterious, said he had something to take care of right before we walked into the cantina, and hasn't been seen since. Which is good, because if he were here, this thing with Regis would be guaranteed to morph into a full blowout.

"Honestly," Regis's voice booms. "I don't know why I spend even a second thinking about how to mess with you, Jasper, when you make it so freaking easy. Hey, Hakim, you smell something?"

Here it comes. I've never felt so naked as right now in this itchy brown frock that looks curiously similar to the tuber storage sacks.

"Yeah," Hakim mumbles. "Trash."

"Worse than trash," Randall says. "Tunneler Trash."

"You reek, Jasper," Regis says.

"Shut your mouth, Regis," I say and instantly regret it.

"You're telling me to shut my mouth? I'm an Earth Force officer, Jasper. You can't tell me what to do."

"You don't outrank us," Cole says, as if that has any chance of steering this conflict in a different direction.

Regis laughs. "Oh, I think I do. I don't see you in uniform. For all I know, you've been booted from Earth Force. After all, Earth Force officers don't have to walk through the trash tunnel. I bet you're no better than Tunneler scum."

"Yeah. Tunneler scum," echoes Randall.

"Go away, Regis," Lucy says.

"You're looking lovely, Lucy."

"I said go away." Her words are loud and slow.

"I told you what would happen if you kept hanging out with these winners, Lucy. Why don't you come sit with me and the guys?"

Lucy stands, puts her hands on her hips, and shouts, "This is harassment! You get away from me right now, Regis, or I will report you personally to the admiral!"

Heads swivel and eyes turn to stare at our table. Great. If anyone happened to miss our Tunneler garb, now we're on full display.

Across the cantina, Edgar Han stands. I think Captain Han is the only person in the world who intimidates Regis. And probably Admiral Eames. She intimidates everyone.

When Han starts heading our way, I exhale and finally glance back at Regis. "Looks like someone's checking up on you."

"We were done anyway," Regis says. "I don't waste my time talking to Tunneler trash."

I'm relieved when they walk away from our table, but I've been around long enough to know we haven't heard the last from Regis today. I spear a small bite of fungus with my fork and let it slide down my throat before my gag reflex kicks in.

Marco chooses this moment to make his grand entrance. He strolls over to our table just as Regis, Randall, and Hakim are out of earshot.

"What did those losers want?" Marco's wearing a brightly colored scarf over his frock. It's adorned with beads I've seen some junior ambassadors wear woven into their fur.

"Oh, just to let us know how lovely we smell," Lucy says. "Where've you been? And where'd you get that ridiculous scarf?"

"Ridiculous?" Marco says. "This is high Gulagan fashion,

Lucy. You should know. I picked it up at the grand market-place. I spotted it earlier today when those Tunnelers rushed our smelly selves out of there."

"Forget the market," I say. "I can't believe Regis knows about the trash tunnel. Everyone knows! Who told?"

"I bet it was your best friend," Marco says to Lucy. "Neeka talks as much as you, and she's always blurting out stuff she's not supposed to. I'm sure she was the one who spilled the beans."

"Don't just throw Neeka under the bus!" Lucy says. "She's *your* junior ambassador, too!"

Great. They're headed for another fight.

I tune them out and try to choke down the rest of my dinner. All the good vibes I had coming into this tour have dried up. Now it seems we're back where we started last tour. At the bottom of the pack. Regis's punching bags.

Mira rises from our table and drifts out of the cantina. She has the right idea. Nothing good is coming our way in here. I chat with Cole and Ryan for a few minutes about *Evolution* and the cheats to defeat the *Alamo*, and then clear my tray.

As I'm headed back to the burrow in my Tunneler frock, trying to ignore the amused looks of everyone I pass, a muffled voice calls, "Hey, Jasper! Over here!"

I look around but can't spot the caller. I jog in the direction of the voice, deeper into the Earth Sector. Someone calls my name again, and I turn another corner. Up ahead is an open chasm. My stomach clenches, and I slow down.

A bridge spans the gap. It's narrow and made from the same slippery mud that makes up most of Gulagaven. No guardrails. Nothing but air separates a solid step and a step to death below. The bridge looks just as deadly as it did the day I arrived on the Tunneler planet. And I know it's especially lethal for me, Jasper Adams, or should I say Jasper "Klutz" Adams.

Mira crouches right in the center of the bridge. From either side, Regis and Randall edge closer every second.

18

"THIS WAY, JASPER!" CALLS THE MUFFLED
voice. Hakim steps out from behind the corner, erupting in
laughter. His hands are cupped in front of his mouth to dis-
guise the sound.

I skid to a stop at the edge of the chasm. "Let her off the
bridge!"

"Look! It's Trash Boy!" Regis shouts. He flinches at Mira,
and she jumps back, throwing her hands to the sides for
balance.

"Stop!" I shout.

Hakim steps behind me and shoves my shoulder, nearly
sending me off the edge.

I dart away from him and stumble over something in my path. Mira's blast pack.

"Yeah, we didn't think she'd be needing that," Hakim chokes out between chuckles.

Mira's mind crackles with adrenaline and hatred. She tries to skirt by Regis, but he blocks her.

"Leave her alone! Let her pass!"

"Come and get her, B-wad!" Regis says.

The bridge looms in front of me, but my feet feel like lead. Challenging those three to a chicken fight on a Tunneler bridge? I might as well have a death wish.

I scan the rim of the chasm, the intersecting hallways, the nearby hovels. Nothing. No one. We're alone.

"What are you waiting for, Jasper?" Hakim jogs past me to join his bad buddies. "We heard you *love* bridges!"

So this isn't about Mira. It's about me. "Let her go, Regis! Now!"

Randall charges Mira. She recoils. Hakim comes at her from the other side. She stumbles to her knees.

Pain.

Fear.

Rage.

Are those my emotions or Mira's? I press my palms against my skull. I have to clear my head, think our way out of this.

"Let's go, Jasper!" Regis shouts. "Now or never!"

I have no choice. I have to go after her. I have to get on that bridge. At least I have my blast pack. It might just save us from a fatal free fall.

On the bridge, Mira darts and dodges, making them work to keep her from escaping their trap.

"Oh no, you don't!" Randall shouts.

While their eyes are on Mira, I grab my straps and race for the foot of the bridge.

Every atom in my body urges me to stop. But this is not about my body. It's about my mind. Mind over matter, right?

My foot hits the bridge.

I feel their eyes on me, but I keep mine locked on Mira.

"Love the dress, Tunneler Trash!" Regis calls to me. "I'll love it even more as I watch you fall."

One step. Another.

Don't look down!

I chance a glance at Regis. His face is lit up like a hungry dog waiting to be fed. When I'm two meters in front of him, he yells, "Now!"

He spins on Mira, and she squares to face him. As soon as she does, Randall darts forward and sweeps her legs. She tumbles off the side, grabbing the edge at the last second.

"Nice!" Regis yells, high-fiving Randall as Mira dangles beneath the bridge. "Are you gonna be a hero, Jasper?"

My legs shake. My eyes are fixed on Mira. She's hanging by

her fingers. Beneath her, the chasm fades to blackness. I can't see the bottom.

My heart slams against my rib cage. My legs threaten to buckle.

Mira's fear weaves with my own. *Slipping! Help!*

I only get one shot. I have to communicate with Mira.

I call up a picture in my mind as crisply and completely as I can. I try to shut everything else out. Mira has to know the plan. She has to read my mind for this to work.

Mira's mind touches mine, then she screams in my skull, *Go!*

I run at Regis then leap off the bridge, twisting in midair to face them, and jamming my fingers on the red buttons of my pack straps. I rocket straight up in the air.

"Hey! What are you doing?" Regis shouts.

High above the bridge, I release my fingers and fling my body flat like Superman. Gravity steps in and pulls me into the chasm. Just as I fall past the bridge, Mira lets go. We collide midair. She wraps her arms around my waist and throws us into a backflip. We tumble through the abyss as the bridge fades above us and the muddy walls rush by faster and faster. I grapple with the controls, but I can't pull us out of the dive.

Panic sizzles through our neural link as we fall. Then a piercing noise rattles my brain.

Mira. She's trying to reach me.

Relax!

I gulp air and try to tune in. In my mind, Mira shows me the manual controls for the blast pack and how to press my fingers.

We soar left. Right. Too far right. Scrape the side. Drop.

It just won't work. I can't fly with these straps!

Close your eyes.

Fly blind through the chasm? *No!*

Do it now!

I close my eyes.

And I can see.

Mira's mental pictures take shape, and I grip the controls. I follow her directions and the blast pack levels out, flies straight. It's like my music teacher showing me how to place my fingers on my clarinet.

We fly through the chasm. I mirror the pictures she makes in my mind until she mentally releases the straps. I drop the controls and—*Bam!*—we land in a heap on the edge.

Opening my eyes, I see we're in the same chasm, although we must have dropped several levels. I try to see the bridge above, but we're blocked by an overhang. "Where are we?"

Mira's mind is blank. She doesn't know either.

The good news: we escaped Regis without falling to our deaths.

The bad news: it looks like we're lost in Gulagaven again, and that was nearly disastrous the first time.

We're about to head up an intersecting tunnel to look for help when a Tunneler comes barreling down the ramp right for us.

Grak. Boraneek. Krag. "Oh! I'm so glad I found you!"

The Tunneler is wearing the same frock as us, but the Earth Force insignia is sewn across his chest, just like Neeka's.

"You were looking for us?" I ask. "Who are you? Are you a junior ambassador?"

"Not here," the Tunneler says. "Follow me. Quickly."

I'm not coming up with a better plan, and Mira isn't offering one either, so when the no-name junior ambassador heads down the ramp and turns into a tunnel, we follow.

When we catch him, he's standing in front of a stone door. "Stick with me," he says, pulling on the handle.

The door opens to a room filled with noise and activity. Dozens of Tunnelers squat on squishy benches like the ones in the Nest, stand around long tables, or hurry among huddled groups. Most of them are kind of short—for Tunnelers, I mean—and almost all of them wear jewelry or have designs buzzed into their fur. In the corner, a band plays the funkiest music I've ever heard. It's like a combo of drums, piccolos, and chanting monks.

"What is this place?" I ask.

The Tunneler we arrived with herds us to some open benches in the corner. Almost instantly a dozen other Tunnelers crowd around him. He deactivates his voice box and chatters anxiously. The others don't look too thrilled to see Mira and me.

Mira squeezes my hand. She senses the Tunnelers' discomfort, too. We don't belong here. We probably would have fared better wandering aimlessly through the tunnels of Gulagaven until someone took pity on us and escorted us back to the Earth Sector. I tug at my frock. I would give anything to be wearing my Earth Force uniform right about now.

A familiar grunt is followed by a very welcome translation: "Jasper? Mira?" Neeka slides onto the bench next to us. "What are you doing here? How did you find the Den?"

I don't know exactly how to answer that question. At this point, I figure less is more. "We were lost, and that guy found us." I point at the junior ambassador who brought us here.

"Grok?" she asks. When we don't answer, she deactivates her voice box and grunts at the young Tunneler. They chat excitedly for a minute, then Neeka gestures and barks at the crowd of Tunnelers who have gathered around us. After a few moments of heated discussion, they back away, leaving me, Mira, Neeka, and Grok alone.

Neeka formally introduces us. "Grok's a junior ambassador, too."

"So that's why you have the Earth Force insignia," I say. "Who's in your pod?"

He turns away, almost like he's embarrassed. "I'm assigned to Captain Han's pod."

"You're Regis's junior ambassador? Is that how you knew to look for us?" Slowly the implications sink in. "Wait a second, did you know what they were going to do? Were you in on it?"

"Oh! No! No! Definitely not! I would never have done such a horrible thing! That's why I came for you. I've tried to do my best as a junior ambassador. I've tried to be loyal to my pod. But I never meant for anyone to get hurt."

"Grok is a good guy," Neeka says. "He's just trying to do his job. We're supposed to stick with our pod."

"Even when that includes nearly getting two Bounders killed?" I demand, but Grok won't meet my gaze. "And let me guess, you're the one who told Regis about the trash tunnel?"

Grok hangs his head.

"Grok!" Neeka says. "I thought we were friends! You can tell my secrets!"

"I'm sorry," Grok says to all of us. "I'm trying to do the right thing. It's difficult. Everyone knows it's hard when you're dealing with—"

"I've told you they're not all like them!" Neeka says.

What was he going to say? "All like whom?"

"Oh! Now, wait a second," Neeka says. "Go easy on Grok. You don't understand. Not all Earthlings are the same."

Was he going to lump all of us Earthlings in with Regis? "She's right, Grok. Most of us are nothing like Regis and his minions. You have to believe me."

Grok looks around. Lots of angry eyes stare back at us.

"It's okay," Neeka says to him.

"Neeka has told me good things about you. And I have met some decent Earthlings. But most are not. Most are bullies."

That's his impression of Earthlings in general? That we're a planet full of bullies? That makes me feel awful. "That's not true," I say quietly. "Thank you for helping us. I hope we can prove you wrong about Earth." Grok nods. The band shifts into a new song. "What is this place?"

Neeka explains that the Den is a hangout for Tunnelers who are no longer kids but aren't quite adults. Kind of like us, I suppose. Grok tells us about his older sister who works at the space dock. I ask him if Neeka talks a lot for a Tunneler. Grok blurts something out in Gulagan, and Neeka slaps him on the paw. They both turn off their voice boxes and jabber away at each other. It doesn't seem like they're mad. In fact, I think they might be flirting.

Slowly other Tunnelers gather round our table. Some of them are junior ambassadors like Neeka and Grok. They activate their voice boxes and translate for their friends. They ask

MONICA TESLER

lots of questions about Earth and the Bounders. One of them asks why Mira doesn't talk. I want to say that I'm kind of like them, that the brain patch is like a voice box, and I'm her translator, but instead I dodge the question.

The music grows louder, and many of the young Tunnelers start to dance.

Come. Mira laces her fingers with mine.

"We should really get back." Showing up late, this time with Mira, may be my last straw with Ridders.

Mira smiles, and her mind touches mine. She doesn't need words to communicate her reaction: Who cares? She tugs at my hand, and I stand. Her energy thumps in time to the music as she weaves us through the crowd.

When we reach the band, Mira slides onto the raised platform and gestures to one of the Tunnelers, who hits a long stone slab with two mallets. He offers the mallets to Mira, and she strikes the instrument. It takes a few tries— and some nasty looks from the room—before she gets the hang of it, but soon she's able to find a harmony line with the rest of the band.

Her brain sparkles in a way I haven't felt before.

I work up the nerve to pick up an extra wind pipe resting on top of a side table. The musician next to me nods, and I blow into the instrument. The sound is definitely foreign, but also familiar in a way, so I'm able to make some consistent sound without much trouble. The Tunneler next to me blows these unbelievable runs. I do my best to match his pitch. It doesn't matter that I sound like a beginner. I'm making music.

I'm making music with Mira. And that's all that matters.

· E⃗ ·

I don't known what time it is when Neeka walks us back to the Bounder Burrow, but I know it's past curfew. Just as I feared, Ridders and Waters meet us at the door.

"We were about to send a search party out for you," Ridders says. "Again."

"I've got this, James," Waters says, touching Ridders's arm. At first I think Ridders is going to protest and put us in all kinds of trouble, but instead he shrugs and heads the opposite direction toward the officer quarters. Waters steps between Mira and me. "Walk with me."

We head to the bathhouse. Waters steers us into the side room—the Nest—and gestures for us to sit. "Lucy told me about your new pod room. I like it."

Mira and I sink down onto the bench. At the space station, Waters fit perfectly in our pod room. He designed it for *us*, but it was *his*. Here, things are different. Waters doesn't belong in the Nest. It's *ours*.

"Do you know this carpet is made from mold?" Waters continues. "Anyhow, I wanted to check in. How are the brain patches working?"

I'm not sure how to respond. I don't think he'd believe me if I said nothing had changed. I drag my toe along the furry rug. "It's going okay, I guess. I think it's going to take a while to really kick in."

"But the two of you communicate now, at least a bit? Can we try it out? Can you translate something Mira says, Jasper?"

"It doesn't really work that way," I say. "It's usually more like an impression than words."

"Well, then what's the impression?"

That it's none of his business, Mira thinks.

"The only impression I'm getting right now, Mr. Waters, is that Mira is really tired. We both are. It's been a long day."

"Very well. But I want you to keep me informed. I may need your help very soon."

Soon? That sounds important. "Why?"

"A critical meeting is about to take place. That's all I can say for now. I've said too much already."

Waters must be talking about the summit. I open my mouth to ask another question, but he shakes his head. The topic is closed.

As we stand up to leave, my mind is whirling. We have to find out about the meeting. When is it? Where is it going down? Our pod needs to execute on our spy mission. And now. I'm certain the summit is the ticket to the truth about Earth Force and its plans for the Bounders.

19

THE NEXT SEVERAL MORNINGS, WE RISE
bright and early to the same routine: breakfast, outfitting,
astrocache. This week, our curfew to be inside the gates is
much earlier so that pods can train with Gedney on the new
technology in the afternoon. We stick with Cole's plan: leap-
frog to targets with bounds and blast packs, then bound back
to base. Next week, the BPS will be rolled out in the Trials, so
we'll have to shift things up.

After finding some plain decals, Lucy hand-lettered them
with our new pod mark, H_2Os5. We refuse to tell anyone
outside the pod what they mean. According to Lucy, psy-
chological intimidation is a key strategy in our social game.

Shockingly it seems to be working. Our pod is the clear front-runner in the Tundra Trials.

Ever since Lucy negotiated terms for our alliance, we've been sharing cache stories and strategy with Ridders's pod. We've even invited them to the Nest a few times, which is fun. It kind of reminds me of a miniversion of the Tunneler hangout Mira and I visited, just a chill place to relax, maybe play some *Evolution*, and not have to worry about the Tundra Trials.

Of course, it's not all fun and games in the Nest. The morning after Mira and I almost plunged to our deaths, we met as a pod in the bathhouse before breakfast. I shared what happened on the bridge, and how Grok brought us to the Den. Then I told them about our meeting with Waters. Despite my growing guilt, I didn't tell them about the brain patches. But I did tell them about the *critical meeting* that Waters mentioned. My pod mates agreed he must have been talking about the same meeting that Ridders unintention-ally revealed.

We need to find out when that meeting is happening.

And we need to be there.

The only problem is we've got almost no time to snoop around, and our few attempts to score scoop have been com-plete dead ends.

I haven't even had a chance to press Waters for information.

He's been acting weird. Every day, as soon as the Trials end, he disappears. I haven't seen him in the Earth Sector at all since that night in the Nest.

Marco's been acting almost as mysterious as Waters. This morning, he left the burrow before I got out of bed. When he finally arrives at breakfast, he's panting and red in the face like he's been out running a marathon. He slides into his seat with a huge grin on his face.

"What?" Lucy says.

"Not here," Marco says, shooting a side glance at Regis's table. "You know, inquiring minds."

"You finally have a payback plan, don't you?" I ask.

He glares at me, but then winks. "I said not here. The Nest. After breakfast."

"You mean you know how to get back at Regis?" Cole asks.

"For the love of the ancient Tunneler gods, Wiki!" he whisper-yells. "What part of 'not here' don't you understand?"

"Sorry," Cole says.

We race through breakfast and blow off Ryan, who has some questions about the day's cache plan. When we finally make it to the Nest, Marco gathers us around and unfurls his palm to reveal a small glass bottle filled with reddish-green powder. "This, my dear comrades, is our ticket to stick it to Regis."

"Ticket to Stick It," Lucy says. "I like that."

"What is it?" Cole asks.

"Foot-warmer powder."

"Huh?" I say.

"It's made from some kind of plant they grown in the greenhouses. I think it's like the Tunneler equivalent of ghost peppers."

Mira lifts the vial from Marco's hand and holds the powder to the light.

"I traded some carob-coated fruit balls to an ancient Tunneler in the market this morning," Marco continues.

"How did you communicate with him?" Cole asks.

"Where did you get the fruit balls?" I ask.

Marco ignores me and answers Cole. "You don't need words, Brainiac, when you speak the language of commerce. Plus, I had some help."

"Yeah, but foot-warmer powder?" Lucy says. "I think that sounds like a good thing. My toes have been freezing by the end of our cache runs."

"Well, a little is a good thing," Marco says, taking the bottle back from Mira. "A lot . . . not so good. If you put more than a sprinkle in your shoes, your feet will be fried. And here's the sinker: it's only activated in the cold. So Regis and his crew won't know there's a problem until they've left the base. They'll have to either take their boots off and freeze their feet, or endure the blistering heat until they make it back."

"How did you find all this out?" Cole asks.

"Like I told you on day one," Marco says. "Our furry friend likes to talk."

"Marco, you didn't!" Lucy says. "I told you to leave poor Neeka alone."

"I think it sounds like a great idea," I say, "but Regis will know it was us, and I bet we'd get in some hefty trouble if we burned their feet."

"That's the best part," Marco says. "Their skin won't really be burned. According to Neeka, it works on the nerves to elevate body temperature in a targeted area. No surface injuries. And as soon as they're out of the cold, the effect wears off."

"So no permanent injuries," Lucy says. "That's good. We probably won't get in too much trouble for the prank. But if we do get busted, you have to promise to leave Neeka out of it."

"I will," Marco says. "But listen to this. They apparently keep a stock of this powder behind the counter at the outfitter so if Tunnelers want to sprinkle a tiny amount in their shoes before heading to the surface, they can. I bet Regis and Company will have a hard time convincing anyone that they're not to blame themselves. Used too much. Oh well."

"Excellent!" I say. "So what's the plan?"

"Wait until they request their boots, then run a distraction while I load the shoes up with powder," Marco says.

"When are we doing this?" Cole asks him.

"No better time than the present. Let's go!"

"Now? But we're not prepared!" Cole says.

"Prepared equals scared. Who needs a plan?"

"That logic sounds a little off," Lucy says.

"It's worked for me so far, Miss Snoot."

Lucy puts her hands on her hips. "Stop calling me names for the rest of the day, Marco Romero, and I'll run your distraction. I'm the master, after all. Don't you remember my award-winning performance when we broke into the cell block to spy on the alien?"

"Who could forget?" I say. "You snotted all over that poor guard crying about your tofu-faced boyfriend, Marco, and how he broke your heart."

"Oooh! That's right! I'm changing my terms," she says to Marco. "You can't call me names, but I can call you Tofu Face as much as I want."

"That's hardly fair, but fine. We've got to go!" He races out of the bathhouse, apparently assuming we'll be following close behind.

We jog to catch up and then chase him through the tunnels. When we get to the outfitter, we head in and request our gear. We're one of the first pods to arrive.

"Isn't it going to look weird that we're just hanging around waiting for them rather than passing into the first antechamber?" I whisper once we get our bins from the Tunnelers manning the counter.

"I don't know. Ask Lucy," Marco replies. "She's in charge of deception. I'm in charge of logistics."

"That is so *not* what we agreed." Lucy shakes her head in a huff and then whispers, "I'll take care of it. Just don't rush to put on your gear."

As Cole, Mira, and I fasten each button and secure each strap in slow motion, Lucy strikes up a conversation with Meggi and Annette. I'm not sitting close enough to hear what they're talking about.

Meanwhile, Marco has positioned himself on the bench directly next to the counter where you pick up your bins. When I sneak a glance in his direction, he turns his hand. His sleeve is pulled low, covering most of his palm; the bottle peeks out the bottom.

It feels like we've spent half the morning putting on our gear when Regis, Randall, and Hakim finally arrive at the outfitter. They act like they're the only people on the planet. They march in, talking at full volume, knocking into anyone in their path. In their minds, they rule the EarthBound Academy, and they probably think they run things on Gulaga, too. They saunter up to the gear counter and bark their names at the poor Tunneler.

"Hey, Regis!" Lucy calls. "I need your expert advice."

This is the moment of truth. I hold my breath. For all of Marco's wheeling and dealing, if Lucy can't distract Regis, the prank's a bust.

MONICA TESLER

Regis turns to Lucy with a skeptical look on his face. He probably can't figure out why she's talking to him, but her request for his expertise must have him intrigued. "Make it quick," he says, waving his buddies over to the other side of the outfitter, where Lucy is standing with a perky smile on her face.

She shifts into full drama mode. "Oh, great, thanks. See, Annette and Meggi and I were just chatting about the aeronaut calendars that Earth Force puts out every year. And you know how every month has its own aeronaut featured in the poster . . ."

As she talks, the Tunneler places three bins filled with weather suits, face masks, and boots on the counter and then heads to the back. With his eyes perma-glued to Regis, Marco slowly withdraws the vial from his sleeve.

Lucy's mouth is moving a mile a minute. She's talking at full volume with lots of gesturing and animation, so that basically everyone in the room is staring at her.

"Of course, Sheek has had more posters than any of the other aeronauts, almost as many as all the other aeronauts combined, so we were just wondering if you think Earth Force is going to start featuring Bounders in the calendars. And, if they do, who do you think the most likely cadets are to be featured?"

Regis laughs. "Do you really need to ask? I'll be the first Bounder featured on the calendar. Obviously. As for girls, it definitely won't be you. Not when you're in the world's worst pod. I'd say Annette has a shot, but not if she keeps hanging out with you."

Meanwhile, Marco pours powder into the boots as quickly as he can, which isn't very quick, since he has to stop and act nonchalant every time someone turns their head.

He'd better hurry. Any second, Regis is going to get bored, or worse, the Tunneler is going to come back to the counter.

Lucy moves on to ask Regis where he'd want to be photographed (he says the quantum deck), what he'd want to be wearing (dress formals), and what month he'd prefer (February). I'm not sure why he chooses February. It's the shortest month, which means his picture would be displayed for the least amount of time. Maybe he doesn't think it through or maybe it has something to do with Valentine's Day.

"Jasper!" Marco whisper-shouts and punches me in the shoulder.

"Huh? Oops. Sorry."

"Let's go!" he says. He nods at Lucy across the room. Mira and Cole are already walking toward the door to the anteroom.

"Thanks for all that input," Lucy says to Regis, "but I just have to say that if you were the very last aeronaut in the entire galaxy, I still don't think they'd choose you as their poster child." She smiles at Regis. "Bye, now!"

Lucy walks away, leaving Regis with a confused look on his

face that slowly morphs into anger. She makes it to the door, and our pod steps through before he thinks up a comeback.

As the door closes behind us, we burst out laughing.

"We did it!" Cole says.

"Shhh!" Lucy says. The room is filled with a few other pods and about a dozen Tunnelers preparing to go to the surface. "Let's not announce it to the world!"

"Play it cool," Marco says. "All we have to do now is wait."

We make it to the next antechamber before Regis comes in. By the time their pod makes it up the ramp, almost all of the cadets are on the surface. Marco and I exchange glances. He pumps his fist.

I'm excited and nervous and impatient all at the same time. "How long does it take to work?"

Marco shakes his head. "Not sure. Just watch."

Waters walks over to our pod for the daily strategy check. I wish he would have waited a few minutes. I don't know if I can keep cool when the prank goes live.

"How are the Waters's Five this lovely morning?" he asks when he reaches us. The spring is back in his step. I haven't seen him this peppy since last tour, before the battle on the Paleo Planet.

"Who told you what our pod mark meant?" Cole asks.

"Don't insult me, Mr. Thompson," Waters says. "I was once an über-informed, science-loving kid just like you. Of course I know what H2Os5 means."

"You seem mighty happy, Mr. Waters," Lucy says.

"What's not to be happy about?" he says. "It's a gorgeous morning. I'm with my favorite pod. I have a—"

"Look!" Marco says. "They seem mighty happy, too!"

Across the tarmac, Regis hops from one foot to the next. "Ouch! Yowch! Yowowouch!" He screams and jumps and shakes his feet like he's rolling out some really bad dance moves.

Next to him, Randall runs in circles on his tiptoes, yelling and waving his arms. Hakim kicks his feet in the air, like he's trying out for a chorus line.

"Oh my god!" Lucy shouts.

"It worked," Cole says.

I elbow him in the rib cage.

"What's happening?" Waters ask.

Regis howls and prances like a lunatic horse.

Randall is on the ground, pedaling his boots in the air.

Hakim crouches over and cries for his mother.

Marco roars with laughter. I can't help but laugh, too.

Waters levels his eyes at us. "What did you do?"

Lucy suppresses a giggle. "Whatever are you talking about, Mr. Waters?"

By now, a group of Tunneler officers surround Regis and the others. Waters jogs over to see if he can help. The air is filled with their hollers and cries.

A sliver of concern creeps in. "You're sure that powder

won't cause permanent damage, right?" I ask.

Marco nods. "Neeka was pretty sure. And the old Tunneler who bartered with us was confident."

"Wait a second," Cole says. "He had a voice box?"

"Not exactly."

Of course that means no. "You don't even know what he said, do you?" I ask.

Lucy swats his arm. "You're going to get us in so much trouble!"

Meanwhile, Regis has escaped from the officers. He sits down on the tarmac and strips off his boots and socks. His feet are bright red. He leaps up and runs down the ramp. Seconds later, the officers escort Randall and Hakim inside, too.

When Waters walks back to us, the spring in his step is gone. He crosses his arms against his chest and gives us the stern-teacher stare. "You have some explaining to do."

Lucy bows her head.

Cole opens his mouth to speak.

I put my hand in the air to stop him.

"They've been after us all year, Mr. Waters," I say. "They're going to be fine. And there's no way to prove we had anything to do with this."

"Well, *I* know you had something to do with this," he says.

When I'm sure I have Mr. Waters's full attention, I rub my

hand against the back of my neck, where he implanted the Youli patch. "There are some things best kept confidential, don't you think, Mr. Waters?"

· E_F ·

When we head out of the burrow for dinner, Neeka practically tramples us. "Oh! Oh! We must discuss!"

"Discuss what, Neeksters?" Marco asks.

She turns her back on Marco and threads her furry arm with Lucy's. "Please! Not here! The baths!"

"It's time for dinner," Cole says.

"Oh, hush," Lucy says. "We certainly aren't in any rush to choke down more forage."

She glares at me, Cole, and Marco. I don't know why she has to lump me in with them. I didn't do anything.

Lucy grabs Mira's hand and hurries with Neeka to the Nest. We follow, but at a distance.

"Let me guess," I whisper to Marco. "You weren't entirely transparent about why you wanted the foot powder."

Marco shrugs. "She never asked."

Once we're safely inside the Nest, Neeka starts chattering and the voice box starts flipping out, just like it did the day we arrived. "Oh! Oh! Oh! No! No! No!"

I bite down on my finger to stop from laughing. From the way Lucy's eyeing me, my hysteria wouldn't go over so well.

Mira approaches Neeka and strokes her arm. Slowly

Neeka's voice lowers to its normal octave, and the voice box stops glitching. "How could you?" it finally translates. "If Father finds out about this, I'm finished with Earth Force!"

"No worries, Furry Friend," Marco says. "He won't find out."

"That's *so* not the issue, Marco!" Lucy says. "You pressed Neeka for information and then tricked her into trading for you!"

"I never lied," Marco says. "Ask her."

"Oh! Oh! It's true. I didn't understand, but he didn't mislead me either. Oh! I just don't know how I always end up in these predicaments."

I guess Neeka is just as gullible with her fellow Tunnelers.

"I don't understand," Cole says. "I thought you said the foot powder is harmless."

We all look at Neeka, waiting for her to confirm what we've been hoping ever since our prank went live.

"Oh! No! They will be fine," she says. "Their feet were slathered with healing ointments, but only as a precaution. And they will have to stay at the hospital overnight for observation."

"But no permanent damage, right?" Marco says.

"True," Neeka says.

"See?" he says. "A successful prank."

Neeka shakes her head. "Still, Father would be most displeased."

"Of course he would, sweetie," Lucy says. "Marco, you owe Neeka an apology."

Marco's not really the apologizing type. Still, he looks from Lucy to Neeka to all of us, sizing up his options. He shrugs. "Sorry, Neeks. Jasper, Cole, let's eat." He turns around and leaves the Nest.

Cole and I dash out after him. I'm not about to stick around for more of Lucy's wrath.

At dinner, all anyone can talk about is what happened to Regis, Randall, and Hakim. By the time Cole, Marco, and I sit down to eat, the existence of the foot powder is common knowledge. As Marco predicted, most people think the burns were self-inflicted—they used the powder without permission and didn't know you were only supposed to use a sprinkle.

"Hey, Zone-Out, are you listening?" Marco asks, spearing a slice of tuber. "I asked how you got Waters off our case this morning."

And it's not the first time he's asked. He's pestered me about it ever since the Tundra Trials this morning. It's definitely not helping my guilt complex. I really should tell them about the brain patch. I have to tell them. But not yet.

"I don't know," I lie. "Let's go. I want to sneak in a round of *Evolution, Gladiator Round*, before bed."

We make it back to the burrow and hang out with some of the guys until Sheek shows up with a *Rah! Rah!* rally speech.

He's been making those on a nightly basis the last few weeks. I think it's how he checks the box for his Director of Bounder Affairs duties. We scoot into our hovel seconds before lights out. By the time Marco, Cole, and I make it all the way to our bunks, they've already flipped the switch.

It's dark when I climb into bed. I settle against my pillow, snuggle under my blankets, and replay an awesome *Evolution* battle in my mind. Just as I'm about to drift to sleep, there's movement in the bunks across from us. Wait a second . . . Did they get released early from the hospital?

"I know it was you," Regis says. He speaks quietly, but those five words seem to reverberate through the burrow. They're low and menacing and filled with absolute determination.

Regis is out for revenge.

WE ARE CLOSING IN ON OUR LAST CACHES,
and now it's all about strategy. Soon, pods will be shut out of
cache tokens. I don't think any cache is maxed yet, but it's getting close. Cache 28 was down to five yesterday. According to
Ryan and the others in our alliance, Cache 11 had only three
tokens left when they snagged theirs just before curfew. That's
where we're headed this morning.

The rule is, we're only allowed to access the BPS twice a
day for caching, and we have to come back to the base to
use it. Opting for a BPS bound first thing in the morning
is risky, because there's often a queue and that means lost
time. Typically we get as close as we can to a fresh target by

leapfrogging between known bounding spots, then fly with our packs the rest of the way. Once we've secured a cache, we bound back to base and grab coordinates from the BPS to bound to the day's second target.

But today, we hover near the BPS as soon as we reach the surface. We can't take any chances. We have to get to Cache 11 right away. Odds are we aren't the only pod missing that token who heard about the short supply.

Six pods rush the BPS once the Trial gun sounds. I think we get there first, but Gedney lets two other pods go before us, probably so it doesn't look like he's playing favorites. When it's our turn, Cole scans the cache coordinates and we bound.

When I hit the ground at the cache site, I immediately see we're not alone. One of the pods who used the BPS before us is combing the area for the box. Mira is already sprinting across the cache zone.

I take a second to size up the competition. Malaina Suarez's pod is nice and very middle of the pack. But just as I'm about to chase after Mira, Han's pod bounds in. Regis hits the ground and takes off running.

When we reach the center of the cache zone—a plain of boulders the size of hovercars—Cole waves us in. "We need to cover as much ground as possible. At this point, it's all about finding the cache first. And with all these rocks and crevices, it could be anywhere. Let's split up. Search your assigned direction."

This is our standard strategy—four of us search the compass points while Cole covers the center circle. I confirm with the astrocache compass and head east.

Even though it's freezing cold, sweat beads on my forehead as I race from boulder to boulder, searching for the cache. Everywhere I look, there's a Bounder crawling through the landscape, turning over rocks, scampering over boulders, leaving no sight unsearched.

Someone should have found it by now. Maybe another pod buried or camouflaged it, or possibly even removed it from the cache zone against the rules.

As I'm about to circle back to Cole for a strategy check, a flutter of movement catches my eye.

Roughly twenty meters south, Suarez's pod is converging. The pod members race toward Lian, a tall girl from Eurasia with black hair that reaches past her waist.

She must have found the cache.

I definitely don't want to alert everyone, but I have to let my pod mates know. It won't matter how quickly I reach the cache if the pod isn't present for the scan. I bound to the center zone and fly to where Cole is searching. He agrees to grab Marco and Mira and tells me to get Lucy and fly for the cache.

MONICA TESLER

I zoom toward Lucy in my blast pack, but halfway there, I bail. Across the field, cadets from Han's pod are rushing for the cache. If I don't get there fast, the tokens will be gone. I think about bounding, but we're so close, my pack is probably quicker. Plus, it would be pretty easy to make a mistake with everyone closing in.

I veer away from Lucy and race for the cache.

"Go, Jasper!" Lucy's voice rises up. She's figured out what's happening, and now she's guaranteed that everyone within earshot has, too. Although with all the cadets racing to the cache zone, it would be pretty hard to miss.

I push myself faster, pressing the connection between my brain and the pack. There are still too many cadets ahead of me. I'm not sure I'll make it in time.

Then I feel a pressure at the base of my skull that builds and balloons like my head is going to burst. The pressure shifts. A surge of power shoots through me, and I explode forward in a sort of minibound. Instead of fifty meters away, I'm standing next to the cache. I pull a token from the cache box while Lian and her pod stand there mystified.

Seconds later, my pod mates arrive, along with every other cadet in the cache zone. Lian hands me the cache tablet. I scan my retina and pass it around my pod.

"We're all set!" I say after Cole completes the last scan. "Let's bound!"

As I lift my palms in the air, a fist rams into my face. I hit the ground hard.

"That's from all of us, you cheat!" Regis yells.

He leaps on top of me, and I brace for more blows.

Marco and some of the cadets from Suarez's pod haul him off me.

As I struggle to my feet, Regis tries to charge me again, but when he gets within half a meter, he freezes. Mira stands beside me, her hands raised against Regis, blocking him with her gloves.

"Call off your magic mistress, Jasper!" he shouts. "Let's finish this!"

I surge forward. Mira's hand whips around. My feet are rooted to the ground by an invisible force.

No! Mira's mind bristles with anger and determination. She's holding me back, too. She doesn't want this snowballing into a full-on brawl.

But she only has two hands, and Marco has other plans. When Hakim rushes me from the side, Marco grabs his atoms and flings him to the ground.

Next thing I know, Lucy and Cole are trying to fend off Randall, and Hakim is back on his feet, making a run for Mira.

Her mind touches mine again. *Bound!*

Even though every ounce of me wants to beat Regis to a pulp, I don't want my pod mates to be caught in the cross fire. Ignoring the pain in my jaw where Regis's fist found my face, I tap in and open a port. Seconds later, I'm lying on the tarmac at the base.

Bam! Mira is there, too. Then Marco. A few seconds later, Cole and Lucy appear.

"Way to start a fight, Ace," Marco says.

"I didn't start it! Regis slugged me!" My speech comes out all garbled. My face must be really swollen. "Why did he go off and hit me?"

"You really don't know?" Lucy asks. "He thinks you cheated! How did you do that superhuman charge at the target, anyhow? We haven't been taught how to do that."

The back of my skull still feels prickly from the surge. I know Mira passed me her energy through the Youli patch, but I can't tell the others that.

"I was so focused on the target, I must have tapped into some additional features of the gloves," I say. "You know Gedney says what the gloves can do is limitless."

Lucy look at me skeptically. "If you say so. It certainly didn't give him the right to hit you."

"Speaking of that," Marco says. "We need to bolt. Odds are Regis will come here next, and if he does, he's coming for you, Fly Guy."

· *EF* ·

Later in the day, after we log a second cache, we meet up with Ridders's pod at our usual lunch spot close to Cache 12, where we ate the first day. Apparently, word is out, because as soon as I bound in, Ryan starts up with the questions.

"Whoa! Your face looks like a rotten banana! Regis really walloped you good, didn't he? How come you guys never told us about the bolt-and-bound move? Are you holding out? Is that like your secret weapon?"

"*I'm* not holding out," Lucy says. "Ask Jasper."

"Well?" Ryan asks me. Everyone else in his pod stares, too.

"What?" I say, unwrapping my BERF. "Nothing happened. Or, at least, I'm not *sure* what happened. My desperation to reach the cache must have given me an extra power surge."

Ryan doesn't look very satisfied with my answer, but he doesn't press me on it.

Annette is a different story. She walks to where I'm sitting and cups her hand against my bruised cheek. "I'm curious, Jasper. How come all the drama at the EarthBound Academy seems to gravitate to you?"

The warmth of her fingers against my skin is distracting. I think it should hurt, but it actually feels kind of soothing, and entirely awkward.

"It seems to me you must be looking for drama," she continues, "sort of like Sheek."

I knock her hand away. "You're comparing me to Sheek? No way! I can't believe you'd say that!"

"Most guys would take it as a compliment."

MONICA TESLER

"Yeah? Well, I'm not most guys."

Annette looks at me with her level stare. "No. You're not."

What's that supposed to mean? Is she insulting me? Should I be flattered? This girl is impossible to understand.

"What about me?" Marco says, thankfully rescuing me from one kind of drama I definitely don't want: girl drama.

"You're worse than Sheek," Lucy says. "At least Sheek is actually ridiculously handsome."

"Come on," Marco says. "I'm hot and you know it."

"In your dreams, Tofu Face."

"What do you think, Meggi?" Marco asks.

Meggi looks like she might faint. She opens her mouth, but no sound comes out.

"You know she thinks you're gorgeous," Annette says.

Lucy slaps Annette on the shoulder.

"What was that?" Cole says.

"I said Meggi thinks—" Annette says.

"Not *that*. Over there." Cole gestures to the huge boulder where we ditched our stuff. "I thought I saw something moving over by our packs."

Everyone stops and stares at the big rock and the pile of blast packs.

"I don't see anything," Marco says.

"Maybe it was a slimer," Ryan says. "Jaron from Amazonas swears they saw one yesterday."

"Yeah, well, Jaron's a liar," Meggi says.

There's been talk of slimers for weeks. The technical Tunneler name is impossible to pronounce, so we call them slimers. According to the junior ambassadors, a slimer is one of the few creatures that can survive aboveground on the Tundra. You can't spot them until you step on them, and then it's usually too late. Slimers can change shape instantly. Usually they spread out real thin along the ground and absorb starlight for energy, but they can also feed off organic matter. So if you step on one, they morph into a giant blob around you. You die a slow, painful death as they take days to dissolve you with digestive fluid. Most cadets think they're not real, that the junior ambassadors are just messing with us.

"We have to go," Annette says. "We have two more caches slotted this afternoon. If there's a slimer by the packs, we'll make sure to let you know."

I think she's being sarcastic—no one really believes in slimers, right?—but I just can't tell with Annette.

Their pod successfully retrieves their blast packs and bounds away.

Once they're gone, Cole asks, "Do you think slimers exist?"

"Of course not, Wiki," Marco says. "But I'll tell you what scary creatures *do* exist—the Youli! And so far we've been pitifully unsuccessful in discovering anything about Earth Force's plans!"

MONICA TESLER

"What about the conversation between Ridders and Sheek about the summit and the military engagement?" Cole asks. "Waters's comments to Jasper confirmed it."

"Great. And what do we know about the summit?" Marco says. "Nothing!"

"I don't think Earth Force is going to offer up any details," I say.

"Of course not!" Marco says. "We need a plan to get the information ourselves! I don't know what 'military engagement' means to you, but to me it means there's going to be a fight. And if they plan to send the Bounders to battle, you better believe I want to know about it in advance!"

"Leave it to me," Lucy says. "It's time I had a heart-to-heart with Sheek."

"Seriously?" Cole says.

"Sure! It will be fun!"

"Okay, DQ, I'll leave it up to you," Marco says, "but if you haven't found out by tomorrow night, I'm in charge, and I'm targeting the weakest link."

"What on earth does that mean?" I say.

"Our furry friend's father is the highest-ranking Tunneler in Earth Force, and his daughter has a hard time keeping secrets."

"Marco, not again! You wouldn't!" Lucy says.

"You bet I would if it means finding out the truth!"

"I'll get the truth from Sheek tonight," she says. "But you leave Neeka alone! After the foot powder, you promised!"

Cole outlines our afternoon cache strategy. We'll bound to a cache site we visited last week and then fly our packs to today's target. Once we secure the cache, we'll bound back to the base before curfew. One by one, my pod mates head out.

I'm just about to bound when Mira bursts into my brain.

Wait!

I pull back from my port and blink. I expect Mira to be right in front of me. Instead, she's running from rock to rock where we ate lunch like she's searching for a cache, and my brain is picking up panic.

Let's go! I think, and just in case she's not paying attention in her mind, I shout, "Let's go!"

Mira is frantic. She's still running, but now she's shaking her arms like she has something super nasty on her hands that she needs to fling off. My brain feels like a glitter bomb exploded all over it.

I dash in her direction. She's basically flipping out—waving her hands, pulling her braid, darting around. When I reach her, I grab hold of her shoulders so she'll stop running. That sends her into even more of a freak-out, so I back away, rubbing the back of my neck as I do. This brain-connection thing is not all fun and games.

"I'm not touching you, okay? What's wrong? How can I help?"

MONICA TESLER

She keeps waving her hands. *Hands! Hands! Hands!*

I have no idea what to do. "What is it, Mira? How can I help?"

My hands! She waves them frantically.

"What about your hands?"

She takes off again, bending down to look beneath every rock.

Her hands . . . *hmmm* . . . maybe that's not the exact word. What I'm feeling from her brain is more the impression of hands. I watch carefully as she shakes her hands by her sides.

Wait a second . . .

I dash to her side. "Mira, where are your gloves?"

There's a wash of relief that crosses her face and my brain. That's it. That's why she's freaking out. The reprieve only lasts a second, though, because the problem itself is extremely grave.

Lost!

21

"YOU LOST YOUR GLOVES?"

A sense of confirmation fills my brain, but it's accompanied by a hoverload of panic.

"Take a deep breath. Try to focus. Where did you leave them? Was it when we were having lunch?"

We race to where we were eating, even though I'm pretty sure Mira already scoured the place searching for her gloves.

I check where she was sitting, and then I branch out in circles, canvassing the area for any sign of her gloves. By the time I've searched a twenty-meter radius, I'm feeling pretty desperate, too.

I also know the others have got to be worried. Seconds later, Marco bounds in, confirming my hunch.

"What on earth?" he shouts. "We've got to bolt, or we won't make it to the cache and back before curfew!"

I lean up against a rock and try to catch my breath. "Mira lost her gloves."

Marco narrows his eyes. "Gloves don't just get up and walk away."

"Yeah, I know, but we've looked everywhere." I throw my hands in the air. "They're gone."

"Maybe one of the others accidentally packed them."

"Good thinking. Bound back and check." The star sinks on the horizon, confirming the dark truth. "If we can't find her gloves, we'll have to fly. And even if we leave this very second, we're cutting it pretty close for curfew. If you haven't found them in five minutes, bring us the astrocache compass."

Marco shakes his head. "I'll be back in three minutes."

Lights glow from his palms, and he vanishes.

Mira sits on the ground with her back to a boulder. I sink down next to her.

Go.

"I'm not leaving you."

Go.

I don't bother responding, by mouth or by brain. Instead, I remove my right glove. Then I untangle her left hand from her right and weave my fingers through hers. She rests her head against my shoulder. Sadness rolls off her in waves. I watch the numbers on my watch tick down.

Three.

Marco and the others must have searched their packs by now.

Two.

If they don't have her gloves, where could they be?

One.

If someone in Ridders's pod mistakenly took them, they could be anywhere on Gulaga. We'll never find them in time.

Marco hits the ground in front of us. My chest surges with hope. He shakes his head and hands me the compass. "We'll keep looking. If we find them, I'll track you down on the tundra."

I nod. "We need to go."

"Good luck. We'll be waiting for you in the Nest." Marco pauses for another moment, then nods, opens his port, and vanishes.

I place Mira's hand on her lap and slip my glove back on. I may have to travel by blast pack, but I'm not willing to give up my sensor straps. Mira knows I'm a disaster with the manual controls.

Mira stands and retrieves her pack from the clearing where we had lunch. She detaches her sensor straps and clips in the manuals.

I buckle the astrocache compass on my wrist and hoist my

pack onto my shoulders. After confirming our route on the map, I nod to Mira, squeeze my grips, and lift off. She flies to my side.

"We have a lot of ground to cover, so don't ease up on speed." Setting our course for the base, I accelerate.

I don't check my watch too frequently because all that does is stress me out. It seems like we've flown for hours over the rocky, monotonous Gulagan plain. Every second that passes brings us closer to the base. I hope. We're working on a very narrow margin of time to make it back before the gates close.

I wish Cole was here to read the map. It's not that I don't know how, but I haven't had much practice. And the way we constructed our routes and staggered our targets, we never had to cross this stretch of Gulaga.

From the map, it almost looks like Earth Force is steering us away from this area. None of the caches are close to here. In fact, none of the caches are even on a flight line between the base and this place.

We glide over a ridge. Beneath us is a big bowl with steep cliffs on all sides. As soon as we crest, the wind picks up. It's hard to cut a straight path with so much turbulence. Typically I would descend, so we weren't flying so far aboveground, but we're very short on time.

Roughly halfway across the bowl, my pack sputters and drops a few meters. A gust of wind tumbles me. I manage to right myself and fly on. Mira's up ahead. I don't think she noticed.

I shake off my fear, sure it's just nerves as we race against the curfew clock.

Sputter. Putter. Putt. Putt.

My pack spurts forward, then stops, then drops.

I gain control again, but can't stop the pack from losing altitude.

It's just like . . .

The trash tunnel . . .

Oh no!

"Mira! My battery!"

My brain's connection with the pack starts to fizzle. I won't be able to stay aloft for long. I focus my full attention on lowering to the ground. I set my course in a sloping arc, trying to capitalize on inertia and not fight too much with gravity.

"Mira!" I shout again, but she continues on her straight course across the valley. She must not be able to hear me over the wind.

Mira! Help!

She slows to a hover and spins her pack.

My battery dies, and I plunge for the valley floor.

No!

Dropping the straps, I flash my palms at the ground and push against the atoms on the planet's surface.

A familiar pressure surges at the base of my skull, just like this morning at the cache site. With the amplified power of my gloves, I repel off the ground, easing my landing. A fraction of a second before I hit, I turn my body, so my back and butt bear the brunt of the impact. Air is knocked from my lungs. I gasp for breath, but none comes. I gasp again, and the sweet taste of oxygen rushes in. I turn over onto my stomach and push my forehead to the cold ground.

A hand on my back. *Okay?*

Mira must sense the pain in my hip. Why am I always landing on my hip?

She moves her hand to the bull's-eye of the pain. I flinch, expecting her touch to hurt, but it doesn't. Instead, I feel immediate relief, like she's radiating warm energy through my body.

I push my chest off the ground and sit cross-legged in front of her. "How do you do that without your gloves?"

Mira shrugs. She cups her palm against my cheek, which is still aching from Regis's blow, just like Annette did earlier.

I lean into her hand, letting her soothing energy run through me.

The cliffs rise up around us, nearly as high as my apartment building back on Earth. I check my watch: 1545 hours.

Fifteen minutes until curfew. No gloves. No blast pack.

The reality starts to sink in.

We're stuck out here overnight.

A shiver ripples through my body. The temperature is

already dropping. We're probably going to freeze to death.

The ground shakes. Or does it? Am I imagining things? Am I just shivering extra hard?

"Did you feel that?"

The next shake knocks me over.

Mira springs to her feet. *Move!*

I scramble to get up, wincing against the pain in my hip.

Move now!

Okay, okay. Geez. The ground lurches, and I fall back to my knees.

The surface of the planet bubbles and curls around me, circling my feet, enclosing my legs in a pool of ooze.

"Slimer!"

Mira kicks at the creature that's sucking me into its blob belly.

I yank my feet, but it oozes tighter.

Gloves! Mira screams in my mind.

I flash my hands at the creature, and it recoils enough for me to pull my left foot out of its grasp.

A second slimer attacks Mira. She lunges. It trips her to the ground and slurps her legs in ooze. *Help!*

I zap my other leg free and spring to where the creature is sucking down Mira. I wrap my arm around her chest and repel the slimer with my gloves. An oozy tendril from another slimer wraps around my ankle.

The entire basin bubbles like a writhing witches' brew. "They're everywhere!"

Run! Mira screams.

I force our feet free, and we dash across the valley. I aim my gloves ahead to clear a path. When we reach the cliffs, we climb until we pull up on a ledge ten meters above the ground, safely outside the slimers' ooze.

"Those things are super scary," I say. "They sounded bad when the junior ambassadors described them, but they're even worse."

Mira's feelings on the topic can be summed up in one word: *gross*.

"What do we do now?"

Mira scans the cliffs. She points to indentations several meters above us that might be caves. *Shelter.*

Good idea. We're getting colder by the second. I try to stand, but a shooting pain bursts across my hip and sends me falling back on my butt. Ouch.

Things are not looking good.

My neck tingles, and an image of the music room at the space station flashes in my mind. Mira must be trying to tell me that everything's going to be all right.

I wish I believed her. The warmth fades, and we're still stranded on the tundra. This is going to be a long night.

Mira ducks under my arm and helps me stand. A pain

shoots down my right leg, but I hobble forward. Seriously, another blast pack fall? How could this happen to me again? Regis would be dying of laughter.

Regis.

Thinking his name is like a magic key to a throwaway memory. Today at lunch, when Ryan was pressing us for details about the cache conflict, Meggi said they'd run into Regis at the base, and he was threatening to track us down on the tundra. What if he figured out where we ate lunch? It's no secret we meet up with Ridders's pod at the same spot most days. One of them must have told Regis. Or maybe Regis bribed someone else to get the information.

It makes complete sense. When we were eating, Cole said he saw something moving by the blast packs. That wasn't a something, it was a some*one*.

"Regis took your gloves," I say to Mira. My voice shakes with rage. Sure, we've gotten pretty nasty with our pranks, but this time he crossed the line.

Climb. She presses my back, urging me onto the cliff. We have another ten-meter climb before we reach a stretch of narrow switchbacks that lead to the caves.

"Did you hear me? Regis took your gloves!"

Climb. Shelter.

"We've got to do something about it!"

Mira shoves me, and I stumble. Her hands hit hard against

my shoulders, but I'm also knocked back by her brain. She thinks I'm a big blockhead for worrying about Regis when we're on the verge of freezing to death.

"Okay! Okay, you're right."

Mira shakes her head and starts up the cliff on her own. She scans the rock face and sets in at a spot where there are lots of grips.

I place my gloved hand on the rock and pull myself up. My hip throbs. I ignore the pain and press forward, trying to match my movements to Mira's.

Every switch in grip, Mira stops and shakes her hands. There's a strange crackling sensation in my brain. I finally realize she's in pain, too.

Since she doesn't have her gloves, her hands are exposed. I didn't even think of that. She had to fly all the way here with just her sleeves for protection, and now she has to grab hold of this ice-cold rock. If we don't take cover soon, she'll definitely have frostbite. She could lose her fingers! What would we do if Mira couldn't use her hands?

I'm fine. Her thoughts sound annoyed.

You could hear what I was thinking?

You're very transparent.

Those thoughts are private, Mira! These patches do not give you the right to barge into my brain whenever you want.

No response. *Well, fine, then. See for yourself how you like it.* I reach out with my brain with the grand plan of probing her thoughts. I feel her mind like a shimmering veil, then— *Slam!*—a solid door bangs shut.

So much for that.

Mira hoists herself up the last half meter of our climb and sets out on the narrow path. A couple of grabs and pulls later, and I'm stepping up behind her. Only a sliver of the star is left on the horizon, and the temperature is dropping at an alarming rate. Mira overlaps the sleeves of her coat so that her hands are tucked inside.

The path couldn't be more than half a meter wide, and there are lots of spots where it's worn away and we have to traverse across by grabbing the rock face. It's slow going, and certainly not made for a klutz like me. Several switchbacks later, we finally near the second ledge. I can barely feel my toes. And when I force a wiggle, it comes with a dull, dark pain that rivals the ache in my hip.

Still, as I scramble onto the ledge next to Mira, an ounce of hope creeps in. If we can get deep enough into one of the caves up ahead, we might make it through the night.

As I set off toward the caves, Mira grabs my hand and pulls me back. When I turn, her brain opens, and words pour out. *Look up!*

Above us, the sky blazes with stars, not Gulaga's primary star, but the stars of the heavens. Just like ours on Earth.

It's amazing.

And I'm transported. Mira and I are on the grass at Waters's lab, lying side by side, staring up at the stars. At first, I'm not sure if this is my memory or Mira's, but soon I see it belongs to both of us.

My breath catches in my throat. I wrap my arms around Mira, and she leans back against me. Her blond hair brushes against my cheek. Together we share a memory and we make a new one. I see what she sees and what I see and it is so much—too much—that I have to close my eyes for a moment before my entire mind is blown to bits from the enormity of it all.

It's a perfect moment, really.

A perfect moment in our far-from-perfect night.

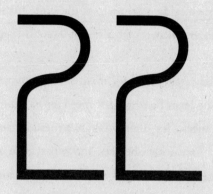

THE MOMENT DOESN'T LAST. MAYBE MIRA
slams down her brain door like before, or maybe the fact that
we're freezing trumps the shared memory magic. Whatever it
is, Mira steps forward and breaks our bond.

She turns around and nods at me. *Light. Gloves.*

Huh? I mean, *Huh?*

Light!

*Yes, Mira, a bit more light would be terrific. And where
exactly do you suggest I find such a thing out here in the tundra?*

Gloves!

Oh. I raise my hands and tap in like I'm getting ready to
open a port. Lights shoot from my fingertips. We make our

way along the ledge, the light from my fingers casting strange shadows along the path and the cliff rising beside us.

Before long, we come to one of the indentations we saw from below. Sure enough, it's a cave. I'm not super keen about exploring a cave in the dark on an alien planet, but it might be our only chance at making it through the night.

I head in first, led by the light of my gloves. Mira follows close behind. The ceiling is low, and I have to duck, which I'm used to after these weeks in Gulaga. With every step, I cringe, afraid that a slimer or something worse is going to wrap around my leg.

We don't go far, just deep enough to escape the wind and anything else that might be lurking on the tundra. Mira grabs my hand and points its light at the wall. She heads in that direction and sits down. I slide in beside her.

Mira pulls her arms inside her coat and huddles tight. I do the same. For the first stretch, my mind wanders. I think about the Tundra Trials and how all the skills we've practiced have primed us for war. I think about what Waters said about intragalactic relations being vast and complicated, and about how more was at stake than we can possibly imagine. Mostly I think about Regis and how I'm going to get my revenge. *Ultio.*

Every few minutes, Mira shifts. I'm paranoid that she's listening in on my thoughts since I don't know how to close my brain door, but she never comments or shows any sign that she's interested.

Then it gets colder, and harder to think. I lean my head against Mira's. At least we're together. My brain sparkles in a way that lets me know she's thinking of me. I call up the time Mom and Dad took us to see the fireworks. I hope Mira knows those explosions of light in my mind are for her.

The notes of a piano trickle into my mind. It's a pretty song. Simple and sweet. It almost feels like we're sitting against a wall sharing earbuds, not freezing in Gulaga with bonded brain patches. When Mira breaks the melody, I imagine my clarinet and echo the song back to her. With each pass, she adds to the harmony, until we've built a beautiful duet.

Then the music fades, and it grows colder still. My mind can't fix on anything except the cold. For what seems like forever, sharp pains shoot up my toes into my shins. But now I can't feel my toes at all. Our breath puffs in little clouds as it escapes our mouths. Mira's teeth chatter. She hums quietly, maybe to keep her mouth still, but it's haunting. I've rarely heard the sound of her voice, even the sound of her hum.

I don't know how much longer we're going to make it. My head aches, a deep throbbing right behind my temples. My brain is slowly freezing. It's kind of funny, really. My brain is worth so much to Earth Force, and it's worth even more now that Waters rigged it up with the Youli patch, but it's not going to think us out of this mess. There are some predicaments no amount of brainpower can fix.

We're going to die here.

Go. There's a calm determination in Mira's thoughts. *Go, please.*

I knew she'd eventually suggest this—that I use my gloves to bound back to the base and try to get them to let me in—and I already have my response planned out. *Just stop it, Mira. There's no way I'm leaving you. It's my fault we're in this mess. My pack wasn't fully charged. If it had been, we might have made it back to the base. Plus, I can't bound into the base anyway. The scrambler would scatter my atoms. So no, I'm not going to bound, no matter what you say. I'm staying with you. We'll get through the night together.*

Go! The determination is still there, but the calm is gone. *Go! Go! Go!* She bashes me with her shoulder. I bash her back. Neither one of us wants to take our hands out of our coats. We must look like bowling pins knocking into each other.

She bashes me hard, knocking herself off balance as she strikes me. I fall back and she falls against me. In that moment, the scarce body heat we have left seems to multiply. If we get as close as we can, maybe our body heat will keep us warm.

I press myself up against the wall and reluctantly unwrap my hands from my body and shake them through their sleeves. I gesture to Mira to sit in front of me, between my legs, and just in case she can't figure out why I'm flailing, I send her a mental picture of my idea.

She crawls over and sits, leaning her back against my chest. I wrap my arms around her in a bear hug, my gloved hands resting against her coat.

Gloves. Warm.

I thought of that before, but the truth is, I don't really know how to make the gloves warm up. Gedney said they were limitless, but I suppose I've hit my limit.

My patch prickles, and then my fingers burn like I'm running them under hot water after playing in the snow.

"Are you doing that?"

Focus.

I sense the connection between my brain and the gloves. Then I feel the river of current Mira is feeding me through our brain patches. Once I get the hang of it, I'm able to warm my gloves. The heat circulates through Mira, and back into me. It's not much, and it's making me very tired, but maybe it's enough to keep our hearts beating through the night. I lose all sense of time, channeling the energy I have left into keeping the heat connection.

Kreek. Arrrgh. Grakakreet.

Breekeet. Karmareek. Arrkkk.

Kargarr. Gareer. Arrrgh.

Mira and I jerk up with a start. My head hurts so much from the sudden movement, I nearly pass out.

Noreek. Arrrgreek. Breeka.

Five Tunnelers wearing headlamps surround us. They're dressed in funny clothes—big, furry hats and coats dyed red and purple and electric blue. They keep grunting in Gulagan. I don't know if they're talking to us or each other. I don't know if they're here to kill us or save us, but since death seemed the only option just seconds ago, my heart leaps with hope.

"What are you doing here?" A robotic voice sounds. "We thought we saw something on the ridge hours ago." One of the Tunnelers steps forward. He has a deep scar by his eye. Barrick.

I can't believe our good luck. "Barrick! It's me! We met our first day! We're Bounders! We're in Jon Waters's pod."

"You won't be in Waters's pod for long if you don't get out of here. You're probably just about frozen already, and it's only getting colder. Get up! We need to move!"

One of the Tunnelers grabs Mira by the armpits and hauls her up. Without the warmth of her body, the cold crushes me.

I'm suddenly very embarrassed. What would the other cadets think if they knew I'd wrapped my arms around Mira to keep us warm? I don't dwell on it. Mira looks too bad off. Two Tunnelers lift and carry her deeper into the cave.

"Don't worry," Barrick says. "She should be okay if we can warm her up. Which means we need to move."

"Where are we going?"

"This cave leads to our tunnel system."

"You mean Gulagaven?"

"Ha! Ha! Ha!" comes through the voice box. "No. We don't live in Gulagaven. You may have heard of us. Earth Force calls us the Wackies."

They're bringing us to the Wacky headquarters? This could be very bad. Then again, it couldn't be worse than what was waiting for us in the cave.

Barrick helps me up and hands me off to two Tunnelers. He barks at them, and they walk with me sandwiched between them deeper into the cave. Their headlamps glow with the silver light of occludium.

A million questions run through my mind, but asking them would be useless. I'm pretty sure Barrick is the only one who's wearing a voice box, and he's way up ahead. The two Tunnelers by my sides are carrying on a conversation in Gulagan. At first I'm paranoid they're talking about me, then I realize I'm probably the least important thing in their world. They check readings on a scanner and every few minutes report into a handheld com device. They're surviving on the outskirts of society in a very inhospitable landscape and climate. Caring for an Earth Force cadet must rank pretty low.

But they *are* caring for me. They're saving us. Even though they don't have to. Even though they probably have good reason not to, since it seems Earth Force hasn't been too kind to them.

They're not what I imagined at all. When Neeka mentioned the Wackies, I pictured them as a couple of old, crazy Tunnelers wandering aimlessly across the frozen tundra. I definitely didn't imagine them as a high-tech search party showing up to rescue us.

Soon, the cave tunnel widens and occludium-powered glow orbs are mounted on the walls. We come to a thick sliding door secured with multiple code locks. It slides back to reveal a bustling city, similar to Gulagaven on a smaller scale.

No guardrails here, either. Ugh.

Barrick tells me they're taking us to their infirmary. As they steer us along the ramps of their city, dozens of Tunnelers rush past. Just like the search party, they're dressed in brilliant colors and styles.

When we reach the infirmary, they lay Mira down on a table and point to the table next to hers. I'm assuming that's sign language for me to get up there. I climb up and stretch out.

A few minutes later, a Tunneler wearing a long green coat comes to check on Mira. She pulls the curtain so I can't see. Hopefully she's a doctor, or at least the Tunneler version of one.

"Is she going to be okay?" I ask.

The Tunneler doesn't answer.

I reach out to Mira in my mind. Nothing. Silence. I haven't felt her connection since the search party found us. How long has she been with the doctor? Why doesn't someone check on me? My hip hurts. And my head. If I only knew that Mira would be okay, I think my head would feel better. The base of my skull is throbbing. A growing blackness creeps along the edges of my vision. Maybe if I closed my eyes for a second . . .

The next thing I'm aware of is Waters's voice. I must be dreaming. I struggle to open my eyes. When they flutter open, I get my bearings. I'm in the Wacky infirmary. The curtain is pulled back. Mira is on the next table. Huge mitts are pulled over her hands. Tubes connect to her nose and arm. That can't be good. I try to sit up. Tubes connect to my nose and arm, too. When did that happen?

But the weird thing is, I can still hear Waters's voice. I close my eyes and focus on his words.

"So you're sure they're going to be all right?"

"Confident." From the sound of the robotic voice box, that must be Barrick. "We got them inside before their temperatures fell to critical. All their vitals are improving. They should be fine by morning."

"Good. These two are special. We can't lose them."

Last tour, that would have made me feel great, proud that Waters thought I was special. Now I don't know if he

MONICA TESLER

genuinely cares about us, or if he just cares about the special technology he implanted in our brains.

He's right to worry about us, though. My brain—Youli patch and all—feels like mush, like I'm missing something very important.

Wait a second . . . Mira and I are miles away from Gulagaven, holed up in an infirmary in the middle of the Wacky compound, which happens to be deep underground across the frozen tundra. Why on earth is Waters here? Did he come because he heard they found us? I thought no one was allowed in or out of Gulagaven after curfew.

"Are we all set for tomorrow?" Barrick asks.

"Yes. The maintenance schedule still shows a power-down of the occludium shields beginning at nineteen hundred hours. The meeting will go forward as scheduled. Which reminds me, I need to scan these coordinates."

"Right here in the infirmary?"

"It's quiet, secure, far off the radar," Waters says. "I think it's ideal."

Barrick grunts. "Fair enough."

I open my eyes just enough to see Waters unlock the black BPS case. That can only mean one thing: whoever is coming to this meeting is going to bound here. It has to be the meeting both Waters and Ridders were talking about. We've got to get more information. Hopefully Lucy had luck with Sheek tonight.

Out of the corner of my eye, there's movement. Mira lifts her hand.

"She's waking up!" Waters says.

"I'll get the doctor," Barrick says.

Mira struggles to sit. Waters rushes to her side.

"You don't need to get up now. Just rest," Waters says, easing Mira back down onto the table.

"Is she going to be okay?" I ask.

He turns to me. "You're awake, too, huh? You kids! Always in and out of the infirmary! You gave me quite the scare tonight!"

"How did you get here?"

"Never mind that," he says. "How did *you* get here?"

Even though Waters is dodging my questions and being super cagey in general, I can't resist giving him the replay of our tale of woe, including my conclusion that Regis is to blame for us being in this mess.

"Well, thank goodness you survived. It's nothing short of a miracle that Barrick and his team found you. And I have another slice of good news—Mira's gloves were found at the outfitters after base closing. Apparently, they were slipped in with some of the returned equipment."

That *is* good news. I was worried Regis might have destroyed her gloves. I have no idea how long it would have taken Gedney to make a new pair.

Waters reaches into a side pocket of the BPS case, and withdraws the gloves. "Of course, you can't use them now. A bound would show up on the tracker, and we can't risk Earth Force discovering this location. Not to mention, the scrambler is activated in Gulagaven. Tomorrow morning, Barrick will walk you back through the occludium mines."

"Our pod mates are probably freaking out," I say.

"Gedney told them you were safe. They know where you are, and they know not to tell anyone. The cover story is that you entered the mines through an exhaust vent and wandered through the night until you eventually made it back to Gulagaven. There are dozens of vents scattered across the planet, so the story is entirely plausible. It won't reveal the location of the outpost, and it has the added benefit of you being able to say you entered the tunnels by curfew, so there's no question you're still in contention for the Tundra Trials. I suspect that's quite important to you kids, seeing as tomorrow is the last day and you're in the lead."

"But I told you Regis stole the gloves. Why can't we just tell the truth? He should be punished! We almost died because of him! He should be kicked out of Earth Force!"

Waters's lips press together in a tight, straight line. "I'm not saying this is fair, Jasper. I'm saying it's our plan. Sometimes it's just not possible to do everything the right way. You have to make choices for the greater good. You and Mira didn't die. The secrecy of this outpost is paramount. And we both know the chance that Earth Force is going to expel one of its cadets—one of its soldiers—is almost zero." He gives me that look my mom uses sometimes, the one that says, *When you're a grown-up, you'll understand.* Then he places his hand on my shoulder. "I need you to do this for me, Jasper. It may seem like a small thing, but it is a very important piece of a much bigger puzzle."

"Like the puzzle piece implanted in my brain?"

"Yes, actually, just like that."

The Tunneler doctor walks into the infirmary, cutting off our conversation. I wish I could have pressed Waters more. But the truth is my head is pounding.

Waters whispers good night and pulls the curtain.

It's pretty clear he's plotting something big. I don't know what it is, but I know Mira and I are pawns in his scheme. Until I discover what he's up to, we might as well play along.

Not like we have a choice.

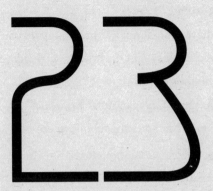

23

"SHE DOESN'T TALK MUCH, HUH?" BARRICK asks.

"No, but she can hear you," I say. "So cut it out with the commentary."

It feels like Mira and I have been following Barrick for hours. I have no idea how he remembers the route. Every tunnel looks exactly the same as the last.

"Fine, I'd rather not talk," he says. "I hate the sound of this stupid box."

"That makes two of us. Why don't you get a new one?"

"And how exactly am I supposed to do that? Waltz right up to Admiral Eames and ask for one? I realize you're a bit slow on the uptake, kid, but the operation we're running is covert."

"I'm not stupid," I say.

"Could have fooled me. I've had to rescue you twice."

"Garr-eek." Cole taught me how to say thank you, although my accent sounds awful.

"Oh, you speak Gulagan now? Fantastic."

Ignore him. Mira adds this choice piece of wisdom to the exchange.

That's easy for her. It's not hard to ignore just about anyone when you don't talk. I guess the downside is that most people ignore you, too. Of course, at this exact moment, that would be an upside.

"How much farther?" I ask.

"One more bend, then that's far enough for me."

"You're not taking us all the way?"

"I don't feel like getting caught this morning, so no."

We walk in silence for the next five minutes. When we reach the corner, Barrick pulls up short. "Straight down this hall, right at the end, third left, straight to the end, right, first left, follow that past the main market. I assume you know your way from there." He turns around and scurries up the tunnel we traveled down.

"Wait!" I shout, but he shows no sign of stopping.

Straight. Right at the end.

"Yeah, that I got. I hope you remember the rest of the route, or we'll be just as lost as before."

Fortunately, Mira's ability to retain Tunneler directions far surpasses mine, and she's able to lead us back to the Earth Sector. We drop our blast packs at the burrow to charge, and then make our way to the cantina.

When we walk in, all eyes are on us. Mira heads straight for our pod table, but I stand at the threshold, scanning the room, looking for Regis.

When I spot him, my heart quickens, and I'm guessing his does, too. His mouth hangs open at the hinges like he just saw a ghost. I suppose he has, in a way. He thought Mira and I were goners. I narrow my eyes at him. I don't want there to be any doubt in his mind that I'm staring him down, that I know what he's done. The realization flashes across his face.

I slowly raise my pointed finger. *You, Regis. I'm coming for you.*

Something collides with my shoulder, pushing aside my revenge fantasies. Lucy wraps me in her arms and squeezes. "Oh, you big goof! I was so worried!"

"It was Regis," I say.

"We guessed as much once Mira's gloves turned up. They had to be planted. We went through all our packs three times to make sure we didn't accidentally take them. Never mind that now. Your poor face. It's purple."

I raise my hand to my cheek where Regis hit me. I'd almost

forgotten what started all of this. "That's the least of our problems. Mira almost lost her fingers from frostbite."

Lucy frowns. "Come sit." She leads me by the hand over to the table. As I launch into the tale of Mira's and my night, Cole is antsy. He's drumming his fingers and squirming in his seat.

"What's with you?" I ask.

"Ignore him," Lucy says. "We have a story of our own, but it can wait until you're done. In fact, it can wait until after you've eaten. We have to be on the surface in under an hour. Go get some food!"

"First I want to hear why he's so fired up. Cole?"

"We found out details about the meeting!" he says.

"Tonight, nineteen hundred hours?" I ask.

"What are you, a mind reader?" Marco says.

"How did you know?" Lucy asks.

Around us, cadets clear their trays and leave for the outfitter center.

"We've got to go," I say. If you're late for the Tundra Trials, your pod is disqualified. "I'll fill you in on our way to the first cache. Now let's eat and go win this thing!" I dart for the food line. Who would have thought a few weeks ago that I'd be racing for a warm meal of furry forage and fungi?

· 𝓔𝓕 ·

We make it to the surface with only seconds to spare and race to join the group of cadets crowded around Commander

MONICA TESLER

Krag for the start of the final day of the Tundra Trials. When Neeka's father sees us coming, he shakes his head and waves us to the side.

"I'm sorry, but rules are rules," he says. "Your pod has been disqualified from the competition."

"Disqualified?" Marco says. "No way!"

This must be about yesterday and what happened with me and Mira. "We had equipment issues! And anyway, we made it into the tunnel system by four o'clock." The lie Waters prepped me with slips out like it actually happened.

"The rule is you'll make it through the base gates by sixteen hundred hours," Commander Krag says. "I'm afraid the exhaust vents do not count."

"But that's entirely unfair!" Lucy shouts. "Today's the last day! And we're winning!"

"There's nothing I can do," the commander says. "I wish there were. My daughter will be devastated."

Cole hits my arm. "Tell him, Jasper. We were set up! We're not the ones who should be punished for this. Tell him!"

I would love to lay the blame on Regis—he deserves it—but there's no guarantee it would change the result. Like Commander Krag said, rules are rules.

But that's not what's really keeping me from telling the truth. Waters's voice rings in my mind. *I'm not saying this is fair, Jasper. . . . It may seem like a small thing, but it is a very important piece of a much bigger puzzle.*

As Commander Krag heads to the departure gong, I grab hold of Cole's coat and corral my pod mates away from the crowd. When we're out of earshot, I whisper, "We need to take the punishment. It's just a stupid contest. If we're disqualified, we won't have such a target on our backs. Think of it this way: we'll have the whole day free. There'll be plenty of time for us to plan our espionage mission."

"I don't understand," Cole says. "All we have to do is tell them the truth."

Mira places her hand on my shoulder. "It's not that simple," I say.

Lucy looks from me to Mira. "Waters put you up to this, didn't he?"

Leave it to Lucy to figure it out. I don't confirm, but I don't deny it either. "All I know is that it's important we don't raise any flags. They can't know the Wackies were involved in our rescue."

"I'm with Jasper," Marco says. "Not because I'm on board with Waters; he's got more secrets than Earth Force these days. I support the Wackies. That guy Barrick helped us when he had no reason to, and none of the stories I've heard about the Wackies from anyone in Gulagaven have ended up being true. So if keeping quiet protects their home, my lips are sealed."

We stare at Cole. He shakes his head and clenches his teeth. He does not like this one bit. I don't know if he's going to agree or explode. "Ohhh . . . ," he grumbles. "Fine."

On our way to the gates, we walk by Regis.

"Thanks for the day off," Marco says.

Regis doesn't respond. He looks freaked. His prank against us worked so well, I know he's worried about payback.

He should be.

· E⫶ ·

We spend the rest of the morning in the Nest. First, I tell the others about Mira's and my adventure last night.

"So slimers *are* real!" Cole says.

"More real than you can imagine," I say with a shudder.

Then Lucy explains how she tricked Sheek into spilling the beans about the meeting. Apparently, he's still pretty burned about not being invited, and he's willing to complain to anyone who asks the right way. All it took was a bit of coaxing. And if there's one thing Lucy excels at, it's coaxing.

"It's all going down tonight," Lucy says. "Parliament Chamber, nineteen hundred hours."

"Parliament Chamber?" I ask. "Waters scanned bounding coordinates for the infirmary at the Wacky outpost."

"Maybe Chic Sheek doesn't know as much as he'd like to believe," Marco says.

"That doesn't make sense," Cole says. "Waters told you he

wants to keep the outpost a secret. Why would he use it for an Earth Force meeting? And usually the word *summit* means a really important meeting involving really important people, like the admiral. Why would they hold a summit in an infirmary?"

I try to match what Lucy told me up against what Waters said. Something doesn't fit, and it's not simply that Sheek has the facts wrong. There's no way Waters would bring the admiral to the Wacky outpost, yet we know the admiral has an important meeting scheduled. Ridders said so. Sheek may not be reliable, but Ridders sure is. That can only mean one thing. "Maybe there are actually two meetings."

"Come on," Marco says. "That's too much of a coincidence."

"Not really," I say. "If Waters's guest is bounding in, the occludium shields have to be down. I heard Waters tell Barrick that the maintenance schedule shows a power-down tonight at nineteen hundred hours. Maybe the shields are scheduled to be down for Admiral Eames's meeting, and Waters is using the occasion to bring in his guest unnoticed."

"Maybe," Lucy says. "But why would Waters do that? Who is he meeting with?"

Now, that's the billion-dollar question. The truth is, I don't know. We don't have all the facts. We're fitting together pieces of a puzzle without knowing what it's supposed to look like. Waters barely told me anything.

"Always more questions," I say. "Why would Earth Force breed kid soldiers? Why are we really at war with the Youli? Every answer leads to another question."

"And another secret," Marco says. "Look, it's all about the pod now. Just like we agreed on the mountain behind Waters's laboratory. If we fight, it's on our terms. We have a right to know their secrets."

Mira places her hand on top of mine. *It's time. Tell them.*

She wants me to tell them about our brain patches? Now? They'll be furious! I pull my hand from beneath Mira's and bow my head to my knees. I wish we'd told them back at the laboratory. Everything would be so much simpler.

Tell them! she insists.

You're sure?

She rests her hand on the back of my neck. *They have a right to know.*

I sit up and take a deep breath. "There's something we have to tell you."

Marco raises an eyebrow. "We?"

Lucy crosses her arms. "You're not going to spring some big secret on us like you did that day in the mountains when you said the Youli communicated with you brain to brain, right?"

"Well, actually, that's not so far off."

All eyes are on me. The Nest is so quiet, I can hear my heart slamming against my rib cage. In the corner, Cole clenches his fists. This is not going to be easy.

"I wanted to tell you before," I start, "but Waters made me promise, and then we left the labs, and . . ."

"Cut to the chase, Ace," Marco says coldly.

Staring at the furry rug, I let it all pour out. "Waters implanted Youli skin cells into Mira's and my brain stems. They're supposed to help us communicate with each other. And with the Youli."

"You're kidding, right?" Marco says. "You're not really saying that you've kept a secret this big all tour?"

I don't look at any of my pod mates as I explain what happened the night Mira and I came in from the field, the same day we agreed to our pod pact.

When I finish, Marco jumps to his feet. "Jasper, you suck! You really truly suck! You are as bad as Waters! You promised you wouldn't keep secrets!"

"Waters made me swear I wouldn't tell—"

"Like that makes it okay?" Lucy yells. "Are you saying you and Mira have been brain-talking about us behind our backs all tour?"

"It's not like that. Sometimes we share words or ideas, but not—"

"How does the brain patch work?" Cole asks. "I didn't know they were developing that technology."

"Shut up, Wiki," Marco says to Cole before turning on me again. "I just can't believe you kept this from us!"

"I'm sorry, okay? I should have told you sooner. I just didn't know what to do." My last words crack in my throat, fighting with a sob I don't want to let out. My eyes swim with tears. "I'm sorry!"

Marco turns away in disgust.

Lucy shakes her head.

Cole looks like he's about to burst. He probably has a hundred questions about the brain patches.

Mira rises and walks into the center of the circle. *Translate.*

No. That is not going to help.

Translate!

"No!" I shout.

"No, what?" Lucy stares at Mira. "Wait. It's happening right now, isn't it? You're brain-talking right now! What is Mira saying, Jasper?"

I shake my head. "She wants me to translate something."

"Brain-to-brain?" Cole asks.

"Excellent," Marco says. "I've always wanted to know what Queenie has to say." He sits down on the rug, crosses his legs, and glares at Mira. "And right now, I say you have some explaining to do."

I close my eyes and try to tune into the picture Mira is showing me in my mind. It takes a while because I have to wrestle against the part of me that wants to burst out crying. I hate having my pod mates so mad at me. And, if I'm being honest, there's part of me that wants to keep Mira all to myself, even though I know that's like the most selfish thing in the world.

Stop! Focus!

Great. Mira's not happy with me either.

"It's not really words," I say, trying to translate Mira's image and its meaning. "It's a picture. Remember that day on the mountain? We built a cairn of stones to symbolize our bond."

"Sure, I remember," Lucy says. "It's all about the pod. That's what it meant, not like you cared, obviously."

"We do care," I say. "And that's still what it means. Mira is reminding us."

Mira grabs my hand and nods me on.

"Look, we were wrong to keep this secret. And we're sorry. I'm so sorry. I didn't know what to do. Waters made me promise, and he made it sound really important that we keep it secret. But I shouldn't have. If I could go back in time and tell you, I would. But I can't."

A sob bursts out, and more come behind it. I swallow them down and take a deep breath. I look at my pod mates. "This is my fault. I'm sorry, but so much is at stake now. We can't let this come between us. Please. It's all about the pod."

A long moment passes. I bite on my finger to stop from crying out loud as tears stream down my cheeks. I have no idea what will happen next. I half expect Marco to storm out of the Nest and never come back.

Finally Lucy stands. "You made a mistake. A big one. Both of you. But the biggest blame belongs to Waters. He can't be trusted anymore. Right now only one thing is clear: it's all about the pod." She extends her hand, and I reach for it.

I look to Cole. After all we've been through, I really hope he's still with me.

He steps next to Lucy and grips her palm. "It's all about the pod."

There's only one more link to the chain.

Mira stretches her out her hand to Marco, who still sits on the moldy rug, his arms crossed tightly against his chest.

"What do you want me to say?" he asks. "'It's all about the pod'? Those are words. We need action. Loyalty. Understand?"

His eyes rise to meet mine. I nod.

Slowly Marco pushes up and seems to shake off some of his anger, though I know regaining his trust will be an uphill battle.

He clasps Mira's and Cole's hands, completing our circle. "Don't think you're off the hook, King and Queenie, but for now, let's move on to espionage. We have two meetings to spy on tonight. And if it's not about the pod, I have no clue what anything's about anymore."

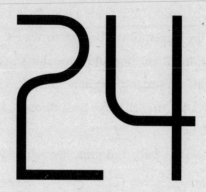

AFTER MUCH DISCUSSION, DISAGREEMENT,
and general disgruntlement over Mira's and my secret keeping, we finally agree to a plan. We're covering the bases by assuming there are two separate meetings. Marco, Cole, and Lucy will hide in the Parliament Chamber. Mira and I will bound to the Wacky outpost. If there's a problem, or if Waters's meeting is a no-go, Mira and I can bound to the Chamber and meet up with our friends since the shields will be down and the scrambler turned off.

"Good luck," Lucy says before she takes off with Marco and Cole for the chamber shortly before nineteen hundred hours.

I wish them luck and watch them go.

"Ready?" I ask Mira as we prepare to bound to the Wacky outpost. I hope our intel is correct, or the scrambler will make this our last trip anywhere.

She nods.

We open our ports and successfully bound to the infirmary where we were treated last night. Our bound site is extremely specific—under a medical cart, behind the treatment curtain—to avoid detection. I overshoot by half a meter, but fortunately, the curtain is drawn. We can see through the curtain, but it's like looking through a hazy filter. I know from last night that it's not possible to see through from the other side.

"Stay still," I whisper.

Stay quiet. She smiles.

I smirk. *Sassy much?*

It feels like hours pass with nothing happening. Nothing except my hip hurting from my fall yesterday, and I can't even stand up to stretch my leg.

There's no one in the infirmary except an actual infirm Tunneler, who's resting on one of the tables behind the divided curtain. He's unconscious, but every few minutes, he moans.

Whenever the Tunneler moans, Mira and I make eye contact and suppress a laugh. It's like our own private joke. They really should up the painkillers for the poor dude. I'm struggling to hold back another round of giggles when footsteps sound in the infirmary.

"Are your guards in position?" That voice belongs to Waters.

Brrrrk. Arrrgh. Kareek. "Yes, just as we discussed." And that's Barrick.

"Good. If they sense anything's amiss, they'll suspect a setup. I don't need to tell you how much is at stake. This meeting must be a success."

"They have the coordinates?" Barrick asks.

"Yes. I transmitted them yesterday and received confirmation."

"I can't believe you got them to agree to come."

"We've been working toward this for years," Waters says. "All my work has led to this moment. Earth's future—both of our futures—depend on it. You know that. How much longer?"

"Five minutes."

The Tunneler patient emits another groan. Waters jumps. I bite down on my fingers to keep from laughing out loud.

"Can someone get him out of here until this meeting is over?" Waters asks.

Barrick barks orders at another Tunneler, and seconds later, two arrive to wheel the patient out of the room. One of them steps behind the curtain, placing Mira and me in plain view. Thankfully he doesn't look down.

A few more tense minutes pass. I'm afraid to move a muscle, even with the pain radiating across my hip.

Then lights flash on the other side of the curtain.

I blink, sure my eyes are playing tricks.

Two Youli stand mere meters from our hiding spot.

I swallow the gasp that jumps into my throat. I can't believe Waters invited the Youli here.

Mira grabs my hand, and a current of fear and excitement runs between us. The last time I saw a Youli in a medical facility, he flung someone across the room. And the last time I faced the Youli, we were nearly killed on the Paleo Planet. I'm not taking any chances. I flex my free hand, preparing to bound or defend us at any moment.

"Welcome to Gulaga," Waters says. "I am so pleased to see you again, friends."

Friends? Waters knows these guys? They're our sworn enemy. They injured our friends, killed our Tunneler guide, and caused the Incident at Bounding Base 51.

We are also pleased. The words sound in my brain. Then a voice-translation box states, "The pleasure is ours."

That was weird. Why did the words get communicated twice? And why weren't they the same?

"We relish this opportunity to speak with you," Waters says. "And we are encouraged by your recent communications. We would very much like to send a delegation to the summit."

Wait a second . . . the summit? I thought this was the

summit . . . or maybe the admiral's meeting . . . but the summit is something else entirely?

Earth does not speak with one mind. "Our understanding is that Earth is not aligned."

Why does that double communication keep happening?

"Friends, it is a process," Waters says. "We are making progress. Those who share our ideals are growing in number."

I release Mira's hand and clench my fists. I don't care what Waters says. The Youli are not our friends. They attacked us on the Paleo Planet. They hurt Marco. They killed Charkeera. They invaded my brain!

Growth is not solidarity. "Despite this growth, there is division in your ranks."

Why do I keep hearing everything twice?

Almost the same but not quite.

Wait a second . . .

First I hear the Youli in my brain, then I hear the translation from the voice box.

The brain-talk is so much clearer than on the Paleo Planet. There, all I could understand was the word *leave*. Now it's coming through in crystal detail. It must be the brain patch!

The young ones? "The children?"

Wait . . . what? I missed something.

"We call them Bounders," Waters says. "And yes, that is who you encountered. We're training some of them to act as translators. We can bring them with us to the summit."

They battled with Youli technology. "We were attacked with our own weapons."

There is a pause before Waters answers. "I can assure you I am now personally overseeing all research and development."

They're talking about the battle on the Paleo Planet! I want to whisper to Mira, but I don't dare make a sound. I sense for her brain. *Mira! They're talking about us!*

As soon as the thoughts leave my mind, my brain erupts in static. A sharp, familiar pain pierces my skull.

The Youli are communicating. My brain can't translate amidst the pain.

But my ears work fine.

"What is the meaning of this?" the Youli's voice box says. "You have these children here? Spying on us? How can you expect trust when you breach our trust in return?"

One of the Youlis starts to shake and radiate a strange glow.

Oh no. This is bad. Very bad.

"I—I—I don't know what you're talking about," Waters stammers. "I assure you. We are the only ones present. . . ."

The Youli flings his arm, and Waters flies across the room. He's pinned to the wall, held there by the invisible force of the Youli's outstretched hand. His comrade thrusts Barrick to the opposite side of the infirmary.

With his free hand, the Youli holding Waters waves back the curtain, revealing our hiding place.

"Liars!" his voice box says. "And that is not all! My ship just reported that another alien craft has entered Gulagan space. You betrayed us, Jon Waters. May you rue this day!"

And with that, the Youli vanish. The pain in my brain fades. Waters and Barrick crumple to the floor.

Bound! In a flash, Mira's gone.

I won't face Waters alone. I open my port and bound.

As soon as I hit the ground, Mira pulls me against the wall.

Quiet!

Ridders's voice rises up from the platform below. "Our guests have arrived, Admiral. The guards are escorting them through the rear tunnel as we speak."

The rear tunnel of the Parliament Chamber? As in the one Mira and I are standing in?

Go! I urge Mira. I can barely stop shaking as we edge along the wall. I've nowhere near recovered from what just happened in the infirmary.

When we reach the secret side door to our carrel, Mira gently knocks. The door cracks open, and Marco waves us through.

"Over here, behind these chairs," he whispers. "And get down!"

"What's happening?" I ask.

"Not sure," he replies. "They keep talking about the

MONICA TESLER

Alkalinians and readying the occludium for the trade."

"What's an Alkalinian—"

"Shhh!" Lucy slaps my arm. "I hear footsteps."

Sure enough, the sound of people passing comes from the hallway. We shrink even lower into the carrel as the entourage passes and descends to the chamber floor.

Four Earth Force guards escort four . . . creatures. Aliens, I should say. They ride upon minihovers that look like flying padded thrones. Their skin glistens with scales and their arms appear robotic.

"What are those things?" Marco asks. "Cyborg lizards?"

"Remember Waters's laboratory?" Cole whispers. "Weren't there some reptilian body parts in one of the cases?"

Whoa. That's right. Could those have belonged to one of these guys?

"Hush!" Lucy says. "We need to listen."

Below, on the center platform, Admiral Eames extends a hand to the alien floating in the center of his group. "Welcome, Seelok. The Alkalinians are among friends here. I trust you'll find your every need attended to."

"Sss-so you sss-say, Admiral Eamesss," the alien in the center hisses in his natural tongue. I'm guessing he's Seelok. Instead of shaking her hand, Seelok circles the admiral on his floating throne. Her honor guard raises their weapons. "But how can we be sss-so sss-sure?"

"You're speaking of the occludium," the admiral says with caution, gesturing to her guards to lower their guns. "Give us the coordinates, Seelok, and we will load the compound onto your ship immediately."

"That sss-simply will not do. My sss-senior offisss-er remained behind. Load the cargo sss-straightaway, and I will give you the coordinatesss."

Admiral Eames nods to Ridders, who rushes out the front doors of the chamber.

"Very well," she says. "But while we're waiting, answer me a few questions. How did the Alkalinians manage to secure this intelligence? The exact location of the intragalactic summit and the Youli docking station must have been extremely difficult to acquire."

Intragalactic summit? Oh my god. *That's* the summit everyone's been talking about. That's why Waters spoke to the Youli. He wanted to send a delegation! Next to me, Cole bounces on his toes. It's probably taking every ounce of control for him to stay quiet.

"Indeed. That is why it comesss at sss-such a sss-steep pricesss." As the Alkalinian hisses and floats around the chamber floor, his long, scaly tail waves like an *S* in the air. His buddies stick near the admiral's honor guard, watching their every move. "Of courssse, we are giving a deep disss-count to our new partnersss."

The admiral bows her head. "Your generosity is appreciated. With your access to intelligence and our military might, I have high expectations of a strong alliance between Alkalinia and Earth for years to come."

My feeling for these aliens can be summed up in one word: *distrust*. With the emotional vibe I'm getting from Mira, her word is *disgust*.

The head Alkalinian speaks into a com device in a strange language of hisses and clicks. "It sss-seems you have met your sss-side of the bargain. I will transss-fer the coordinatesss."

"What about the map?" the admiral asks.

"It is there, too. But first I have another requessst."

"We spent weeks negotiating terms, Seelok. The time for requests has passed."

"Thisss is not a demand, it is an invitation," Seelok says as he circles the admiral. "I know you are training cadetsss. We invite you to sss-send the young Boundersss to Alkalinia for training, to sss-solidify our allian-ssse."

Alkalinia must be their home planet. The thought of sending Bounders there makes my skin crawl. I can't imagine visiting those lizards on their home turf.

"Thank you for your kind invitation," Admiral Eames says, although something tells me she's not too grateful. "The cadets are returning to Earth shortly, but we will discuss the possibility for a future tour of duty. Now, Seelok, I must insist you transfer the coordinates."

One of the Earth Force officers steps forward and lays the BPS case on a table set up on the platform. The Alkalinian flies his minithrone over and scans something into the coordinate sensor. The officer checks the BPS and nods at the admiral.

"Thank you, friends," she says. "My officers will see you out. Safe travels."

When the guards lead the Alkalinians to the rear tunnel, we cower in the cover of our carrel. As they fly by, I peek, catching a glimpse of the last Alkalinian's scaly tail waving behind him.

Down below, the admiral and her honor guard wait in silence until the Alkalinians are safely outside of earshot.

"Thank goodness that's done," she says. "I couldn't stand another minute of their slime."

Ridders reenters the chamber and confirms that the Alkalinian vessel immediately departed Gulagan airspace.

"Excellent," the admiral says. "It is time to test the Bounders in battle. Tomorrow we launch Operation *Vermis*, our offensive against the Youli. Primary target: intragalactic summit, Youli vessel."

She starts toward the ornately carved doors and stops. "Make sure to lift the shields. Now that we've partnered with the likes of the Alkalinians, we have to watch our backs."

MONICA TESLER

· E_F ·

We wait until everyone leaves the chamber before sneaking back to the Nest. When we finally arrive, I tell Marco, Cole, and Lucy what happened with Waters and the Youli at the Wacky outpost. They pepper me with questions, but I don't have much to say. I've already told them everything I know.

Mira rocks in the corner with a furry blanket wrapped around her. Lucy bites her lip as a lone tear snakes down her cheek. Marco paces back and forth. Cole sits on the bench jiggling his knees, with posture so straight he looks like a pole is stuck to his spine. Every few seconds, he asks another question I can't answer.

Eventually I can't stand the questions anymore, mostly because I'm pretty sure he's asking because he thinks I'm keeping secrets. "No! I don't know what Waters planned to do at the summit! I don't know anything about the history between Waters and the Youli! And I don't know what Barrick and the Wackies have to do with it!"

"Rebels," Marco says.

"What?" I ask.

"Call them rebels. Wackies is derogatory. They're rebels, not Wackies. And it's the rebel outpost, not the Wacky outpost. This is a rebellion, Jasper. And it appears we're caught in the middle."

"I'm not caught in the middle of anything," Lucy says.

"You said it yourself the other night, Marco. Waters has been keeping secrets all tour. Now we know why. He's been meeting with our sworn enemy. I may not love Earth Force, but it's clear whose side I'm on."

"How can you say that?" Marco jumps to his feet. "Tomorrow they're sending kids—us—on a life-threatening military operation! You may be on Earth Force's side, but they're not on yours!"

"They're trying to protect the planet!" she screams. "You're just looking for an excuse not to do your duty!"

"I did not sign up for this! The entire Bounders programs is built on lies! You know that, Lucy! You're just not willing to give up your Bounder star status!"

Just as Lucy is about to skewer Marco, the door to the Nest flies open and Waters storms in. His hair sticks up in clumps, and there are mud stains on the knees of his pants. He's breathing heavily, like he ran all the way here from the rebel outpost.

He marches into my space and jabs a finger into the air between us. "I spent the better part of a decade laying the foundation for today's meeting, and you go and blow it to bits! How could you do this?"

My brain pulses. I know Mira is trying to tell me something, but I'm not listening. I've had enough. Enough of the secrets! Enough of the expectations! Enough of everything!

I leap to my feet. "How could *I* do this? How could *you* do this? We're at war with the Youli!"

"Jasper Adams, you are way out of your depth," Waters says.

"If I'm out of my depth," I say, "it's because you've been keeping us in the dark!"

"You know so very little about what's happening," Waters continues. "We were seconds away from getting invited to the summit! They were going to give us the coordinates!"

"It's the coordinates you want?" Marco stands and walks toward Waters with a stone-cold stare. "No problem. Now lay off Jasper and Mira. You're the one who has explaining to do. Like Jasper said, you're the one with the secrets."

Waters narrows his eyes at Marco. "What exactly do you mean *no problem*?"

"I mean we have the coordinates. Or we will tomorrow, when Admiral Eames gives us the down and dirty on our mission."

Waters's face goes slack. "What mission?"

"Well, you see, Mr. Waters," Lucy says, "we just so happened to be in the Parliament Chamber when this very important meeting took place between the admiral and these scary reptile aliens. And it turns out we have a new alliance with the Alkalinians where basically they sell us secrets in exchange for occludium. So now we have the coordinates for the intragalactic summit and the Youli docking station, which, according to Admiral Eames, is good news because she's planning to send the Bounders to battle there tomorrow. So that's what mission."

Waters's face is stuck, like he's replaying what Lucy says over and over but it doesn't compute. "Are you saying that Alkalinians were *here*? On *Gulaga*?"

"This was classic military bartering, Mr. Waters," Cole says. "The Alkalinians sold us secrets. They must be intelligence brokers."

"To put it more than nicely," Waters says. "The Alkalinians are bottom of the barrel, scum, worse than fleas on fleas on dogs. I simply refuse to believe what you're telling me. Even Eames wouldn't stoop so low as to fraternize with the Alkalinians."

"Oh, she has," Marco says coolly. "Just as she's stooped so low as to send kids to their deaths in the interest of Earth Force. There's that. And let's add to the list that Admiral Eames—and you, Mr. Waters—have withheld information from the planet Earth about the existence of not one, but at least two alien species. There's that, too. And let me take a wild guess and say that you didn't plan to tell Jasper's and Mira's parents that you implanted alien technology into their brains. I really hate to say that, Mr. Waters, because I can't believe you'd stoop so low."

Waters sinks to the ground. He buries his head in his

hands. Lucy looks at me. I shrug. I have no idea what to do. I'm not about to apologize for busting up his meeting. Or for telling my pod mates about the brain patches. Just like Eames, he planned to put us in harm's way without our true consent. Waters might have the right motives, but his methods fall far short.

Waters presses his hands against his knees and stands. "I . . . I don't know what . . . I need to find Gedney." He staggers out of the Nest.

"It had to be said," Marco says once Waters is gone.

"I know," I say. "It just sounds really awful when you say it out loud."

Cole sinks onto the squishy bench. "I can't believe tomorrow we're going to war."

"Remember, it's all about the pod," Lucy says.

"The pod doesn't mean that much if we're dead," I say as I sit on the furry carpet and lean back against the bench.

Mira rests her head on my shoulder, and the notes from the song we shared on the tundra snake their way into my mind.

THE NEXT MORNING, THEY WAKE US TWO
hours earlier than normal. Senior officers bark orders, instructing us to dress in operations gear and prepare for a postbreakfast briefing with Admiral Eames in the Parliament Chamber.

"Fun and games are over, kids," Marco says, swinging down from his bunk. "Time to report for soldier duty."

"I knew they'd send us to our deaths sooner or later," Regis says. "All hail Earth Force."

I laugh then cough to cover up the fact that I'm laughing. Did I just have a moment of solidarity with Regis? This is proof that I'm viewing this as us versus them.

Cadets versus officers. Bounders versus typicals. Kids versus grown-ups.

I'm just not used to being on the same side of *versus* as Regis.

I have to shake that mind-set. If we're going to stand a chance at carrying out our mission and arriving home safely, I need to be on the same side as Earth Force. Earth versus Youli.

After breakfast, we're marched to the Parliament Chamber. It's noisy with chatter, grunts, and voice-box translations. Many Earth Force officers—both Earthlings and Gulagans— are already present.

When we walk in, Neeka rushes to our side. "Oh! Oh! I'm not sure what's happening, but I had to find you! Father has been chattering about an important mission! I'm so worried! Even for you, Marco!"

"Thanks, Neeksters." Marco lowers his voice and extends his hand. "I'm sorry again about you-know-what."

"Oh! You are most forgiven!" Neeka grips his palm with her paw. "I can't stay! I'm not even supposed to be present! They only let me in because I said I had a message from Father." Neeka hugs each of us with her furry arms then scurries from the chamber.

"Do you think we'll ever see her again?" Lucy asks as we watch Neeka go.

"Of course we will, DQ," Marco says, but his voice lacks its usual confidence.

Minutes later, Sheek arrives flanked by cameramen from EFAN. They're going to film this? You must be joking. Sheek takes the podium as the cameramen get in position. He lifts his chin for a right-side angle then tips his head for the left.

"We're about to go to battle, and he's posing for the cameras?" Marco says.

As it turns out, the filming is quick and limited. Sheek gives some *Rah! Rah! Go Bounders!* cheers for the camera, along with some crowd shots. After, Ridders announces Admiral Eames, and there are more crowd shots of everyone standing at attention. Then the EFAN crew is ushered out of the chamber. Gedney slips in just as the doors close on the camera crew.

The admiral gestures for silence. I don't need a brain patch to sense that the room sizzles with anticipation. Even though we don't know the specifics of the mission, we know it's serious. And we know it involves the Youli, which means it's dangerous.

"In three hours we will be commencing Operation *Vermis*, our formal counterstrike against the Youli for their attack on the Paleo Planet. This military operation has been months in the making.

"We just received intelligence indicating the exact coordinates for an intragalactic summit between the Youli and their allies in the Outer Arm. Captain Han will review the battle plan."

Han steps to the podium and activates a projection of the Milky Way galaxy in the center of the Chamber. He zooms in on the Outer Arm, and then zooms again to the coordinates, revealing a relatively clear zone. That must be the location of the intragalactic summit.

"An advance team will bound to the coordinates and detonate a *diruo* pulse to disrupt their shields and systems. Then our quantum fleet will bound to the coordinates and act as a decoy, engaging in disruptive maneuvers to confuse and distract the enemy.

"At the same time, a small stealth unit will bound directly inside the Youli vessel. The specifics of that mission are classified, but the potential impact could permanently change the course of the war in our favor."

Han goes on to explain the decoy maneuvers in detail. I really should pay attention, but I can't help thinking about the stealth unit bounding inside the Youli ship. It sounds just like the Navy SEALs, the old American military units trained in small, insular groups to carry out deadly missions in complete independence.

Which sounds kind of like a pod.

And kind of like what we've been preparing for all tour in the Tundra Trials.

When I tune back in, Ridders is standing at the podium. "Officers, cadets, please proceed directly to the space elevator. Your captains will explain the mission in more detail at the staging area. Waters's pod, please stay behind for a secondary briefing."

Marco catches my eye. "Stealth unit?"

Could that be it? Are they ordering our pod to bound to the Youli vessel?

As Regis walks by our carrel, he laughs. "I'd be jealous, if I didn't like living so much."

Chants rise up as the cadets march out of the chamber:

"Birthright, Bounders fight!"

"Birthright, Bounders fight!"

"Birthright, Bounders fight!"

When the other cadets and officers have left, and the chamber falls silent, Ridders waves us down to the floor. Only Gedney and a handful of elite officers remain.

Admiral Eames leaves the podium and joins our pod. "You've been selected for the stealth operation aboard the Youli vessel." Her voice is quiet, concentrated. It's the same tone I've heard her use with her inner circle, Ridders and Han and the other aeronauts. I feel myself getting sucked in by her attention. There is no mystery why she's admiral. She makes you want to please her.

"I am not going to parse words," she continues. "What you're being asked to do is extremely dangerous. I can't guarantee

MONICA TESLER

your safety. But I can assure you that you've been chosen based on your skills, and that we have every reason to believe that the mission will be a success. You will bound by quantum ship piloted by Captain Han to the summit coordinates. As soon as you arrive, Captain Han will detonate the *diruo* pulse, and you will free-bound to the Youli vessel. Once there, you will make your way to the systems room. When you locate the bio server, you will install a patch carrying a preloaded virus."

Patch? Like . . . ? Mira lifts her hand to the back of her neck. Yeah, like that.

The admiral turns to Gedney. "Kindly explain the patch placement."

"Yes, Admiral," Gedney says. "The patch contains Youli prime cells. When the patch is fused with bio material, the cells contained in the patch merge with the host cells and start to create new pathways. The technology was intended to create pathways for growth and development—"

"Mr. Gedney," the admiral interrupts. "Please simply explain the logistics of the patch placement."

Gedney shakes his head but continues, "We've imprinted a viral worm on the patch that will forge pathways into the Youli systems and degrade those systems over time. Once the patches are planted, the subsequent degradation should be system-wide."

"So this patch will shut down the Youli systems?" Cole asks, his eyes as big as dinner plates.

"Not right away," Admiral Eames says. "In fact, once they get their systems back online from the *diruo* pulse, the Youli should perceive no difference whatsoever. That's the beauty of Mr. Gedney's patch. By the time the damage starts, we'll be long gone."

The admiral beams at Gedney. You'd think he'd be basking in her praise. Instead, he hangs his head.

The door to the Parliament Chamber flies open and Waters rushes in. "Admiral, a word?"

"We're in a closed session, Jon. I will speak with you after today's successful operation."

"About that—"

"I'm not sure how you got past my guards, Jon, but this meeting contains classified information above your clearance."

Waters opens his mouth like he's about to shoot back a retort. He pauses, looks around at the bevy of soldiers holding guns, and shakes his head. In a quiet voice, he asks, "If I can just have a minute with Gedney and my pod."

The admiral sizes up Waters, and I'm not sure whether she'll agree. She waits until Waters drops his head like a dog cowering before an alpha. "One minute, Jon. The cadets need to get to the space elevator right away."

"Yes, of course, Admiral."

Admiral Eames and the other officers head for the doors.

Seconds later, it's just Waters, Gedney, and our pod

standing in a circle on the chamber floor. If it wasn't for the horrible circumstances, this would be a nice remember-when moment.

"If you just give me the coordinates—" Waters starts.

"No," Gedney says.

"I could probably convince one of the aeronauts—"

"No."

"There is still time to save this!"

"No, no, no!" Gedney shouts at Waters. He rises up to nearly twice his size. Waters steps back.

I kind of like the new Gedney. That is, until I remember he masterminded the virus that will probably leave me dead by day's end.

"I don't understand," Waters says, shaking his head. "How could everything have gone so wrong?"

"I'll tell you how," Gedney says. "You're one man, Jon. You can't expect to take down Earth Force and broker a peace deal by yourself. Being right is not enough."

"But if I was able to get to the summit . . . explain what happened to the Youli . . . if only—"

"Enough! There's no way you could convince the Youli that you didn't betray them. Not to mention, I would never let you risk the kids' lives."

Waters tips his head and narrows his eyes. "What exactly is the offensive?"

"*Diruo* pulse, perimeter attack, followed by a secret mission aboard the Youli vessel," Gedney says.

"What secret mission?" Waters asks.

Gedney steps in front of us, almost like he's shielding us from Waters. "The admiral was quite intrigued by your report on the prime cell patch technology development. While you've been running around on secret errands all tour, she had me upload a degradation virus to one of the patches. These kids—your pod—are bounding directly to the Youli vessel to plant the patch on their biotech systems."

"No." Waters's face droops, then his whole body deflates until he's on his knees on the chamber floor.

"I'm afraid your minute is up, Jon," Gedney says. "I need to escort these kids to the space elevator."

· *EF* ·

Earth Force officers and cadets fill the space elevator. The atmosphere buzzes with adrenaline and reeks with the sharp smell of sweat. Even though the elevator is packed, it's nearly silent. I'm guessing most Bounders are too nervous to talk. Maybe the aeronaut captains are nervous, too. The truth is, I have no idea whether they've been in combat before. I never thought to ask, which now seems incredibly stupid. But with the Earth Force code of silence, they probably wouldn't have told me much anyway.

Out the window, Gulagaven shrinks as we zoom away. I

can barely pick out the entrance to the occludium mines or the aeroport or the giant leaf structures where they harvest forage for food. Soon we pass out of the atmosphere, and the planet is just a giant rock beneath us as we climb toward the space dock.

Will we make it back? Will I ever see my family again? Will Addy be forced to train at the EarthBound Academy with the memory of a dead brother fresh in her mind?

Above us, the space dock grows bigger as we close in. I can't believe only five weeks have passed since Addy tried to convince Cole and me to hack the apartment lift. What will she think when I tell her about the space elevator? If I'm allowed to tell her. If I'm *alive* to tell her.

I've got to get rid of these thoughts. They're too distracting for me to focus on my mission. I wish I could talk to my pod mates, but I don't dare break the silence.

Wait. All this talk about the virus patch, and I almost forgot about my brain patch. I reach out with my mind and brush against Mira. *Hey, you okay?*

She doesn't respond with words. I get snippets of feelings and memories. Sadness, fear, helplessness. An image of the Youli prisoner in the space station cell block. A replay of yesterday, when the angry Youli flung Waters against the wall, convinced of his betrayal. A picture of Waters today, when he realized his plans lay in shambles.

Are you afraid? I ask.

Sad. This is not my choice.

What do I say to that? It's not my choice either. But there's one thing I know about being a Bounder: you don't have a choice.

Three tones sound and a voice comes over the intercom, first in Gulagan, then in English: "We will be arriving at the Gulagan Space Dock in two minutes. Please prepare to disembark."

Our choice or not, here we go.

26

WE LOAD INTO HAN'S SHIP, DONNING OUR
gloves and blast packs, and strap in. Lucy has the virus patch
tucked into her uniform. The BPS is strapped to the center
platform.

I review the mission in my mind. Our quantum ship,
piloted by Han, bounds to the summit coordinates. Han sets
off the *diruo* pulse. Our pod uploads the Youli vessel coordinates from the BPS and free-bounds. Han bounds back to the
Gulagan Space Dock, triggering the decoy maneuvers. The
quantum fleet bounds to the perimeter of the summit and
engages in war tactics devised to distract the Youli and their
allies. The Earth Force ships stay out of range of precision

weaponry and focus their attacks on the security buffers while engaging in a random bounding sequence—using both quantum ship bounding and cadet free-bounding between ships—to throw off the Youli's manual backup trackers. Once our pod locates the Youli systems center, plants the virus patch, and bounds back to the dock, Admiral Eames issues the retreat order.

To our enemies, our operation should look like a ditched effort by Earth Force. What they won't know is that the patch placed by our pod ensures long-term degradation of the Youli systems.

If all goes as planned, we'll be safely back at the dock and down the elevator in time for a disgusting Gulagan dinner and the Tundra Trials victory celebration.

Han conducts a final systems check. He was our pilot the first time we rode in a quantum ship. I can still remember how he told us to picture a ride at a summer fair, how he said the bound was just like that but over in a millisecond. There is nothing about this flight that will feel like a fair ride.

A million things could go wrong. Has the BPS ever been tested with a ship? It could malfunction, and we'd fail to manifest, just like what happened to the aeronauts in the Incident at Bounding Base 51. Or if the BPS works fine, the coordinates could be off. We could bound into the middle of a planet or a star or a black hole. We could manifest right next to a security ship and be fired on before we have a chance to set off the pulse. Even if we make it safely to the summit, the vessel coordinates could zoom us right into the middle of a Youli mess hall, or bunk room, or bathroom!

Even if we make it undetected to the Youli vessel, we've got to navigate through the ship to the systems room using a pirated map that may or may not be correct, plant the virus patch (something that's never been done and may set off like a zillion alarms), and then, if we haven't already been killed or taken prisoner, bound back to the Gulagan Space Dock.

That's a lot of room for error.

"I'm scared," Lucy says.

"Me, too," I say.

"It's all about the pod," Marco says. "We've got this, Bounders."

I hope so, Marco. I hope so.

The spider crawlers remove the scaffolding. Han pulls up the visual of the quantum field. "Commencing the bound in five, four, three, two, one."

Puffed!—Stuffed!—Slammed!—Bammed!

"Go! Go! Go!" Han shouts as I open my eyes.

We struggle with our harnesses. Every second matters.

"Did we make it?" Lucy asks.

"Do they see us?" Cole shouts.

Han doesn't waste time answering. He keys in the sequence

for the *diruo* pulse as soon as the exterior visual comes into focus on the monitors.

In front of us, an enormous cylinder, ten times the size of the Gulagan dock, pivots in space. Six spheres rotate and slide on an intersecting axis. Circling the spheres are at least a dozen gigantic spaceships, most of them bigger than a bounding base. Some of the ships look like huge passenger crafts. Others look like jets or saucers. One is even shaped like a cube.

Our tiny quantum ship is so small compared to those monster crafts—like a fly on a hover windshield—that it's hard to imagine they'd even notice us. But until we detonate the *diruo* pulse, our ship will show up on every single security system. Guaranteed.

Han is right. We need to move.

"Brace for the pulse," Han says as he enters the command. Weird vibrations run through me and the body of the ship, then ripple out across space like circles spreading from a stone dropped in a pond. On the monitor, lights flicker at the perimeter of the summit zone and domino inward. In the seconds before the backup power ignites, everything is black, like the summit and all the ships were suddenly swallowed by space itself.

"It worked," Han says. "Stage two. Move!"

Mira, me, Cole, Lucy, Marco. That's the order.

Mira presses her hands to the scan pad, opens her port, and bounds.

I'm next. If Mira wasn't waiting on the Youli vessel, I might chicken out.

Cole crowds me from behind.

I lay my hands on the scan pad, sense the coordinates, and bound.

Bam!

My feet shift beneath me, and I fall onto my hands and knees, sinking into a world of glowing orange mush. I'm overwhelmed with the smell of overripe cantaloupe. Did these coordinates land us in the Youli compost?

Hands grab my shirt and yank me to the side of the strange passageway I've arrived in. I raise my palms to defend myself, but then see it's Mira. She ducks inside a compartment built into the wall. I follow her in and sink into a pit of slime up to my waist. A grate allows us to see the hallway from our hiding spot. So far the orientation is exactly as described on the Alkalinian map.

She points through the grate. *Watch for the others.*

"No brain-talking!" I whisper. "They might hear us!"

Cole emerges a second later.

"Get in here!" I whisper-shout.

He looks around, trying to locate my voice. Lucy appears. I slide open the grate and wave them both into the compartment.

"Yuck!" Lucy says, wiping slime from her hands. "What is this stuff?"

Mira puts a finger to her mouth, reminding Lucy to be quiet.

Marco bounds in. He dives into the compartment seconds before two Youli pass in front of us.

"That was close," Marco says.

"Too close," I say.

"What's up with all the mush?" Marco says.

"I think this is the section of the ship that gets compressed when they bound," I say.

"Shhh!" Lucy says. "Where's the map?"

"I uploaded it to the astrocache compass." Cole activates the compass on his wrist, pulls up the map, and twists the image for a different angle.

As I peer over his shoulder, a high-pitched alarm pierces my brain. I press my hands against my skull. Beside me, Mira does the same.

The alarm must mean Earth Force has commenced the attack. "The battle's on!"

"How do you know?" Marco asks. "What's wrong with you?"

I adjust to the constant ringing in my head and lower my hands. "There's an alarm. I can hear it in my brain."

"The patch?" Lucy asks. When I nod, she adds, "Creepy, but probably convenient for our mission."

"What's taking you so long, Fun Facts?" Marco asks Cole. "Like Jasper said, the battle's on! We need to move!"

"Quiet!" I say. "Let him concentrate."

Seconds pass before Cole speaks. "If this map and the coordinates are correct, we're close. There are two hallways and a connecting bridge. From there, we should reach the systems room."

"What are we waiting for?" Marco asks, his hand already pressing against the grate.

Mira throws her arm in front of him. A second later, Youli voices fill my brain.

"Someone's coming," I whisper.

We stay absolutely still as a group of Youli rush by our hiding spot, brain-talking about an attack.

Our attack.

Mira catches my eye. I shake my head—my reminder not to brain-talk. The Youli might hear us, and that would be a fast track to busted.

When the Youli turn the corner at the end of the hall, I nod at my pod mates.

Marco pushes back the grate, and we climb out of the wall compartment. As soon as I take a step, I slip, landing on my butt in the middle of the mushy orange passage. My feet are still covered in the slime from our hiding place.

"Let's go!" Marco says. He gives me a hand and hauls me up.

It's hard to walk in the mush, but I can't let my klutziness put the mission at risk. I place my feet carefully and follow Cole down the passage.

The hallway glows like we're outside in the sun, but there's no light source in sight. The walls, floor, and ceiling are all made of the spongy orange stuff.

"This building material is fascinating," Cole says. "I believe it's organic living matter."

"All I know is it stinks!" Lucy says. "Seriously, why does it smell like rotten fruit?"

"Bounders!" Marco says. "Let's go!" He shoves Cole ahead.

Cole jogs down the hall, with us close behind. When he stops short, we nearly crash into him. "We're approaching the turn. We need to confirm it's clear."

"I'll do it." Marco creeps to the corner and peers around. Meanwhile, Lucy guards our back. Without taking his eyes off the next hallway, Marco waves us forward.

We swing around the corner into a passage that looks almost exactly like the one we came down except there are lots of intersecting hallways. We have to check each branch before scuttling across. I'm aware of the distant sound of Youli brain-talking, but it doesn't seem to be coming closer. I glance at Mira; she shakes her head. The sound fades.

With the next turn, the bridge Cole described is up ahead. It doesn't look much different than the hallways we've already traveled, except one side is lined with windows looking out into space.

Although the Youli alarm has faded to a constant hum in the back of my brain, the reason for the alarm slams into focus as we step onto the bridge.

We're drawn like magnets to the window and the scene outside.

From where the Youli vessel is docked on the axis, we look inward toward the pivoting cylinder. We can see past the cylinder all the way to the outer edge, past the rotating spheres and the other docked vessels, past the guard stations providing security for the summit.

Beyond the buffers, barely visible from where we stand, an outer ring of small vessels flash in and out of view. The Earth Force quantum fleet. Lights spark through space as crimson and aqua lasers target the bounding ships. The ships vanish a millisecond before impact then—*Pop!*—reappear on the other side of the space station, like popcorn jumping through the dark expanse of space.

"Are we winning?" Lucy asks.

"It's a decoy, remember?" Cole says. "We're not fighting to win."

"A decoy for us, Super Friends," Marco says. "Let's go!"

Blast! An explosion rips through space like a starburst.

"No!" The word escapes my mouth much louder than it

should. I cover my mouth and hope the Youli didn't hear.

Mira slams her hands against the windows. Currents of rage and misery radiate from her mind. The Youli vessel shakes, knocking me off balance. As I steady myself against the spongy orange wall, debris ricochets off the windows.

"Tell me that wasn't one of our ships!" Lucy says. "Tell me there weren't Bounders on board!"

"Don't let that be for nothing," I say quietly. "We need to go."

We pull away from the window and follow Marco the rest of the way across the bridge. I'm careful not to let my eyes wander back to the scene outside. I can't afford to be distracted right now. Too much is at stake.

When we reach the systems room, Cole peers through the entrance then jumps back. "There's someone in there."

"Let me see." Marco peeks his head around the door.

Lucy looks at me then back at the window where Mira has drifted. Next to Lucy, Cole hops on his toes. I point to the door. We need to stay focused, keep our heads in the game. She nods. Cole blows out a long exhale. Mira steps away from the glass.

Marco ducks back and huddles up. "Here's the deal. There's a Youli in the corner working at a souped-up monitor. His back is to the door. I'll take him out."

"You'll what?" Lucy says.

"You heard me. I'll take him out." When Lucy opens her mouth to protest, Marco keeps talking. "Look, it's not like I'm going to kill him. I'm just going to knock him unconscious. Jasper said they freak out from physical contact. Right, J?"

When I tackled the Youli on the Paleo Planet, he went into sensory overload. "Yeah. It could work. But we need a better plan."

They all stare, waiting for me to cough one up.

"Let me get a look at the room." I creep to the doorframe and slowly lean forward. It's just as Marco described and consistent with the intelligence we got from the Alkalinians. The room is circular and made from the same spongy orange stuff, but there are bright-colored ribbons running through the walls and floor, all leading back to a center core that looks like an enormous green tree trunk. All those colors feed into the trunk like a root system that not only powers the Youli computer systems and their ships, but also, at least according to the Alkalinians, provides some kind of sustenance for the Youli themselves.

A dozen screens are built into the wall on the far side of the systems room. Some of them show the exterior of the vessel and the battle beyond. A Youli is standing in front of one of the screens, probably watching the battle. Hopefully that will be enough of a distraction.

I pull back and gather my pod mates. "How's this? Marco

and I subdue the alien. Cole and Lucy, you head to the center pillar and get the patch planted." I turn my eyes to Mira. "The Youli's mind will go haywire once we tackle him. I won't be able to focus on anything else. You need to flag us if you get word on the brain waves that his buddies are coming. But remember, no brain-talk!"

Marco doesn't wait for anyone to weigh in. He rushes into the room, assuming I'll have his back when he takes out the Youli.

In *Evolution of Combat*, there's this thing that happens when your army is about to be defeated in battle. Everything moves in slow motion. It's this special feature that gives you extra time to set up your last-ditch defense, but it also brings everything into hyperfocus. You might be fighting in a field of poppies and not even notice, but when the slow motion kicks in, you suddenly see each bright red petal of a particularly tall flower.

That's what it's like when I enter the systems room.

A second before impact, the Youli turns around. Marco is nearly on top of him, but the Youli's eyes find mine. They're big and black and bottomless. Even though I'm still moving, I feel frozen. And as I brace for the Youli's onslaught of feelings, expecting to sense rage or confusion or maybe even fear, I'm overwhelmed with curiosity and kindness, like that's the place from which the Youli operate. Curiosity and kindness.

330   MONICA TESLER

Marco knocks the Youli to the ground and punches his face. I kneel on his shoulders and keep him pinned while his brain floods mine with blurry thoughts of the battle and the summit and the crazy Earth kids who have just attacked him.

Cole races around the center pillar. Lucy fishes the patch from her pocket. Mira stands at the door. Her arms are wrapped around her body. She rocks her chest forward and back as if tilting on an internal pivot.

"Have you got it?" I shout to Cole and Lucy.

"Not yet!" Cole hollers back.

"Hurry!" Marco yells.

"You're not helping!" Lucy snaps.

The Youli struggles, and a new wave of words and emotion rushes over me. *Stop! Peace! Please!*

He pushes against my brain. My patch twinges. It takes all the focus I have not to respond with my mind. I squeeze my eyes shut and press my hands against the Youli's chest.

"Almost there!" Cole shouts.

Stop! Peace! Please!

I funnel all my energy—mental and physical—into restraining the Youli and keeping him out of my brain.

"Jasper!" Lucy yells like it's not the first time she's called for me. "What's happening? What's going on with Mira?"

I open my eyes. Mira stands at the door. Her face is filled with frustration. She's clapping her hands.

Why would she be . . . ? Oh . . . of course . . . she has no way to communicate.

She throws up her arms, and glares at me. Her voice reaches my mind. *They're coming! They're coming!*

As soon as her words touch me, the Youli jerks. He heard her, too.

"They're coming!" I yell to our pod mates.

"All set!" Lucy says. "Next stage. Go!"

Marco slaps my leg. "Bound! Now!"

I open my port and—*Bam!*

My feet hit solid ground: the Gulagan Space Dock. My pod mates surround me on the flight deck. We made it!

My brain is finally free of the Youli's grasp. All that's left is a memory, a lingering trail across the cosmos.

Mission accomplished.

And that's when it hits me. The Youli's sensors may not be able track our bounds, but thanks to the patches and our brain-talk, their minds sure can.

SECONDS AFTER MY FEET HIT THE DECK,
I'm airborne. Strong hands grab my thighs and hoist me up.
As my head crests above the crowd, I see the entire flight deck
is crushed with people—humans and Tunnelers, all celebrating an Earth Force victory. Voices chant my name and the
names of my pod mates. The shouts swell so loud, I cover
my ears.

I'm propped on the shoulders of two officers. Not far
from me, Marco barely stays balanced on the backs of two
Tunnelers. He pumps his fists in the air then tips his head
and howls. When he catches my eye, he turns up his thumbs.

Captain Han steers through the crowd with Cole on his

shoulders. Lucy stands on the bounding ship scaffolding, waving to the crush of people below. She looks like a star. She even blows kisses.

Everyone's cheering. They're cheering for us. They're cheering for victory.

None of them knows a Youli attack is imminent.

Maybe it's not. Maybe I'm being paranoid. The only person who can help me figure that out right now is Mira.

Where is she?

I scan the crowd but can't find her. "Mira! Mira!" It's no use. There's no way she could hear me over the hoots and hollers and Gulagan grunts.

I could be wrong. If the Youli tracked us, Earth Force would know, right? We wouldn't be celebrating. We'd be preparing to defend the space dock, the quantum fleet, Gulaga.

Something catches the corner of my eye, and I turn. A few meters to my right, two officers have Mira in their grasp. They're probably just trying to lift her, but she's having none of it. She pushes one of them in the chest and shakes free of the other.

I focus on her with all my might. *Mira!*

Her eyes dart around until they find mine. Her gaze is drenched in panic. Then she thinks the same words she used on the Youli vessel. *They're coming!*

She sensed it, too. The Youli are coming. They traced us. And it's all because of Waters and his stupid brain patches.

We need to do something.

"Put me down!" I shout. "The Youli are coming!"

No one can hear me over the din. I kick the officers in the chest, knowing I'll probably pay for it later, until they're forced to lower me. I slip through their grasp and duck into the crowd, desperate to shield the space station before it's too late.

But now that I'm down, I'm not sure what to do. How on earth can I convince this horde a threat's on the way?

I run toward Lucy who still clings to the scaffolding. When I reach the metal rungs, she waves at me with an enormous smile on her face. I climb up and spin around, linking my arm around a vertical bar for balance.

As I scan the crowd, Lucy sidles up beside me. She presses a giant kiss on my cheek. "We did it, Jasper!" she speaks into my ear.

Below us, Earth Force officers and Tunnelers cheer. Their shouts converge on a single chant.

"Birthright, Bounders Fight!"

"Birthright, Bounders Fight!"

"Birthright, Bounders Fight!"

"They're coming!" I shout back at Lucy.

"What?"

I twist on the scaffolding so I can shout in her ear. "The Youli! They tracked us! Through the brain patch!"

Lucy pulls back as a wave of concern sweeps her face. "No."

I lean close. "Yes! Help me find Mira! Then grab Cole and Marco and head for the elevator!"

Lucy scans my face. First she shakes her head. Then, when she's convinced I'm serious, she nods. We search the crowd. Seconds later, she grabs my forearm and points. Mira is making her way through the masses, heading for the large, elevated platform near the doors where Admiral Eames stands, flanked by Captain Ridders and Suarez.

I grab Lucy's hand and squeeze. She squeezes back, then we both descend the scaffolding and are swallowed by the crowd. I can only hope she finds Cole and Marco in time. My job is to intercept Mira.

I keep my eyes locked on the admiral. From her post on the platform, she claps and waves to the crowd. She's obviously just as oblivious as everyone else.

A large Tunneler in front of me refuses to budge. He grunts in Gulagan. I try to ignore him and scoot by on the side, but he blocks me, still talking. Doesn't he understand I have no clue what he's saying? He sounds happy enough, for a Tunneler at least, so he must be congratulating me. I give him a thumbs-up. He nods and slaps me on the back. I duck around him and continue on.

Someone catches my sleeve, and I'm jerked to a stop. I spin around to find Ryan standing there with a huge grin. He gets inches from my face. "You rock, Jasper!"

"Thanks! Gotta go!" I don't bother explaining. I rip my arm from his grasp and spin back. I take one step and slam straight into Maximilian Sheek.

He is the last person I want to see right now. Sheek swings his arm around my shoulder and bends over. "The heroic Jasper! I knew my pointers would pay off. Let's try for a photo op!"

"I have to find the admiral!" I shout.

"Excellent idea! EFAN is sure to run extra coverage if the admiral is in the shot." Sheek presses his hand against my back and steers us into the celebration. It turns out running into Sheek was a stroke of luck. The crowd parts when he waves his hand. Don't they know he's a total phony?

Mira reaches the platform seconds before us. She's already climbing when I grab the rungs and haul myself up.

Captain Suarez is on us immediately. "Whoa! Back off, cadets! You can't be up here!"

"I need to speak with the admiral!" I shout.

Suarez levels a cool stare at me, then shifts to Mira, who pulls at her braid and looks like she's about to bolt.

"It's important!" I cry. "High-level intelligence about the mission!"

She hesitates but then alerts the admiral, who waves us to the back of the platform.

The admiral smiles and spreads her arm wide. "Miss

Matheson, Mr. Adams, our very own heroes. If it weren't for you and your pod—"

I can't waste time with this. "Admiral, I'm very sorry—I know interrupting you is against like every Earth Force protocol, but you have to listen to me. The Youli tracked us. They'll be here any second."

The smile leaves the admiral's face. "The *diruo* pulse rendered our ships untrackable. The only thing you're right about, cadet, is your violation of protocol."

"Listen, it's hard to explain, but I had this sort of brain connection with the Youli, and—"

"Brain connection?" the admiral interrupts. She shouts to be heard over the cheers below.

"Yes, and there was this Youli in the systems room—"

An alarm sounds, and it's not in my head like on the Youli ship. This alarm is loud, piercing, and capable of calling every one of the soldiers celebrating below to attention.

The admiral lifts her com link to her ear to hear over the siren.

A tense moment passes. All eyes on the flight deck are on the admiral.

When she lowers her com link, her face is drained of color. "It seems you might be right," she says to me before turning to Suarez, Ridders, and her honor guard. "We've detected an incoming bound in Gulagan space. Get everyone off this space dock now!"

The admiral issues orders, then her guards rush her off the platform. Suarez and Ridders swing down and guide the panicked crowd toward the dock doors.

When Mira and I get off the platform, we link hands. We're about to join the evacuation when a hand seizes my forearm.

"Not so fast!" Sheek shouts. "What happened to our photo op?"

"What? Don't you know what's happening? The Youli tracked us. We're under attack."

Sheek's face contorts as he processes this information. Then he roughly shoves us aside and runs for the door. "Stand aside! Coming through!"

Mira rolls her eyes then takes off after him, dragging me behind her.

The crowd funnels toward the narrow door opening until we're all stuck and jostling in a human traffic jam.

Screams ripple through the crowd. Someone ahead of me points. I spin around.

Just off the flight deck, a Youli ship has just bounded in. The space surrounding it still shimmers with the aftershock of the bound.

The ship looks just like the one from the Paleo Planet, except now it's reversing the bound sequence. First, it's a ball about the size of our quantum ships, then it starts to unfold, so that by the time we finally reach the doors amidst the crush of people, the disk is wider than the flight deck. Shots fire from the craft and ricochet off our shields.

We press forward and squeeze through the doors. Inside, the space dock is jammed with people, and the air is thick with smoke. The floor rocks, and we're thrown down. A Tunneler falls on top of me, and his fur rubs against my face. I push off with my feet, trying to stand. The ground shifts. But it's not the ground—there's a person beneath me. He shifts out of the way, and my shoes find a solid surface.

I shout for Mira, but I can't even hear myself over everyone else's screams. Smoke burns my throat as I suck in a breath.

Mira finds my hand and laces our fingers. *Don't let go.*

I'm grateful she can reach my mind, even if it's what led the Youli to our doorstep. Fear rolls off of her in big waves. I can only imagine what my brain must feel like right now.

We creep forward until the crowd thins and we're running for the space elevator. Dense smoke clouds the main passage, so we reroute through a generator room. A narrow bridge spans the engineering center, a four-story drop to the floor below. I don't even think about falling when I dash across.

When we're nearly at the door, the space dock reels from another hit.

We're launched forward, away from the pit. The sound of

MONICA TESLER

bending metal echoes through the cavernous room.

Mira and I scramble to our feet amidst the screams.

"Help!"

Mira pulls against my hand. *Stop!*

I jerk forward. We have to keep going. There's no telling how much time we have before this place blows apart. We have to make it to the space elevator.

"Help!"

Mira releases my hand. I skid to a halt and spin around. The narrow bridge we crossed has collapsed, but its center support still stands. Perched on the narrow platform, completely stranded above the engineering room, is Regis.

"Help!" he shouts. "Please!" He sees that we've stopped, that we've heard his call. His face lights with hope. But when his eyes meet mine, his face falls.

Everything in me wants to turn my back. This is the guy who left us for dead on the tundra. He tried to push us off the bridge in Gulagaven, and now he expects us to save him from a bridge that collapsed?

Payback, Regis. *Ultio*.

I take a step backward and will myself to turn around and run for the space elevator, but I just can't do it. Regis is stranded with no blast pack and no hope of rescue other than us. I grab the straps for my pack. Mira pushes off, and I follow, flying across the pit for Regis.

I send Mira a mental picture, and we execute, gliding behind him from either side.

"Hang one of your arms over each of our shoulders," I shout to him. "We'll fly you back."

Regis hesitates. "How do I know you won't drop me?"

"Now or never," I say. "If you don't want to trust us, suit yourself."

He spreads his arms across our shoulders and steps off the platform. His weight threatens to pull us down, but Mira and I hold steady and steer us back to the ledge. Regis leaps as soon as we clear the pit. He takes off running without a glance back.

"Nice of you to say thanks!" I call after him.

The sudden shift knocked Mira off balance. *Fungus Butt!* she brain-screams after Regis.

No kidding, I think as I help her up.

We stumble out the door and into the crowded hallway.

When we're steps away from the bay, the news reaches us.

"The elevator just left without us!"

"They hit capacity! We have to wait for the next trip!"

"The Youli will shoot us out of the sky!"

"This is a death sentence!"

Wait . . . no . . . the elevator left? What are we going to do?

Everyone crowds into the bay. Sure enough, the elevator

has already started its descent. Tunnelers work feverishly at the controls. Commander Krag grunts orders. Every few seconds, he activates his voice box and assures us that they're running the cab on an emergency speed setting, that it will be back for us in less than twenty minutes.

Twenty minutes? How on earth do they think we'll last twenty minutes with the Youli firing on the space dock?

There's nothing we can do but wait. I scan the bay but can't spot my pod mates. I hope Lucy, Cole, and Marco made it onto the first elevator. We probably would have made it, too, if we hadn't stopped to rescue Regis.

The bay is packed and still more people pour in. Smoke seeps in, too. It's getting hard to breathe.

"Please stay calm," Commander Krag says. "The first evacuation trip has already reached the atmosphere. The cab should arrive for a second evacuation in eleven minutes."

"Eleven minutes!" someone shouts. "We won't be here in eleven minutes!"

Mira squeezes my hand.

"Do not panic," the commander continues. "We've raised traditional force fields. We've implemented auto defense measures that should keep the Youli ship off our immediate perimeter. Where you're standing is the most secure location on this dock. I have no doubt we'll weather this attack. At least for another eleven minutes."

The elevator bay is so packed, it's hard to see. The only place that's clear is down. Down through the transparent floor, past the occludium shield, all the way down to the Gulagan surface. Down to safety. All we can do is look down and watch as the elevator now makes its way back to where we wait.

Minutes pass like hours. We have no idea what's happening outside, but it's hard not to imagine the worst each time the floor shakes or the lights flash in the reflection of the windows beneath our feet.

I clench my fist and feel the link between my brain and my gloves. It's so tempting to bound. It would be so easy to visualize the Nest, open a port, and step through. But if even part of the occludium shields around this dock or the planet remain intact, or if the scrambler is still activated in Gulagaven, we'd never materialize.

Mira's brain touches mine. *They followed us.*

I circle my arm around her shoulder. *I know.*

Is this our fault?

Will she know if I'm telling the truth?

No, I lie.

I know you're lying.

Even in the eye of this awfulness, a smile teases my lips. At least I'm with Mira. It's not like our connection makes the brain patches worth it—particularly since the Youli just used them to track us—but since I can't change the past, and there might not be a future, I might as well smile at the one positive result of Waters's folly.

As if she read my mind—which, I guess she did—Mira wraps her arm around my waist and douses us in her sparkly energy. But beneath the sparkles, I sense her mind is poised to spring. She's ready for battle.

"They're beneath us!" someone shouts.

I shake my head, thinking I've somehow missed the elevator cab crossing the remaining distance to the bay.

But no. That's not it.

The Youli ship glides beneath the space dock. As it passes, I see the reflection of all our waiting faces in the ship's metal surface.

As soon as the ship passes from view, it turns around and crosses again. A beam of light trails behind the ship and slings around the elevator shaft with each turn.

Cries rise up around us. "What are they doing? What is that light?"

Oh . . . my . . . no. The Youli ship is wrapping that light beam around the elevator shaft. They're trying snap the shaft in two like a dry twig.

Everything shifts back into that *Evolution of Combat* mode again. The Tunneler on my left sniffs and bats at his whiskers. I think he's crying. The officer next to me crouches and bangs at the floor with his fists. The air smells of smoke and wet cat and dirty gym clothes.

Commander Krag barks furiously into a receiver that looks oddly like an old-fashioned telephone back on Earth.

The Youli ship swings around for another pass at the elevator shaft with its light cable.

Is the guy Marco and I tackled on that ship?

Are our pod mates watching from the surface?

Will I ever see Mom and Dad again?

Will they tell Addy I died a hero when she reports for her first tour of duty?

"No!" I shout, but I can barely hear myself. The bay is filled with screams and cries and smoke and fear. I pull Mira close and force myself not to close my eyes.

With one final tug, the Youli ship breaks the shaft of the space elevator.

28

THE DOCK PITCHES AWAY FROM THE SHAFT
as it's jettisoned from its anchor. We're launched into the air.
Mira slips from my grasp. My back slams against the center
console, and I tumble down the clear floor, now tipped on its
side. Landing in a pile of Tunnelers and humans, I grope for
Mira. My brain nearly bursts from fear—mine and hers. That
must mean she's conscious, which means she's still alive.

I shove past a Tunneler, and wiggle to the top of the body
pile. At the center of the dock, Commander Krag shouts into
the phone and jabs at the control panels. He's tied himself to
the console with long strips of brown burlap ripped from a
Tunneler frock.

Beneath us, the elevator cab continues to rise, unable to stop its propulsion. It shoots up the shaft and off its tracks, heading straight for us. The cab slams into the space dock. I'm thrown back in a heap with the other struggling survivors.

Debris from the collision rains down on the planet below.

Lights blink on and off then shut down completely. Seconds later, emergency lights ignite. The dock starts to level, and I scramble to my hands and knees and crawl to the corner of the dock where I sense Mira.

Here! Here! She knows I'm coming. A delicate, gloved hand pushes up from beneath an Earth Force officer slumped against the wall.

I reach the officer and roll him off, unsure if he's dead or just unconscious. Mira pushes past the body and throws her arms around my neck.

Are you okay? I ask her.

She doesn't answer, but the fear that floods my brain is laced with relief and determination. I can't see how we're getting off this dock alive, but at least we're together.

"Attention!" Commander Krag says over the intercom. "Help is on its way. Please proceed quickly but orderly to the flight deck."

Help is on its way? How?

"Look below!" someone shouts.

From the surface of Gulaga, a passenger craft blasts

MONICA TESLER

through the atmosphere and glides through the occludium shield.

"They're coming for us!"

Go! Mira darts forward, clenching my hand.

We rush and shove through the bay door and into the narrow hallways that connect with the flight deck. Our hands are clamped like a lifeline, and we press forward in the wave of the crowd.

We spill onto the deck just as the passenger craft touches down. There's a huge gouge in the right wing, and smoke billows up from the tail. The ramp lowers, and the crowd swells aboard.

When we enter the cabin, the craft lifts off. Mira and I are thrown to our knees. I haul myself into a seat and help her in after me. We fasten our harnesses as the craft banks into a 360-degree turn straight into a spiral dive for the surface.

"Whoa!" the Tunneler beside me shouts. "Who is flying this thing?"

"I have a guess," comes a voice from behind. I turn around to find Captain Han in the next row.

"The only person I know who can fly a passenger craft like this is Admiral Eames," he continues. "And that means we just might make it."

The admiral is at the helm? Everyone always says she was the best pilot in the Earth Force fleet. I hope she still is.

The ship rocks left, jerks right, then drops. Smoke fans in from the side. We gun ahead then circle back, maneuvering through the Youli lasers that flash like fireworks out the front windows.

Mira squeezes my palm. I squeeze my eyes shut. Our lives are out of our hands now. All we can do is wait and trust in the admiral to fly us to safety. And that's probably a long shot.

Every moment takes a minute. Every minute takes an hour. My mind races back over the last six weeks.

The Youli battle. The night in the cave with Mira. Regis and the bridge.

Our pod. The Nest. Neeka. Grok and the Den and the Tunneler band. Connecting with old friends. Building alliances.

And so many secrets. The Youli. The Alkalinians. The summit. The brain patches.

My mind speeds all the way back to Addy's room. She was furious at me for keeping secrets. *You're loyal to them. To Earth Force. Not to me.*

I see it so clearly, now, at the end. Everyone demanding I keep their secrets. My parents insisting that I keep quiet about being a Bounder. Earth Force commanding us to keep the Youli war confidential. Waters making me shut up about the brain patches.

Everything is built on secrets. All the way back to the

Incident at Bounding Base 51 and the Bounder Baby Breeding Program. The war we're expected to fight is waged on secrets. And secrets led the Youli to our doorstep.

But that's not what really matters right now, in my last moments. What matters is me. My role. My responsibilities. Why am *I* keeping secrets? Why am *I* hiding the truth from the only people in the world who truly have my back?

My sister.

My pod.

Sometimes even myself.

I may never make it back to Earth. I may never even reach Gulaga. But if I do, I make this vow: I am done with other people's secrets. My loyalty lies with my pod and with my sister and with my fellow Bounders. If I ever keep another secret, it's out of my loyalty to them.

Cheers erupt in the cabin, shaking me back to the present moment, speeding everything up.

I open my eyes. The window is clouded by a silvery haze.

"We've passed through the shields," Admiral Eames's voice says over the intercom.

Oh my god. We actually made it?

More cheers. And claps. And whistles.

Mira hugs me. Han slaps me five.

We're descending to the surface, safe beneath the shield.

Seconds later, the passenger craft lowers onto the tarmac

on Gulaga. Crews rush alongside, spraying down the fires from the Youli attack.

Once the craft is deemed safe, the ramp is lowered, and we're waved off. Tunnelers cover us in fur blankets and urge us to hurry. The temperature on the surface is so cold, we could be compromised in minutes without the proper gear. The icy air fills my lungs and slaps the exposed pockets of skin on my face and hands. They rush us across the tarmac and down the tunnel, through the antechambers and the outfitter center, and into the tunnels of Gulaga.

Hurry, hurry, hurry, deeper and deeper into the bowels of Gulagaven.

When we reach the central chasm, I grind to a halt and gaze out over the bottomless pit. I can't believe we actually made it.

Mira slides in beside me. *No more secrets.*

She knows what I was thinking. She must have been walking with me through the memories. "You've got to stop peeking into my brain like that!"

She rests her head on my shoulder, and our minds hum with a sparkly energy of possibility and promise.

· *E̶F̶* ·

The five of us huddle in the Nest. I didn't know it was possible for our pod to be so quiet for so long, but it turns out having so much to say and nothing to say are very close cousins.

MONICA TESLER

The truth is, we're lost in our memories of the day and the tour.

There were casualties.

Six Tunnelers died when the cab was launched from the elevator shaft.

Eight Earthlings and thirteen more Tunnelers, including Neeka's father, Commander Krag, didn't make it off the space dock.

One of the new aeronauts was killed in the quantum ship explosion we saw from the Youli bridge. A cadet was also lost in the explosion. Lian had just initiated a bound and failed to materialize. She's presumed dead, just like the aeronauts from the Incident at Bounding Base 51.

My mind keeps returning to the Youli ship, probably so I don't have to think about everyone who died today. Even though we're at war, even though their attack led to the death of my comrades, I can't shake the feeling that there's more to the Youli than we know.

Three words echo in my mind: *Stop! Peace! Please!*

I close my eyes and see us trudging along the squishy orange hallway. I know it's crazy, but I wish we could have explored the ship. I want to see where the Youli sleep, what they eat, how big their flight deck is, if they even have a flight deck. Before, when all I knew about the Youli came from the space station prisoner, or the Paleo Planet attack, or the Earth

Force tales of our alien enemy, the Youli could be contained as a story in my mind.

Now, since I've hid in *their* ship, walked down *their* halls, heard *their* voices, I want to know more. I want to know how the Youli *live*. They're not a story. They're real. And as different as they are from us, I'm starting to think we're more the same than we've been led to believe.

Waters called them *friends*, and as wrong as Waters has been, I still think he's basically right. After all, today we attacked first. They asked us to stop. They wished for peace. They even said *please*.

Marco paces across the furry fungus rug, unable to sit still for more than a minute at a time. Gulagaven has been on full lockdown since Admiral Eames piloted the passenger craft to the surface. Even though the planet is shielded, we're under strict orders not to venture beyond the lower sublayers. If the Youli manage to penetrate our defenses, we have a better shot of surviving a ground attack in the lower levels.

Last we heard, no Youli ships have been spotted in Gulagan space since two hours after the space elevator disaster, thank goodness. If the coast is still clear by tomorrow morning, they'll shuttle the Bounders off the planet.

A knock at the door makes me jump. The handle twists, and Gedney steps in.

"I'm so relieved you're all here," he says, entering our

temporary pod room. "I knew you made it back, of course, but it feels better to see you with my own eyes."

"Did the virus patch work?" Cole asks.

Gedney rubs his forehead. "It's too soon to tell. I have no reason to think it won't."

"That was quite a summit you shipped us to," Marco says. "Waters wasn't kidding when he said intragalactic relations are complicated. There were a lot of aliens there, Geds. A lot more than Earth Force has told us about."

Secrets. I don't know if we'll ever get to the bottom of Earth Force's secrets.

"Where *is* Waters?" I ask. I have words for Waters. Lots of words about his handy-dandy little brain patches, which led the Youli right to our doorstep.

Gedney stares at his shoes for a long moment before speaking. "He's gone."

"What do you mean 'gone'?" Lucy asks.

Gedney sits beside me on the squishy bench. "I mean, I don't expect he'll be back. It was time for him to part ways with Earth Force. Past time, really. He's a good man, and a great friend, but even good men make mistakes. And even great men can let the end goal get in the way of the proper path."

"Riddles, Geds," Marco says. "Those are no more than riddles."

"Not riddles, Mr. Romero. Just an old man too tired to speak plainly. I wanted to see you kids before I go. I'm leaving for the laboratory on an early shuttle." He pushes himself up. He looks half-Tunneler the way he's hunched over.

"I'm so glad you're safe," he continues. "We'll be back together in a few months. Hopefully a few things will have changed. Some cadet behavior this tour was inexcusable."

"You heard about the bridge?" I ask. "The stolen gloves?"

Gedney nods. "That's not something I can let stand. I only wish Waters had told me sooner."

"You're booting Regis from the Force?" Marco asks.

"Nothing is certain, except it looks like I'll be in charge of your pod."

"You're going to be our pod leader?" Cole asks.

Gedney smiles. "And I bet you thought you had bad luck with Waters. Wait until those new cadets meet me!"

It's hard to believe a new group of Bounders will be joining the EarthBound Academy next tour. When I ship out for my third tour, Addy will be with me. She'll start her training to be a soldier.

"Will they be sending us to battle when we return?" I ask. "What about the new cadets?"

"Ah yes, Jasper, your sister will be joining us." When I nod, he continues, "The new cadets will need to master the glove

356   MONICA TESLER

technology. Much is up in the air. The admiral . . ." Gedney lets his words fall off.

"The admiral what?" Marco says.

Gedney doesn't answer.

"Please, Mr. Gedney," Lucy says. "If there's something we should know about our third tour, please tell us."

Gedney purses his lips. "Very well. I've been informed that the Alkalinians invited the Bounders to train on their planet. During our post-battle briefing, Admiral Eames discussed sending an advance delegation to assess the risk. The admiral is aware of your pod's skills. Depending on what she hopes to accomplish, I wouldn't be surprised if you were selected."

So the admiral is going to accept Seelok's "invitation." Whoever gets sent to that snake den is walking right into peril, I'm sure of it. I really hope Gedney's wrong, and it's not our pod. Regis would be an excellent choice, unless Gedney somehow manages to get him expelled from EarthBound Academy.

Either way, we'll be expected to report back to duty in a few months. Addy will be with me, and the stakes will be even higher.

29

THE CROWD IN THE PARLIAMENT CHAM- ber is rowdy and loud, kind of like the mood on the flight deck once our pod bounded off the Youli vessel, but now the celebration contains a thread of darkness woven with the deaths of our friends and comrades.

Sheek is hamming it up for the cameras again. Pose right. Pose left.

"How did he get to be the face of Earth Force?" Lucy asks. "He didn't even see action in battle."

"They can't risk tarnishing his pretty face, obviously," Marco says.

When the admiral's honor guard enters, we take seats in

our carrel. The admiral herself soon follows. Butterfly bandages close a cut on her left cheek that she must have gotten when she flew the rescue mission to the space dock. At least she fought alongside us.

Ridders silences the crowd as the admiral steps to the podium. "Greetings, fellow officers and cadets of the EarthBound Academy. You have served your planet well. You have acted with courage and heroism. While our thoughts are with our fallen comrades, who gave their lives for our cause, let us honor their memory by standing together in solidarity and victory. I am pleased to confirm that Operation *Vermis* was a success."

All around us, cadets and officers jump to their feet, cheering and clapping. I slowly rise with my pod mates.

Soon one cheer crystallizes above all others:

"Birthright, Bounders fight!"

"Birthright, Bounders fight!"

"Birthright, Bounders fight!"

The admiral gestures for quiet. "Yes! Bounders! When you're back next tour, there will be much work to do. With the Youli weakened, our offensive will be in full force. You will again be asked to defend your planet. And you will again rise to the challenge!

"Tomorrow," the admiral continues, "you will be heading home as the second tour of duty of the EarthBound Academy draws to a close. But today we have even more reason for celebration! The tokens have been counted, and we have a winner of the Tundra Trials! Let me turn the podium over to Captain Sheek, who will announce the victor."

Sheek strides to the podium and strikes a few more poses. "Thank you, Admiral. And thank you to everyone who helped make the Tundra Trials a great success. The competition was fierce, and a late disqualification of a top contender led to some last-minute drama—"

"A completely *unfair* disqualification," Cole mumbles under his breath.

"But I am pleased to announce," Sheek continues, "that we have a clear champion. Before I announce the winning pod, let me announce the prize. As many of you know, Earth Force is days away from launching the Paleo Planet tourism initiative. The winning pod will accompany *me* on the first public tour. That's right. We'll be flying out together on the brand-new, custom-built 770 passenger crafts, and it will all be featured on my Paleo Planet EFAN special."

"That is so unfair!" Lucy says.

"Why?" Marco says. "That prize stinks. We've already been to the Paleo Planet. We almost died, remember?"

"Now, I won't keep you in suspense a moment longer," Sheek continues. "The winners just so happen to be my very own pod, now led by Captain James Ridders! Captain, cadets, will you please join me down here?"

"Yes!" I say. "Our allies won!"

Everyone claps as Ryan, Meggi, Annette, and their pod mates meet up with Ridders and Sheek at the podium. The EFAN crew is ushered back in to snap shots of the victors, and Sheek, of course.

Shortly after, the admiral leaves with her honor guard and Ridders explains the logistics for our return to Earth. Tomorrow morning, we'll fly by passenger craft to the nearest bounding base. From there, we'll free bound to the Ezone at the space station and transfer to smaller crafts for the trip back to Earth. Cole and I are grouped with the other cadets from Americana East.

When Ridders wraps up, we head to the floor to congratulate our friends. Soon, the only people left in the chamber are the Bounders and their junior ambassadors. Sadly Neeka is nowhere to be found.

"I wish she were here," Lucy says. "I want to give her a big squeeze and let her know how sorry I am about her dad before we leave Gulaga."

"I have an idea," I tell her. I track down Grok talking to some other junior ambassadors. "Hey! Argotok! Any chance you can get us into the Den tonight?"

· E⊢ ·

A few hours later, we meet up with Grok and Ridders's pod and wind our way through the tunnels to the Den. As we're about to enter, an old Tunneler with a scar across his face steps from the shadows. Barrick.

Grok stops, but Marco waves him on. "It's cool. Give Jasper and me a minute. We'll meet you inside."

At first, Grok hesitates, but then he pulls the door open and ushers the rest of our group into the Den.

Marco and I duck around the corner where we spotted Barrick.

"Hey, kid," he says to me then turns to Marco. "You one of the lost boys from day one?"

"Yeah," Marco says. "You bolted before I could say thanks."

"As one does in unfriendly territory," Barrick says.

"Speaking of that," I say, "why are you here? Isn't it risky?"

"Less risky for me than for the one who wants his message delivered."

"Huh?" I say.

Barrick shakes his head. "Still aren't quick on the uptake, kid. Jon Waters asked me to find you."

Waters?

Marco clenches his fist. "Where is he?"

"Relax. He's safe. And he's relieved to know you are, too. He cares about you kids."

"He has a funny way of showing it," I say.

"There are a lot of things at play, kid," he says.

"Yeah, yeah, yeah, intragalactic relations are complicated," Marco says. "Look, Barrick, we've heard it all before. You can call us kids all you want, but the truth is we're soldiers. And we're smarter and far more skilled than most adults you'll ever know, including the infamous Jon Waters. So give us the message or don't. We have somewhere to be."

"Fair enough," Barrick says. "Waters will be watching and trying his best to keep you safe. When the time is right, he'll reach out. He's on your side. We both are. But trust no one in Earth Force."

"Anything else?" I ask.

"Yeah, kid," Barrick says. "He's sorry."

"A little late for that," Marco says.

"It's a little late for a lot of things," Barrick says and takes off down the passage.

Marco stuffs his hands in his pockets and gazes into the shadows.

"What was that all about?" I ask once I'm pretty sure Barrick is out of range.

Marco shrugs. "I believe him. And I believe Waters."

"Why?"

"Because I trust Barrick. He hasn't given me a reason not to trust him. Unlike most people."

He means me. "I get it, okay? No more secrets. Not to you.

Not to any of the Bounders. In fact, I can't wait to get home. I have a lot of things I need to tell my sister before she comes to the Academy next tour."

Marco turns to me with a cold stare. "Make sure of it, Jasper. I'm all about second chances. But not third." Once he lets his words sink in, he nods at the door to the Den. "Let's head in."

When we enter the Den, we're greeted with the same loud and joyful atmosphere I remember from my first trip here with Mira. Grok waves from a table in the corner packed with our pod mates and allies and some junior ambassadors. As soon as we sit, a Tunneler arrives with bowls of something dark and foamy.

Marco raises the bowl to his lips. "A bit earthy, but it beats what they serve in the cantina."

"That's a pretty low standard," Annette says.

"What's in the box, Jasper?" Lucy asks, twirling a hot pink ribbon around her finger and nodding at the black case by my side.

"You'll see," I say.

The music picks up, and the crowd swells. We grab another round of drinks for the table and reminisce about the Tundra Trials.

"I never got to see a slimer," Ryan says.

"Be grateful." I shudder with the memory of that creature oozing its way around my legs.

"I'll be happy never to sink my teeth into BERF again," Meggi says.

"I'll drink to that." The bowl leaves a foamy mustache on my top lip.

"Do you think they're going to send us to Alkalinia next tour?" Cole asks.

"What's Alkalinia?" Grok asks.

"It's nothing!" Lucy says, giving Cole an evil eye. "We are so not talking about that tonight." She springs to her feet. "There's Neeka!"

Lucy races to Neeka's side and leads her to our table. Our Tunneler friend stoops even more than normal.

When they reach us, Neeka switches on her voice box. "Oh! Oh! I'm sorry I didn't make it to the briefing. It was a difficult day. I wanted to see you before you left Gulaga, though, so I'm glad you came."

"Sorry about your dad," Marco says. The rest of us nod and tell her how awful we feel about what happened.

I can picture Commander Krag tied to the controls on the space dock, confidently barking orders until the very end. "He was very courageous," I say.

"Oh! Thank you. He served Earth Force, he did his duty, but I will miss him very much."

"Of course you will, sweetie," Lucy says. "If there's anything we can do, even after we leave Gulaga, please ask."

Neeka sits with us for a few minutes, and then excuses herself to be with her family.

After she leaves, we toast and take turns sharing stories. Cole asks a gazillion questions about the occludium mines and the aboveground leaf structures. Amazingly one of the junior ambassadors is just as pumped to provide endless answers. Lucy isn't the only one in our pod to find a kindred spirit among the Tunnelers.

"I wasn't going to bring this up," Lucy announces to the table. "You know, with the battle, and the deaths, and everything. But now since we're hanging out, and having fun, and it is our last night here after all, and so I was just thinking—"

"Cut to the chase, DQ," Marco says.

"Okay, fine, I will. Does anyone know what day it is?" Lucy grins at all of us like the answer is so obvious we should be jumping in line to be the first to answer.

"Umm, the day we almost got killed by the Youli?" Ryan asks.

"Yes, and?" Lucy says.

"The last day of our tour?" Meggi says.

"Yes, and?"

"The day you stopped being so dramatic?" Marco says. "Just tell us!"

"Here's a hint," Lucy says. "It's October twelfth."

"So what?" Annette says.

366   MONICA TESLER

"It's Lucy's birthday," Cole says. "She told us back at the labs."

"Yes! Yes! Yes!" Lucy flings her arms around Cole and plants a huge, wet kiss right on his cheek. Cole turns as red as a ripe tomato.

We sing happy birthday to Lucy. Grok brings over a basket of creepy crawlies as a birthday treat. I almost barf on the spot. But once I get over the grossness, it's immensely entertaining to watch the Tunnelers eat the nasty things. Even Ryan chokes down a few.

As we sip on another round of foamy Tunneler brew, Marco raises his bowl. "It's all about the pod!"

We all lift our drinks. "It's all about the pod!"

Mira slips away to join the band. The beat picks up, and I can't help but sway to the music. Most of the Tunnelers leave to dance. Lucy, Meggi, and Annette follow.

I grab my black case and cross to the back of the room, where the band jams. My brain sparkles when Mira sees me coming. I fit together the pieces of my clarinet and join the song, enjoying another perfect moment in our imperfect Bounder world.

Acknowledgments

There are so many people behind the scenes who have contributed to the success of the Bounders series and helped bring *The Tundra Trials* to bookshelves.

I have so much gratitude for my editor, Michael Strother, who believed in me and my characters. These books will always have him in their pages.

The entire team at Simon & Schuster/Aladdin has been awesome. I am so fortunate to have them ushering my books into the world. I am especially grateful to Sarah McCabe, who took this book by the hand and helped it across the finish line.

My agent, David Dunton, championed the Bounders series from the beginning and found these books a great home, for which I'm so grateful.

One of the best experiences of the past year has been meeting and corresponding with readers. Thank you so much for your e-mails, letters, handshakes, and high fives. I love knowing that readers are connecting with my stories.

Writing may be a solitary profession, but I'm blessed with an incredibly supportive community of authors, many of whom have terrific books of their own. Special thanks to Melissa

Schorr, Lee Gjertsen Malone, Bridget Hodder, Victoria J. Coe, Dee Romito, Jenn Bishop, Jen Maschari, Abby Cooper, Janet Johnson, Jen Malone, MarcyKate Connolly, Marilyn Salerno, Julia Flaherty, Lisa Rehfuss, Debbie Blackington, and all the Sweet Sixteens.

I greatly appreciate the fabulous authors who took time out of their busy schedules to read and blurb *Earth Force Rising*: S. J. Kincaid, Shannon Messenger, and Wesley King.

I have a wonderful community in which to live and write, and the support I've received has been truly sustaining. Special thanks to my south shore friends and family and my Oechsle colleagues.

When I visit schools, I always talk about my childhood and active imagination. More than ever, I'm grateful to my parents, Richard and Lynne Swanson, for creating a home environment that allowed my creativity to flourish.

Of course, my heart bursts with love and gratitude for the three main guys in my life: Jamey, Nathan, and Gabriel. Thank you so much for walking with me on this journey. You are all a source of comfort, inspiration, and joy.

Gabriel, second only in birth date, your passion and focus are both incredible and familiar. This book is for you.

ACKNOWLEDGMENTS

Don't miss Jasper's next great
adventure in the EarthBound Academy!

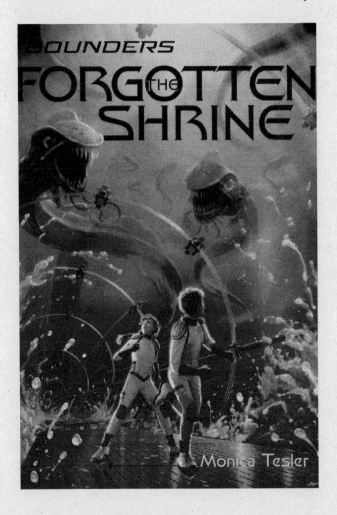

OUR KNEES TOUCH AS ADDY AND I SIT ON crates in the dirty storage room. The place is packed with boxes and piles of papers that fall to the floor in a cloud of dust every time I shift my weight. In the corner there's a crate filled with electronics like the ones they sell at the antiques shop—old swipe screens and these odd contraptions people used to wear on their ears for sound. Near the door is a stack of dolls with plastic heads and thick, stuffed bodies. Their lips look like tiny flowers the color of blood. They stare at us with cold, perfectly circular eyes.

Whose stuff is this? Who collects dolls and old headphones?

"Are you even listening to me, Jasper?" Addy runs a hand

through her sandy hair as she rolls her eyes. From the sound of her voice, it's not the first time she's asked.

I swat away some cobwebs. "How did you find this place again?"

She shrugs. "I was bored during your last tour. Mom said I couldn't go outside after curfew, so I explored inside."

"You're not supposed to be in the basement." I lean over and pick up a pair of purple headphones. My movement launches more dust into the stale air.

"Neither are you, yet here we are." Addy grabs my knees and forces me to look at her. The way her green eyes drill into mine, I'm worried she can read my mind. She's always been intense, but since I got back from the EarthBound Academy, she seems to have taken it to a new level.

"Can we get on with it?" she continues. "I have a group chat in twenty minutes."

By "group chat" she means an online meeting of her supposed-to-be-secret Bounders' rights group, which I'm sure Earth Force is monitoring and recording. During my last tour of duty, Addy connected on the webs with some other Bounders to talk about Earth meet-ups and in-class support for potential cadets. While I think a Bounders' rights group might make sense, it's hard to care too much about help at school when you're being asked to defend your planet against the Youli, an advanced alien race.

"So skip it," I say. "This is a lot more important than your group chat. Plus, tomorrow we'll both be shipping out to the EarthBound Academy. You'll have more Bounder buddies than you can count."

A sneaky smile lifts the corners of Addy's lips. "Speaking of shipping out, am I finally going to meet your girlfriend?"

This again? "For the millionth time, Addy, Mira is not my girlfriend." I'm not exactly sure what Mira is to me, and I'm not sure how I'd ever explain Mira to Addy. I definitely don't want to tell her about the brain patches and the actual mind-reading part.

"Sure." Addy's voice is laced with sarcasm. "Either way, once we blast off, there's no more secrets, which brings us back to the whole reason we're down in this dump."

Right. I made a promise at the end of last tour that I'd stop keeping secrets from my pod mates and my sister. I'd planned to tell Addy the truth when I returned, but the news was blitzed with rumors about aliens and Earth Force lies. The Force responded swiftly, arresting a handful of protestors who tried to land their vessel at the aeroport training facility. They said anyone caught disparaging the Force would be punished.

I'm sure our apartment is bugged. It certainly didn't do much to calm my fears when an officer showed up unannounced last month to review my "confidentiality commitments" to the Force. I wonder if they suspect a Bounder of the leaks?

After all, Earth Force managed to keep the Youli war a secret until they launched the EarthBound Academy. Anyway, it was just too dangerous to talk to Addy.

Still, I'm not going back into space without keeping my promise and cluing her in, and it's not like Addy would let me. She suggested we meet here in this old storage room in the lowest subfloor of our apartment building. And from the condition of the place, I'm guessing the only people to have set foot in here for the last fifty years are Addy and me.

I pluck a discarded mobile phone from beneath one of the dolls. "The person who put this stuff here has to be dead, don't you think?"

Addy shrugs. "Maybe."

I drag my finger across the dusty phone screen, drawing an *E* and an intersecting *F*, the Earth Force logo. "I can't decide whether this stuff is vintage or trash."

Addy's gaze morphs into a glare. "Jasper!"

"Huh?"

"You're avoiding the topic, the whole reason we're sitting on a stockpile of discarded electronics. What's the deal with Earth Force? You promised you'd hold nothing back if I found a safe place to talk! Look around. I held up my end of the bargain."

That's true. There is no way Earth Force bothered to bug this place. It's probably one of the most secure spots in all of

Americana East. If Addy and I died in some freak accident, like say if the box of creepy dolls tumbled over and crushed us, they probably wouldn't even discover our bones for another fifty years. Still, I wish I had time to stall. As much as I want to tell Addy, as much as I've committed to tell her, it's still hard stuff to say out loud. And I'm not sure how she's going to take it.

But her eyes sear me like lasers. There's no turning back.

I take a deep breath. "So, you know how we've always been told that Earth Force needs the Bounders to expand the quantum bounding space exploration program?"

"Let me guess," Addy says in a bored voice. "There's more to it." She waves her hand in a circle for me to continue.

"Well, yeah, there is. Earth Force's agenda is not exactly what you hear about on EFAN." I pause, waiting for her reaction.

"Obviously, J!" Addy throws her hands in the air, sending a dust cloud directly at my face. "Are you going to tell me what's going on or not? It's bad enough Earth Force thinks they can make me join their ranks without disclosing the truth about my mission. Now you're acting just as cryptic as them, when you promised you'd tell me the truth!"

I don't know how to do this. I don't know how to tell Addy she's signed up to fight in an alien war. She's already angry. That might throw her over the edge.

"We've always known we're Bounders, Addy," I say in a

quiet voice. "I don't understand why you're so mad. What's changed?"

"What's changed? Really? You have no idea what it was like while you were gone! Everyone knew I was a Bounder, but I didn't get to go to space! I had to face all the stares and questions on my own! Thank goodness I found the chat group. They've been a lifeline for me."

"I guess I didn't know it was so hard on you."

"Forget it. I'm fine. But where have you been since you got back from your last tour? Did you bury your head in that beanbag of yours? The rumors are rampant, and they all come back to the Bounders! What is Earth Force hiding?"

What rumors about the Bounders? The gossip I heard was about aliens. "Where'd you get this stuff? In that chat group? I thought you talked about Bounders getting help at school."

"Please, Jasper. You are so naive. That's just what I tell Mom to keep her off my back."

Naive? Hardly. If she knew how I spent my tours of duty, she wouldn't say that. The way she's talking reminds me of Barrick and the Wackies, the group of rebels we met on Gulaga. It turned out Waters was closer to them than he was to Earth Force. If what Addy's hinting about her group is true—if they're anything like the Wackies—she's lucky she hasn't been arrested. I need to tell her the truth. It may be the only way to keep her safe.